EMILY KOCH

Emily Koch is an award-winning journalist and graduate of the Bath Spa Creative Writing programme. Her debut novel *If I Die Before I Wake* was shortlisted for the CWA Ian Fleming Steel Dagger. She lives in Bristol with her husband and daughter.

EMILY KOCH

If I Die Before I Wake

VINTAGE

5 7 9 10 8 6

Vintage
20 Vauxhall Bridge Road,
London SW1V 2SA

Vintage is part of the Penguin Random House group of companies
whose addresses can be found at global.penguinrandomhouse.com

Penguin
Random House
UK

First published in hardback by Harvill Secker in 2018
First published by Vintage in 2019

penguin.co.uk/vintage

A CIP catalogue record for this book is available from the British Library

ISBN 9781784705718

Printed and bound in Great Britain by Clays Ltd, Elcograf S.p.A.

Penguin Random House is committed to a sustainable future
for our business, our readers and our planet. This book is made
from Forest Stewardship Council® certified paper.

MIX
Paper from
responsible sources
FSC® C018179

For Matt

The Brain—is wider than the Sky—
For—put them side by side—
The one the other will contain
With ease—and You—beside—
Emily Dickinson

No one knows how dark the night is until you can't speak into it.
Julia Tavalaro

She still smells of sleep. I lean back against the dishwasher, holding her against my chest, looking down the line of her spine – the striped black and white T-shirt rippling where it meets the waistband of her denim shorts; her pale legs curving towards her ankles. She doesn't put her arms around me. I hook a finger under her chin, trying to lift it so that I can kiss her. If only she'd let me – then this would all be over, I know it. She hesitates, pushing her jaw down against my hand: her breath is warm against my skin. I think I feel her starting to give; she is tired of this, too. I can't even remember what started it. Can she?

But I'm wrong. She puts her palm against my stomach and twists her face away from my fingers, her blonde hair falling across her eyes. 'Don't,' she says.

She pushes me away, turns towards the kitchen table and picks up a spoon. Her small hands work quickly to finish making her sandwiches, scooping coleslaw onto the ham, pressing the second piece of white bread down firmly over the top. She makes a sharp slice with the knife diagonally across the middle. She won't look at me, but she knows I am watching. She gives the knife an unnecessary second push downwards with the heel of her hand, her mouth set in a grimace.

'Don't be like this.' I duck down, trying to get my face level with hers, trying to catch her eye. Her cheeks are flushed peach-pink.

'Come with us. We'll do some easy routes, you can have another go. You enjoyed it last—'

'It's your thing, Alex. I don't have to do it too.' She wraps her sandwiches tightly in several layers of cling film, squeezing the life out of them, and drops them into her rucksack. There's a bottle of water in there, too, and the bright orange of the OS map of the Quantocks I saw her pull off the bookshelf last night.

'It would just be nice to have you with us,' I say, stretching my arms out behind me, rolling my shoulders. I feel strong, ready for a good session in the Gorge. I'm looking forward to that ache I know will come later, the familiar feeling of a body well-worked. 'You don't have to climb, if you don't want to.'

She zips up the rucksack, walks over to the cupboard and pulls out her trainers, knocking mine onto the floor.

I bite my tongue to stop myself asking her if she is going to bother picking them up. Instead: 'Please. I don't want to leave it like this.'

Maybe, by this evening, she will have softened. A long walk will help clear her head.

I think about the letter. I need to tell her about it, but not when things are like this. I need to pick my moment.

She is kneeling down now, pulling on her trainers, stamping her heels down into them angrily – nearly rocking herself off balance in the process. I'll wait a bit, give her time to decide she likes me again, try and get her when she's in a good mood. She stands up, looks at herself in the mirror by the front door and puts some lip balm on, without smiling at her reflection.

Or should I do it now, when things couldn't get much worse?

'Bea, there's something—'

She walks in my direction but doesn't look at me, grabs the rucksack from its spot on the floor by my feet, and I follow her gaze as she looks at the clock on the wall above the sink. No – this isn't the right time. I said I'd pick Eleanor and Tom up before half-eight. And *anyway, I don't want to have to think about it. I need a break. I'm sweating at the thought of that envelope, the accusatory words. My mind flashes with the questions that have been distracting me from my work, making me edgy around Bea, and interrupting my sleep. What have I done?*

Later. I'll do it later.

With the rucksack over her shoulder, she picks up her car keys from the bowl under the mirror and opens the door.

'Have a nice time,' I say, still trying, although part of me would like to make a snide remark, or walk over there and stand between her and the door until she acknowledges me. Why is it always me who has to make the first move to make up? It's certainly not because it's always my fault. 'Looks like it should be a hot one. You sure you've got enough to drink?'

She pauses, rests her head against the door frame, her back to me. Then she walks out and pulls the door closed behind her.

Not even a goodbye.

1

'What's your intro, then?'

That's what my news editor used to ask me as soon as I walked into the office. He'd say it without turning his gleaming bald head away from the computer screen. His unnervingly delicate fingers would be spidering across his keyboard, his bottom lip sticking out and wobbling as he mouthed the words he typed. I'd be expected to rattle out my answer straight away. The top line of the story. What you'd say to your friends at the pub to catch their attention. The most important part to tell the reader, so that if they stopped there, at least they would know the gist.

As a cub reporter I stammered out a few answers, staring down at the brown carpet tiles, sweating in my suit and tie, hoping for someone to step in and tell me how I should start. Before Bill could bark at me, I might try and beat him to it and ask, 'What do you want me to go in on?' It worked a few times but then he got irritated. He'd drag his eyes from the monitor, wheel his office chair out from under his desk with a push of his feet, place his hands gently on his medicine-ball stomach, and say, 'I don't know, Alexander. You tell me. You need me to hold your hand, sweetheart?'

In those days, I thought it would be impossible for me to ever despise a person more than I despised Bill, or for anyone to deliberately humiliate me more than he did. I have been proved wrong on both counts.

I'd attempt another answer, mesmerised as always by the disturbing pink smoothness of his flabby face. Then he'd add his pet catchphrase, which he delighted in shouting across the newsroom even after I learned to file perfect copy, 'Want me to wipe your arse as well?'

Given my current condition, the irony of that final question is not lost on me. I heard it about once a week for four years but I never dreamed that I would actually need someone to clean up my shit on a daily basis before I turned thirty.

I learned to work out my intros as I walked back from press conferences, or drove back from interviews. What most excited me? What was the most important, the most arresting bit of information? How could I pull two, maybe three, elements into it and still keep it under twenty-five words? ('Keep it short, keep it sexy,' Bill used to growl.) That way, when I came through the doors of the *Bristol Post* offices, I could just sit down and write, knowing where I wanted to go.

But I'm struggling with the intro for this. I've got Bill's voice in my head – he's telling me to go straight in on the drama. How I ended up in hospital, the injustice, the heartbreak, the deceit and so on. But as far as I'm concerned, that's the obvious stuff. The story I really want to tell boils down to one question. What will happen to me next?

The opening lines for the article Bill would want would be easy. But the version I want? That's harder. The trouble is, you can't write your intro until you know how the story ends. So I have two versions ready:

A BRISTOL man has been hailed a medical miracle after waking up from a two-year coma to enjoy an emotional reunion with his family.

6

Or:

A BRISTOL climber, who had been in a coma since a fall in the Avon Gorge two years ago, has died.

Everyone thinks that behind my eyes there is darkness.

They think that when I wake up they will have to fill me in on months of lost time. They believed, of course, that I would wake up. At first. But after a year or so had passed – when I heard nurses discussing their New Year's Eve plans for the second time since I'd been in this place – I knew. My family were turning. When they visited my hospital bed, I picked it up in their voices. Hope and determination were becoming weariness and doubt.

Hope For An End – whatever end – raced head-to-head with Hope For A Sign Of Life. Would the race have been run differently, if they'd known the truth about what happened when the starting gun was fired? Who knows? As it was, Hope For An End was edging it.

And who can blame them? I must look totally lifeless. I can't talk, I can't move. I can't tell them that I hear every word they say.

My life as I knew it was stopped shortly after I turned twenty-seven. Now hours, days and months merge together into a trick of time, so all I know for sure is that I've been conscious for two Christmases – you can't miss it when carol singers visit each bed on the ward – and I assume that makes the length of my imprisonment a couple of years so far. The words the doctors and nurses use include 'coma' and 'vegetative state'. They have no idea that I am awake; no tests show them the activity in my brain that I'm desperate for them to see.

I don't know what is wrong with me either. How can I be paralysed but still able to feel when a nurse touches me? How can I seem to be a vegetable but actually understand everything that's going on? Sometimes my eyes open of their own accord. The doctors tell my family: 'it happens – nothing to get excited about'. But how would they explain the fact that I can see, in those random, thrilling, moments? A coma patient can't see, surely? Okay, so I can't see *properly*. I see shapes, shades of grey. Changes in the light. Not people's faces or features. Not colours. But still – this isn't what I thought being in a coma would feel like.

I wonder if I'm the only one of me in the world. A medical phenomenon they don't even know exists.

All of this leads to one place: a decision my family must make about whether they should pull the plug. From what the doctors say, I know I'm not attached to any kind of life-support machine. So, strictly speaking, there's no plug to pull – but I have learned that there are other ways to let someone like me fade away. I am fighting for my life, fighting to be kept alive. I have to prove there is something worth saving.

I've tried moving: nothing. I can't even make myself blink. I've tried talking: nothing. The doctors never notice any physical progress. But what if there is some other way I could show them that my mind is working? If I can keep my brain ticking over as much as possible; if I can think and think and think; if I can train my mind to keep active and moving; then maybe things will change. My brain might jump-start my body. Or perhaps they will see something when they next wheel me into the MRI scanner for tests.

Maybe then they will grab me by the hand, or by the collar of this hospital gown – I don't care which – and pull me out of this hole. Give me back my pile of clothes, hand me my release papers, open the doors and let me walk out. Maybe they will talk to me, treat me like a proper human being. There must be a way.

So, here I am: telling myself my own story, to keep my mind moving. Back in the day I'd have been delighted to land this assignment. There's a lot of meat, plenty for me to get my teeth into – both in the darkness of my time in hospital, and the darkness of what put me here.

There are details that I'd have had to phrase carefully to get past the editor. There would have been legal hoops to jump through so that I didn't risk prejudicing the trial. The paper would have splashed on it; maybe even for two days in a row if I'd found enough angles. It would have been picked up by the nationals and won me some awards. This is the kind of scoop that could make a career.

I feel like I used to when I called in to a copytaker, back in the early days before they were all made redundant. Before we all started emailing our articles straight in to the newsdesk. Every now and then I am tempted to use a bit of the lingo – add an extra level for me to concentrate on and exercise my brain that bit harder. I could say 'Point' to indicate the end of each sentence. 'Par' for a new paragraph. 'Ends' for the end of each piece. Point. But I'm not sure I can be bothered to do that the whole time. Point. This story isn't just a quick fifty-word NIB. Point. It could get tedious. Point. Par.

But I like to let myself run with this scenario, sometimes. Allow myself to believe I'm not so alone, and that I'm not talking to myself. I imagine it just like the old days. I'm sitting in my car, parked up next to a murder scene: a pot washer in a Fishponds café has stabbed his boss over unpaid wages, in front of horrified customers enjoying their fry-ups. I have spoken to a barber from across the street, who tearfully told me the dead man was a 'top guy, the kind of person who always stopped to say hello'. The usual kind of thing.

Murder, I learned in my years as a reporter, affects the lives of the most ordinary people. Not just those you might think deserve it. No one ever thinks it will happen to them, until it does.

'Put me through to a copytaker,' I say. She answers the phone brightly with a thick Bristolian accent, 'Morning! Where you to, then?' She's wearing her headset, tapping away on the keyboard with painted false nails, as I read to her. She stops me every now and then to check a sentence, tell me I've used the same word twice, or that it's too windy to hear me, but otherwise all she says is, 'Mmm. Yep. Go on,' before she eventually signs off. And that's what I want now: I don't want questions, demands. I want to explain how everything I felt sure of was thrown into doubt, how horrifying it is to find out that someone wants to do you harm. I just want to talk.

That's a lie. I don't 'just' want to talk. It hurts – physically hurts – to think about all the things I want to do.

Had I known this whole situation was on the cards I would have done so much more. Led on the most difficult climb in the Gorge. Pitched to present a TV show where I explored remote deserts and interviewed indigenous tribes living half-way up desolate mountainsides. I would have scaled Everest. I would have enjoyed the small stuff, the everyday things, too. I would have looked at the sky more.

If I could get out of here, I would spend a night asleep in my own bed under a duvet that didn't smell of starch, lying however the hell I wanted to lie – not where a nurse had arranged me, propped up with cushions. If I woke up to a sound in the night, I wouldn't be terrified of the dark, because I'd be able to defend myself. In the morning, I would roll over to face Bea, and watch her sleep for a few minutes before waking her up. She would climb on top of me and take over my lips with those starving kisses. One thing would lead to another, and afterwards I wouldn't make the bed.

I would eat a bacon sandwich – crisp salty meat on slices of soft white bloomer. Brown sauce. There would be fresh coffee in the cafetière filling the flat with the smell of toasted nuts and sugar on the edge of burning; there would be ice-cold apple juice; Bea would hand me a bowl of bright pink fresh grapefruit so sour it would make me wince. I would walk – no, run – through the streets in the rain. I would talk and talk and talk.

Since being struck dumb, I have so much to say.

2

I've always been fighting, since the moment I woke up in hospital. But I haven't always been on the same side of the battle lines. For a while, before everything started to go crazy with Bea and the police, I stopped wanting to live. It wasn't that I gave up. In my mind I was still fighting, just for a different outcome.

After what must have been months and months of doing my best to show the doctors my mental alertness, of attempting to move different parts of my body, of straining to speak – or even just grunt – I stopped. When they ran tests, I didn't bother to try and respond. I had a new goal: death. I hoped that if they thought I was unresponsive for long enough, they would let me go. After listening to conversations between doctors and my dad, I knew they could. They could stop feeding me, or let me slip away the next time I got an infection.

I had many reasons for thinking this would be for the best. I would be doing everyone else a favour. I could give Bea, Dad and Philippa the chance to move on with their lives. Even if I woke up from this nightmare, who could say whether I would be able to walk? Look after myself? Feed myself? I couldn't burden them with that.

I looked at it as the kind of life-or-death decision I'd heard about people making when a climb went badly wrong; it was rare, but there were still stories. You had to keep your cool, make the best decision for you and your partner. It would be horrendous to cut your friend's rope and send them to their probable death, but if it meant the difference between one or two people crashing to the ground, then you'd do it. And, theoretically, the same applied if you had to make the call on cutting the rope above you, knowing that the fall would kill you, but save your partner. That's how I looked at it. I was cutting my rope. It was the best decision I could make in the circumstances.

A feeling that I deserved to die had slowly built up over the months of lying here. This had all happened for a reason. My body and my guilt locked me into my sentence. There was no question in my mind that this was a punishment: and my biggest crime had been killing my mum.

That's what Philippa said I had done – my sister wasn't known for mincing her words. Is it any excuse to say that I was 'only eighteen' at the time, when Mum found out the cancer was back? While Dad lobbied our mother with reasons for hope and life, in the face of her second round of radiotherapy, I held her hands, looked into her eyes and let myself be carried away by her desperation and pain. If I hadn't taken her side and let her slowly surrender, we all knew she would have had more skin-blistering treatment. She would have listened to me.

But she had such convincing arguments. She was so sure of what she wanted. 'Was hospice nurse,' she reminded me, writing her stilted messages on the notepad she carried everywhere. Talking was too embarrassing because of the slur she was left with after they removed part of her tongue, and too painful because of the dryness the hours of radiation had bequeathed her. 'Saw hundreds of people die,' she wrote. 'Know what I want. No more treatment. Help me explain to your dad.'

How was I going to break it to him that she was giving up? He was already a shell of his old self. My voice felt loud those days, in a house where no one else seemed to speak. Dad had retreated into crime thrillers, guitar practice, and piles of geography coursework marking – the once-open door to his study now firmly shut. He hated talking to Mum through the notepad, so he avoided it as much as she did and they moved politely around each other, hiding from difficult conversations in their separate quiet worlds. How was I going to tell him that his wife wanted to die? Philippa had followed his lead and sunk into a bitter, seething silence. Mum got ill when she was fourteen, and died when Philippa was sixteen – it was hard to know how much of her reaction was down to Mum's illness and how much would have happened anyway as she embraced her teenage moodiness. She swung from sulking in her room to screaming at any one of us. Mum was not spared, and in fact seemed to get the worst of it. It was hard to watch them together, with Philippa refusing to hug her, looking at her with undisguised hatred, deliberately making her life difficult by insisting different clothes be ironed, or different food be cooked for dinner, or that she wanted to watch a different DVD to the one we'd chosen for our monthly family movie night. Mum's capacity for patience was astonishing, and when I glanced at her eyes to check for tears, they were always resolutely dry.

I didn't have quite the same level of tolerance. One evening Mum pushed a note over the dinner table, asking Philippa, 'How's Jenny?'

Out of nowhere Philippa had rolled her eyes and sneered, 'Screw you. Seriously – screw you.'

I followed her upstairs to her bedroom, fuming. Mum didn't deserve this. Ignoring her protests, I slammed open her door. 'What the fuck, Phil?'

'Leave me alone.' She was crying, wiping her face with the sleeve of her hoodie.

'Why are you treating her like this?'

'Do you even know who Jenny is?' she asked, sitting down on her bed, picking up a magazine and flicking through its pages. 'She was my friend from debating club. Which I don't go to any more because Dad has to take Mum to her acupuncture session on Tuesday nights instead. Doesn't she get it? I haven't seen Jenny for months, because of her.'

I looked around her room – at her *Cruel Intentions* and *Never Been Kissed* film posters, her old teddy bears kicked off the bed onto the floor, the history textbooks on her desk – looking for something that would help me understand her selfishness. 'You think debating club is more important than Mum getting better?'

'It's all right for you. You don't care that everything has changed since she got ill. I caught Dad crying the other day. Have you ever seen him do that before? He didn't even cry when Nana and Grandad died. Mum's made him miserable.' She slapped a hand down onto her magazine's cover – as if this fact was sure to convince me.

'It's not her that's made him like that,' I said, sitting down in the chair at her desk, smoothing over the open pages of her textbook. 'It's not her fault. It's the cancer. If you need to blame something, blame that.'

She tore the cover of her magazine off, ripped it into small pieces and tossed them into the bin by my feet. 'But I can't touch the cancer, can I? I can't shout at it. I can't see it.' She looked up at me, tore out another page without glancing down, screwed it into a ball, and held my gaze until I had to look away.

The next day I was helping Mum do weeding in the garden – she tended it devotedly right up until the final weeks of her life – and she pulled her notepad out of her apron. 'Sun cream?' she wrote, and I got up from my kneeling pad to fetch her some from the house. In the August sun she needed to apply a high factor to the long scar running down her neck, the result of the surgery to remove her lymph nodes which had been done at the same time as they removed part of her tongue. I had started walking away across the lawn, when I heard her speak – a rasping, garbled word, but unmistakable. 'Alex.' I turned, and she beckoned to me. As I made my way back to her, she started writing again. 'Ask Phil to bring it to me,' she wrote. 'You take a break. She can help me.'

I winced. 'I don't know if she'll come, Mum.'

'Ask,' she wrote.

I sighed. I didn't want her to be disappointed.

'It's okay,' she wrote, smiling up at me from her spot on the ground at the foot of the apple tree. 'It's just her way. I understand. Ask her. She might come.'

But Philippa wouldn't leave her desk when I passed the message on. She rolled her eyes and told me she was too busy with her homework.

This was how she was for the whole two years of our mother's illness. How would she take it when I told her that Mum was going to refuse more treatment? Part of me was worried that she'd be glad – worried she might even tell Mum that she would be pleased to see the back of her.

I spent several days agonising over how I was going to tell them. I'd always been a procrastinator, particularly when it came to sharing bad news. I could have saved myself and the people around me a lot of pain if I hadn't been. And there were things I should never have put off telling Bea, things that happened in my final weeks. I've paid for that cowardly delay these past few months.

In the end, it was taken out of my hands. While she was in the shower, Dad leafed through one of her notebooks. He found the page that read, in fat blue felt-tip pen, 'No more treatment. Help me explain to your dad.' I was watching TV in the living room when he strode in, threw the notebook in my lap and asked: 'When were you going to tell me?' His face was red and shiny with sweat, his breathing fast and shallow. 'I won't have it,' he said, when I didn't reply. Snatching the pad out of my hands, he walked back out of the living room. The door to his study slammed. 'I won't let her!' He shouted the words this time – it was the loudest noise I had ever heard him make. I muted the TV, walked quietly out into the corridor and put an ear to his door. All I could hear was the sound of sheets of paper being torn from their spiral binding – Mum's notepad. 'You can't do this to us, Diane,' he shouted, before the house went silent again. When Philippa appeared at the bottom of the stairs, wondering what was going on, I dragged her into the living room and sat her down next to me on the sofa. She wasn't glad after all. 'She can't do that,' she said, her eyes wide. 'The doctors won't allow it.'

'They'll have to.' I put my arm around her. 'And we have to respect her wishes.'

She pulled away. 'We do not,' she said. 'You're not going to go along with this?'

I nodded, without looking at her.

'What's wrong with you? You can't let her die. The radiotherapy will make her better this time.' She spoke rapidly, standing up. 'Dad will know how to talk her round. You can't let her do this. Please.' She started crying. 'I just want my old mum back,' she whimpered. I still couldn't look at her face. 'I want everything to go back to how it was before.'

Over the first months I had spent in hospital, my mind stormed with these painful scenes. I was convinced I was being punished.

By choosing death I finally accepted my fate: I had to pay for everything I had done.

3

I remember the last time Bea visited me, before everything changed for both of us.

The nurses had positioned me on my left side, propped up with cushions to relieve my back and prevent the pressure sores that they constantly checked me for. This meant I was facing the window; my eyes were closed but I could feel dim sunlight on my skin. I listened to the sirens as the ambulances sped by on the road outside, their pitch changing as they passed.

The door to my room whined, and someone padded up behind my back. I recognised the scent: citrus and cigarettes. Bea walked around to stand between me and the window, and I felt the soft touch of her lips on my forehead – her usual greeting.

'Only me,' she said, her sing-song voice drowning out the chatter on the ward. 'Oh.' She touched my face. 'Hang on, I'll sort that out.'

Footsteps. Then the soft rip of paper from near the foot of my bed. Footsteps approached my head again. Bea dabbed a tissue to the corner of my mouth, where saliva was dribbling out and dampening the pillow under my turned cheek.

Don't, I thought. She wasn't my nurse. I didn't want her to see me as her helpless patient. *Don't do that.*

'There we go. That's better.' She walked around to the other side of my bed and leaned in to kiss my right ear, then pressed her cheek up to mine and asked, 'Are you dreaming in there?'

She paused.

'That would be nice.'

I felt the cold frame of her glasses against my skin, then she lifted her head away from me and her weight sank the mattress as she climbed onto the bed, curling her small body around the back of mine.

'Then maybe, when I go to sleep and I dream, we could meet up, you know? Dream-me and dream-you. Hang out.'

Her bent knees dug into the back of my thighs as she breathed into my neck.

'Sorry,' she sighed. 'It sounds stupid. But I had a weird dream about you this morning and it would be nice to think it was really you, somehow.'

She put a hand on my back.

'I dreamed I was in bed, about to get up. Then a cat jumps in through the window and starts clawing at my back, like this.' She scratched her nails through the thin material of my pyjama top in long, deliberate strokes down my spine. It was the best thing I had felt in days. 'God, Al. I swear you're still losing weight. These ribs.'

She gently dragged her fingers upwards towards my neck.

'Anyway, so then it starts drawing circles on my shoulder blades. Like a little, I don't know, a little cat masseuse or something.' She laughed without a sound – but the slight movement of her lips on my neck set the fine hairs of my back and shoulders on end. She inhaled, and reached her arm around my stomach.

'Outside I could hear someone moving their bins around. I think that was real. I could hear someone laughing.' She rubbed my abdomen. 'And I was pissed off because – well, you know what I get like when I'm woken up before my alarm goes off.'

I did. A smile flickered through my face without moving any of my muscles. I remembered my dopey, puffy-eyed Bea, her face creased from the folds in her pillowcase, rolling over and groaning at me if our neighbours dared to slam the door to their flat before seven o'clock. If I ever needed to get up before her, I had to be absolutely silent. Although, strangely, if it was the other way round, she was allowed to make as much noise as she wanted, and switch all the lights on.

'Then this cat starts pinching my fingers,' she said. 'And I'm thinking, how is this cat pinching me? Then there's more laughing, but this time in our bedroom. I hear this voice, saying: "You're so cute when you sleep. Sleepy little Honey Bea."'

She had always pretended to hate it when I called her that.

'I know that voice, I'm thinking. And I say: "You've been gone a long time." I smile, I reach out to touch your face.'

She lifted her hand to my cheek.

'And I say: "You're back. You came home."'

Bea.

'It was vivid. You were right there, pinching me, stroking my forehead. You were kissing my scar.'

I saw her. That perfect scar, a little dent that tugged her lip gently up towards her nostril, the only visible remnant of a mild cleft lip. After several years of me kissing it, she had eventually stopped trying to hide it behind her hand.

'I was happy,' she whispered, the laughter gone. 'But then you weren't there. You know how in dreams the edges slide away? I rolled over and reached for you, and you weren't there any more.'

She held her palm tight against my stomach, thumbing my protruding lower ribs instead of the muscles she used to stroke.

'And then I woke up and I remembered. You couldn't have been there.'

She sniffed, and her head moved away from me.

My body may have been paralysed, but I could still feel when my heart twisted for her, as it did then. I wanted to lift my needled hand and put it on hers, and tell her it would be over soon.

That was my hope. I wanted to put an end to it, knock the weight from her small shoulders and push her forward into better days. I was making progress, I thought. They would soon start to talk about letting me die.

Before my hospital confinement, we used to talk about our three future kids. Two boys, one girl. They'd all be climbing (taught by me) and learning to draw (taught by Bea) from a young age. They would learn guitar from my dad, and we'd name the girl after my mum. Bea had never met her, but it was her idea. I remember exactly where we were when she suggested it – on holiday in the Algarve. The beach at Praia de Odeceixe was a spit of golden sand, bordered on one side by a river and lagoons where smaller children paddled, and on the other side by the sea, where older children played in the surf. Bea was sketching me as I lay on my back, propped up on my elbows, while I tried to work out how the black, jagged cliffs of schist overlooking the river mouth had been formed and shaped – and, more importantly, whether they could be climbed.

'There's a little girl over there, who keeps throwing her brother's toys into the water,' Bea said, putting her pencil down. 'She's a terror.'

I turned to see. 'Where?'

'Don't move!' she said. 'I haven't finished yet.'

I shook my head and laughed.

'Sorry.' She picked up her pencil again. 'I didn't mean for you to look. I was just saying.'

With my head back in the desired position, I resumed my study of the cliffs.

'I was thinking, if we had a girl, one day,' she said. Her pencil scratched at the paper, and I looked at her out of the corner of my eye. She tilted her head, squinting her eyes at the sketchbook, assessing her progress. 'We could call her some-thing to remember your mum. Maybe not Diane – it sounds a bit dated now, don't you think? But what about Didi?'

I smiled. Little Didi. Using my mum's name had never crossed my mind, but now that she mentioned it – yes. It would be the perfect way to keep her memory alive.

'What do you think?'

'Am I allowed to talk?' I asked. 'It would involve moving my mouth – it could mess up your masterpiece.'

She threw her pencil at me and laughed. 'You may speak.'

'In that case, I think that would be a great idea. Mum would have loved it.' I handed her pencil back, trying not to move the rest of my body too much.

'What was she like?' Bea asked.

'I've told you, haven't I? I feel like I've told you everything.'

'There must be more.' Bea put her sketchbook down and moved her towel closer to me. She sat down at my side, pulling her pale green kaftan over her knees. She'd insisted that she wanted to go somewhere warm, where the sea was bright blue and the sand was golden – somewhere I would be forced to walk around without a top on and show off my climber's shoulders, she had added with a grin. She picked up a handful of sand and let it slip out in cascades between her fingers. 'Tell me little things about her,' she said. 'I wonder if our children will be like her in any way, even if they never meet her?'

'Little things?' I repeated, tilting my head back and closing my eyes against the glare of the sun. 'She didn't know how to say no to people.'

'A good or bad thing?'

'Good,' I said. 'Mostly. But sometimes people took advantage.'

'Like Philippa?' I nodded. Bea understood a lot about our family dynamic, considering she hadn't been around when Mum was alive.

'She loved roses. Always wanted a new one to plant in the garden, for every birthday. She never wanted anything else. She preferred pink ones, and she liked to keep a list of the names in her gardening diary. I got her one once called Gertrude Jekyll.'

Bea laughed. 'That's Didi's middle names sorted.'

I could see Mum clearly now, crouching in the garden to plant one of her new roses, the hem of her patterned skirt sinking into the muddy earth. I felt a tightness begin to form in my chest, so I moved on. 'And she liked blue cheese with caramelised onion chutney. On chive crackers. No butter.'

Bea put a hand on my shoulder and the tightness forming around my heart slunk away. 'I wish I had met her,' she said.

'Because of the cheese?'

She laughed. 'Yes. Because of the cheese.'

We had lots of conversations like that.

But now I wasn't around to have those kids with. Bea had amazed me with her determination to stick at my side. I had worried that her visits might tail off over time. That the draw of real life and real conversations would start to pull her away from me. But still she came. Would I have done the same? Surely, by this point, part of her thought it would be better if I could die. Better for me, but also better for her. She would be able to move on.

Bea laid her head back down next to mine. 'There are times when I miss you so badly. Like last night – I convinced myself there was someone watching me from the garden. I really freaked out. You'd have said something to make me feel better, you know?' She paused, and sighed. 'Maybe I'm spending too much time on my own.'

I felt her lips against my neck.

'Wake up, wake up, wake up,' she whispered. Then: 'Go to sleep, go to sleep, go to sleep.' She couldn't decide which she wanted. My Bea. Breaking with too-painful love.

After she left, I could still feel her there, tucked up behind me. We weren't in a hospital bed, but back at home. I was just pretending to be asleep, as I had done so many times before with her, challenging her to stir me. She lay behind me, kissing my shoulder blades. She wrapped a smooth leg around me, rolled the weight of my body back onto her so I could feel her nakedness press into my back. 'Come on, Alex. Wake up,' she murmured, as she used her nails to lightly circle over my chest, down my stomach. She flicked the elastic of my boxers. 'Wake. Up.'

As the fantasy continued, my body responded for real. It's another quirk of this condition of mine – I can still get it up. Not necessarily when I want to. It doesn't happen every time Bea is here, or every time a nurse touches me. I don't get hard every time I think about Bea naked – not like I used to. The first time she noticed the sheets moving unexpectedly I heard her breath stutter and change. She touched my leg, moving her hand upwards – then she hesitated and pulled away. She stood silent for a moment before calling Dr Sharma in.

'Look,' she said. 'What does that mean?'

'It's unlikely to mean anything at all,' Dr Sharma said. 'Alex will still be able to get erections – parts of his body will still function in a similar way to how they used to.'

'But it seems so strange that his body would do that. What if it's the sound of my voice?'

'I know it's confusing for you. I'm sorry. But I'm not convinced that it is. I don't think this is a result of him reacting to outside stimuli.'

I briefly imagined shoving him up against the wall and asking him what his game was. I was desperate for her to touch me. Why wouldn't he let her try it? What harm could it do?

'Look, Bea – can I call you Bea?' Dr Sharma asked. 'What I think we are seeing here is a bit like what happens with Alex's eyes. You know how sometimes they are open a little bit, and sometimes they are closed?'

'Yes. But this. What's happening now. This is different, isn't it?'

'Less frequent, perhaps. But it's that same kind of scenario. His body will do some things – open his eyes, or even cry – without him having control over it, and without him necessarily reacting to you being here. Some things he does are just reflexive.'

'But how can you be so sure?'

'We've done lots of tests. We've watched him. In the very rare cases when we find out that a patient like Alex is conscious, it's because one of the scans shows up certain kinds of activity in their brain, or because we notice they are blinking or moving their eyes in response to things we say. Alex isn't doing any of that.'

'I thought this might mean something,' she said quietly.

'I know, I'm sorry. The same goes for some other things too – if you notice his heart rate changing or him getting goosebumps when you touch him. It makes it look like he is awake, but he's not. If you see his eyes follow you, or you think he blinks at you, then that's different. Tell me if that happens.'

'You're saying he has no idea I'm here.'

'I'm saying that, for the moment, we don't think he is conscious. But it's still good to visit him. Just try not to get your hopes up.'

There was an awkward silence.

'While you're here,' Bea said, finally, 'there's something else I've been wanting to ask.'

'Of course, go ahead.'

'If he comes round, how much will he be able to remember, from before?'

'Bea,' Dr Sharma said, a warning in his voice. 'You know that we are not predicting that he will come round, don't you? You understand the prognosis?'

'Yes, but hypothetically speaking. If he did?'

'You're worried he might not remember you?'

'No, I ...' She stopped, sighed. 'More like his immediate memory. The weeks before, the day of his fall. That kind of thing. I've heard with head injuries, sometimes they can't recall—'

'You must be very keen to know exactly what happened to make him slip. He was an experienced climber, I heard?'

'Very.'

'He might remember, he might not. I'm not sure I should really—'

'Hypothetical situation,' Bea cut in. She sounded frustrated – one beat short of losing her temper with Dr Sharma and his evasiveness.

'Someone with these injuries probably wouldn't remember the day of the accident itself. Before that – it's too hard to say. It would depend on a number of things.'

'Fine, I understand,' she said. 'He might remember, he might not.'

At the time I assumed she was asking these questions because she hoped I *would* have full recall. It's only now, looking back, that I wonder if she was hoping the opposite.

4

As the months passed after my hospital admission, I had become increasingly sure that Bea didn't think I could hear her. What I deduced from the way she spoke to me was that she liked the idea that I might be listening, but that's all it was – an idea. It wasn't reality, not as she saw it.

Sometimes she would ask me something, and wait for a second as though I might answer. But mostly she spoke to me as if I was a diary to be filled with her daily activities and thoughts – and a few confessions thrown in here and there. Her monologues were journal entries, or letters to an old friend. But – no, they weren't quite like that. There was something unnerving in the way she threw the words out into the room as if they'd never matter. I couldn't quite put my finger on it, my mind wouldn't make the link. But Bea made it for me. It wasn't long after her dream about me appearing in her bed, when she visited again.

She was pacing. Her voice swung from one side of the room to the other, following the noise of her footsteps.

'So, what have I done today . . . ?' she began. I couldn't concentrate on what she said. The nurses had moved me onto my back, leaving my arm twisted. They were well trained in this inadvertent torture technique – leaving their victim in excruciating stress positions.

'. . . then I went for a run . . .'

Not only could I not concentrate, but I didn't have much interest in what she was talking about, either. All I wanted her to do was rearrange me, and get me comfortable.

My left arm, Bea. Can you straighten me out?

Pins and needles bit into my hand, spreading up past my wrist. She stopped still next to my bed, and stroked my tingling fingers.

'. . . new trainers were good but I'm not sure they have as much support as I'm used to and I'm sure I'm still over-pronating . . .'

Still rubbing across my knuckles, she leaned in to kiss my forehead. The pain eased in my arm, and I willed her to talk about something more interesting. I wanted to listen to her – it was better than the mind-numbing silence I usually had on repeat – but sometimes the banality of what she chose to tell me did my head in.

'If I'm honest,' she said, and paused. 'I was running for a reason. To straighten something out in my head.'

I felt the gentle tickle of her nails on the back of my thumb.

'There's this group.'

She walked away from the bed, her shoes padding softly on the floor.

'A grief counselling group. I went to a grief counselling group.' The words tumbled from her mouth in a rush.

'It was Rosie's idea. I thought it was stupid.'

I didn't understand. Who had died?

'She suggested going to the same one Tom went to when his dad died – he said it wasn't just for people who have been bereaved. A life change is enough.'

So nobody was dead. Which meant – was she talking about me being in here? Was that her life change? She was right, it sounded stupid. There must have been other counselling available for someone in her position.

There was a crinkling sound, and when she next spoke she

had something in her mouth. 'God, Al,' she garbled, and the smell of spearmint hit me. 'It was a disaster.'

Her footsteps came closer again, and I heard her scratching at her head as she walked. She used to run her fingers up through her short, blonde hair when she got stressed, over and over. I could see it now. I had always loved the way it fell across her khaki green eyes and the freckled skin of her forehead.

'It started when I called the guy to find out about it. He asked me why I wanted to go, and I don't know why I did it, but I said –'

She paused and made a funny noise, as if she had remembered something embarrassing.

Then she rattled out, 'I said my boyfriend died nearly two years ago in a climbing accident.'

I wanted to laugh out loud. The kind of laugh that makes you spit out your tea.

'And then, from there, I couldn't take it back. When I went to the session they were all so nice about it. I felt awful.'

I listened to her feet, still padding back and forth across the room.

'And I cried. It was awful. The woman leading the session asked us all to remember something – "go back to a time when Alex tried to cheer you up when you felt sad" she said. "What would he say to you when you were sad?"'

What would I say? I would hold her, or try and make her laugh. I never felt like I said the right thing, but I could usually make her smile if I did something ridiculous enough.

'"Tomorrow will be better." That's what you always used to say. So I told them that, and they smiled and patted me on the back and I cried and it was awful.' She sighed. 'They all thought I was talking about my dead boyfriend.'

Bea wouldn't have told me all of this if she had really thought I could hear her. She didn't like admitting her mistakes, and hated it when I found out about something that gave me cause to tease her.

If I could have laughed, I would have. When you're in my position you take your kicks where you can get them. Then a latch abruptly clicked into place in my brain. I imagined Bea, sitting around, discussing my death with other grieving men and women, and suddenly I knew what her style of talking to me brought to mind: a bereaved relative, visiting the grave of a loved one.

5

A strange combination of smells. Something like solvent, reminding me of gloss paint, mixing with another, more aromatic scent – aftershave of some kind. This particular doctor's visits always started like this: the first sign was always the smell. Often that was the only hint I had as to my visitor's identity, as he wasn't much of a talker. He was a specialist of some kind, and he visited less frequently than the other doctors – every few months or so. Over the time he had been tending to me, I hadn't managed to work out his name – no one had addressed him within my earshot. So I called him Quiet Doc.

Normally he checked me over and muttered a bit. It was always a shock when he had more to say – like he did a few days after Bea's visit.

I spent several minutes listening to him rove around, picking up my charts, sliding my vase of flowers along the table. He sighed frequently as he did it, as if it was all a huge effort.

He continued his usual checks, putting a hand to my forehead, his scent getting stronger as he moved closer to me. He held it there, then slid it down to my left cheek, pushing it away from him – presumably checking the movement of my neck, or looking in my ear. Then he held my jaw and pulled my face back towards him.

I knew what came next: arms. He pinned my right elbow

joint to the bed, and lifted my right wrist, checking my range of movement. He repeated the test on my left side. He did all of this slowly and silently, not in a rush as most of them usually were.

It should have been reassuring to have someone take their time. It should have felt like he was doing his job properly, taking care over everything. But despite his thoroughness, he didn't seem very pleased to have to look after me, with all his huffing and muttering. And there was something unsettling about the way he touched me – his hands lingered and slid from one part of my body to the other, in contrast to the perfunctory movement I was used to from most of the other medical professionals.

I sized all of this up as he checked the movement in my leg joints and investigated the flexibility of my fingers, one by one.

All look okay?

He took my pulse by holding my wrist for a minute or so, before inspecting the tracheostomy tube sticking out of my neck, tugging it this way and that.

I knew the drill. He usually said a few things when he finished his check-up. He talked quietly, as though the words were more for his benefit than mine.

'Good, Mr Jackson, you're doing well.' He paused. 'No improvement.'

This was his style. He seemed encouraging, but at the same time he never noticed anything that suggested I was getting better.

This was his cue to scrutinise the charts a few more times and leave, without another word.

Not today.

'You're determined to survive, aren't you?' he said, almost under his breath. He sighed again.

'You've had pneumonia how many times?' He walked down to the end of my bed and I heard the clatter of my chart's clipboard as he picked it up again. 'Enough,' he said. 'And yet, you're still with us.'

It wasn't the kind of thing I would have wanted to hear from a doctor in my old life – but feeling as I did, I agreed with him. How was I still alive?

'You're a symptom of the totally fucked healthcare system this country has,' he said. His language shocked me – I hadn't heard any of my doctors swear. Even though they had no idea that I was listening, they generally acted professionally.

'There are so many more people surviving injuries like yours these days than there used to be, because medicine gets better and better.' He put my charts back and walked over to the window on my left. 'But what's the point? Perhaps it would have been better if you had died.'

If you don't want to be here, don't let me keep you.

He must've turned suddenly. Without warning, I felt a tug on the plastic tube which ran into my stomach, through which the nurses administered drugs and food.

This wasn't part of his usual routine.

I listened as he fiddled with something at my side; it sounded like the plastic fitting at the end of the tube.

What are you doing?

What was he doing? Giving me medicine? Not food – that would be a job far below his pay grade. What if he was poisoning me? Ridding the world of this burden?

My face grew hot and my heart began to thud as the tube dropped back down by my side.

What have you given me? Morphine?

Was he my ticket out of here? Did he think I was enough of a drain on their resources to actually end my life?

His footsteps moved away from my bed, but his smell lingered as the door clicked open, shut, and he left me alone to wonder what he had just put into my system. If anything.

33

Could this man be my ally?

No, he wouldn't do that. My imagination was running away with me. I couldn't feel any change in my body, and the drugs usually worked quickly when they were pumped straight into my stomach. He was a doctor. He wasn't going to euthanase me, no matter how much he resented my existence on his ward, even if he thought it was the best thing for me.

My doctors were there to look after me, not kill me. I never imagined I'd be thinking those words and feeling disappointed.

6

El Cap, Whareapapa, Meteora, Les Calanques: climbing meccas that I've never seen. Lying mummified in my bed, I can't identify with the person that said: I'll go next year. Next year. Next year. I'll go one day. Why did I do that?

But at least I climbed in the Canadian Rockies – and in many ways it all began there, ten years ago. In the Rockies I became obsessed with the sport – more than I ever had when climbing in the Avon Gorge and at the indoor walls back home. And also in the Rockies, I met Bea – in that camp by the gates to Banff National Park. For those few months we lived among pine forests and startling turquoise glacier-fed lakes, overlooked by huge snow-capped mountains: Ha Ling Peak, Grotto, Mount Lawrence Grassi, the Three Sisters. Waking and looking up at them made me want to grab my ropes, chalk up, and climb. And I did – on my days off – but I spent the rest of my time hiking with groups of teenagers, assisting the climbing instructors when they introduced the kids to the easier spots, and running activities at the camp.

I have no idea how Bea got the job. She wasn't anywhere near as sporty as the rest of us, and she made it clear that she didn't want to be there. But her mum had forced her to apply – 'I told her she wasn't going to get many opportunities in life like that,' Megan later told me. 'I wanted my daughter to do everything I never did.'

It took another two years for us to get together, although if I'd had the balls I would have made my move much earlier. As always, I procrastinated. We didn't stray beyond friendship that summer – but we were still inseparable. Bea and Rosie, another camp counsellor, bonded over their outrage at the no-alcohol-in-camp rule, and picked me up as their ally. They liked to look after me, seeing themselves as my big sisters, or something, even though they were only a few months older. Every morning, Bea made sure I put enough factor thirty on to stop my fair skin burning, and on a couple of occasions she put lemon juice in my red hair to try and bleach it. I didn't get much of a say. Rosie attempted to improve my fashion sense, forcing me to throw away what she called my 'offensively dreary' T-shirts. They coached me in a futile effort to get another girl at camp to go out with me, suggesting chat-up lines and engineering situations for us to be alone together. I didn't even like the girl particularly, but I went along with it because they seemed to enjoy themselves so much.

Bea and I would stay up late sometimes after Rosie had gone to bed, and she listened as I tried to make sense of what had happened shortly before we arrived in Canada. In the winter, my mum's wish to die had been granted. It was her idea that I should take a year out before university. 'You'll need some time off after all this,' she scribbled on her notepad, in one of her 'when I'm not around' written lectures, which I actively avoided. Bea listened for hours as I tried to get my head around it, and the few things she said always made me feel much better. It started as a shy drip of memories and obvious thoughts – 'how is it fair that someone who never smoked in her life could get mouth cancer?' and 'my dad says he's fine but I don't think he is' and 'what do you think it feels like to die?' But the drip became a burst main in September, when one of the children died in an accident in the camp swimming pool just before we were due to go home.

In the last evenings at camp, everyone was upset. We'd sit against the wall outside the back of the counsellors' dorms, my arms around both Rosie's and Bea's shoulders, and their heads on my chest. We'd drink our smuggled beers and take it in turns to share a set of headphones to listen to our favourite songs of the summer. We've got to live like every day is our last, I'd say, and the girls would nod their heads against me, wiping away tears. I didn't take that advice. I wasted far too much time before my accident: whole days spent hungover in front of the TV, weeks moping around the flat when I failed to get my act together and book a holiday during my annual leave, not to mention the years coasting as a reporter when I could have been pursuing my ambition to make documentaries.

Years later, our little gang of three was reunited when I moved back home to Bristol after graduating from UCL. By that time Bea and I were going out. She had been studying graphic design here while I was in London. Rosie ended up joining us after travelling through Europe as an English-as-a-foreign-language teacher. ('If I'm coming back to the UK, I may as well live near you two.') Our knot tightened when she got together with one of my climbing buddies, Tom. During my hospital incarceration the two of them were always welcome visitors – an entertaining double act. Before my accident, Bea would say to me that she wondered how other couples behaved behind closed doors. Were we different? Did we argue more? Did we have as much sex as everyone else? I got exactly the chance she would have loved – to be a fly on the wall in another relationship – when Tom and Rosie came in.

Not long after Bea told me about her grief counselling session, they visited me. My eyes were creased open for a few hours that day – only a slit. I didn't have the control to open them wider or close them. I could make out greys, blacks, whites.

Amorphous shapes, light and dark. But I couldn't focus on anything. When they walked in, they interrupted me listing all those climbs in the world I hadn't done and never would, if my plan to die worked. *El Cap, Wharepapa, Meteora, Les Calanques*: a list of places I needed to say goodbye to, mentally. I could make out movement to the right of the room in front of me as they flung the door open; I could see the darkness of Rosie's long black hair and Tom's tall lanky figure, but I couldn't see their faces.

'. . . you said you were going to do it,' Rosie was saying.

'And I will,' Tom said. 'When I want to.'

What was it this time? The weekly food shop, perhaps. Or painting the spare room.

'You promised me that you would help me out. I've taken over so many extra classes since Janice left. I don't know how I'm supposed to get all this done with the lessons I have to plan.'

Tom's grey shape approached the left side of my bed, his flip-flops smacking on the floor. 'Look at him,' he said, as he sank down into the chair. I smelled familiar lemony-sweet climber's balm as he put his hand on mine. He was never a big talker, but I'd really noticed it in the last year or so. He could say what he needed to say in about a third of the words it took Rosie to express herself. 'How do you think he looks? A bit better?'

'He looks no different. Absolutely the same. Come on.' Rosie's voice came from further away, and I could make out shifts in the light at the end of my bed where she stood.

'Come on what?'

'He looks the same as always, and I don't know why you ask that every time we come here. It kills me. Stop doing this to yourself.'

'What do you mean?'

'You. Thinking he's going to come out of this.'

'What?'

'It's not going to happen. He can't hear us – you know what the doctors have said. He doesn't know we're here.'

'I guess.' Tom didn't sound convinced. I heard a rattling noise. 'But does he look comfortable?'

No. I'm really hot. And I'd kill for a beer.

'Huh,' Tom said. More rattling. Some tapping.

'What're you doing?' More rattling. 'Tom?'

More tapping. A thud.

'Tom, I know you can hear me. I'm a metre away from you. Tom?'

'Arm of this chair's a bit loose,' he said. 'Remind me to bring some wood glue next time.'

Typical Tom. Fixing stuff. Always tinkering with things – and far better at DIY than me. 'It's an engineer thing,' he used to say to me, when I'd resort to calling him over to help me put shelves up, or unstick a window. 'I can't string a sentence together like you,' he'd say. 'Just like you're a total fool with a hammer.' Bea had quietly resigned herself to the fact that she'd picked a dud man-of-the-house. I'd become used to coming home to find Tom fixing a tap or mending the dishwasher. Bea called him before even bothering to tell me there was a problem.

Rosie sighed. 'It's not your job to repair the furniture. We'll just tell the nurse. Or something. Stop fiddling with it.'

He didn't say anything, but I knew he was actively ignoring her. He'd bring the glue next time. She couldn't stand in between him and a project – no matter how small.

Rosie's footsteps moved around the right-hand side of my bed, opposite him. Her petite shape dropped into a chair. The coconut fragrance of her perfume hit me, mixed strangely with the pungent scent of whiteboard markers; she always smelled a bit like that after a day of teaching. I braced myself for the usual conversational ping-pong that occurred when they sat either side of my bed like this.

'You okay?' Tom asked.

'Not really,' she groaned.

'Is this still about Bea?'

'It was awful.'

'What was?'

'Tom!'

'What?'

'I told you last night. Weren't you listening?'

'Don't talk to me like I'm one of your students.
I was knackered.
Alberto made me try some
really tough sections.'

What routes did you do? Any new ones?

Rosie didn't say anything. I tried to see what she
was doing, but I was lying on my back, sitting up slightly
and facing the wall at the end of my bed. She remained
on the periphery of my vision.

'She was so massively pissed off with me,
but could I honestly call myself her friend if I
didn't tell her she needs to move on?'

Had I just heard her right?

'You know what I think about this,' Tom said.

I hadn't heard about anyone confronting Bea like this before. Feeling as I did about the course of the rest of my life, I was glad Rosie had had the guts to raise it.

'He's not going to come round,' Rosie said gently. 'Come on, you know what the doctors have said. Not now he's passed the twelve-month point.'

'He might.'
Tom pulled his hand away
from mine and started cracking his knuckles.

I'd never have guessed how deep Tom's loyalty went. I almost felt bad for throwing it back in his face, but I wished he would let go.

'Okay then – when will it happen? And in the meantime Bea is there, what? Waiting? What about her? What about kids?'

'Kids?'

'Children, a family, all that kind of stuff. Everything is totally on hold for her. On pause.'

Tom stopped cracking his knuckles.
'Do *you* want children? Now?'

'No. Not now.'

'Just checking.'

'But soon.'

'How soon?'

'A couple of years?'

'Just checking.' Tom exhaled.

When are you going to grow a pair? Count yourself lucky
you can be a dad.
They sat in silence for a few minutes and I could make out his
fidgeting from the corner of my eye. My room was really warm.
Airless. My pyjamas were damp under my sweaty skin,
between my back and the mattress. Weren't they hot too?

Eventually Rosie started talking again.
'It didn't help that I mentioned
that random girl – you know, in London?'

What? Why remind her of that?

'Why would you bring *that* up?'

'I was trying to say that maybe
Alex didn't have such strong views on loyalty
as she did – I don't know. I thought
maybe it would help persuade her.
I didn't think it through.'

I hated to think about Bea remembering my mistakes.
That first year we were together – me in London finishing

my degree, her in Bristol – felt like a lifetime ago, but I could
still see her eyes as I told her what I'd done.
I was an idiot to have risked everything.
We'd been over it, she'd forgiven me. It was forgotten.
Why bring that up again?

'Obviously not,' Tom said.

                          'Don't, please – I know. I can't believe
                                    I thought it would help.'

'Would you up and leave if it was me lying here?'

                                        'She's
                   thirty next year, and she's sitting
                       here waiting for something
          that won't happen. She knows that, really.'

'What about all the stuff with his dad?
How did she take that?'

                        'Mmmm . . . she wasn't impressed
                      that I'd spoken to Graham about it.'

Tom coughed.

                           'I knew she wouldn't like it.
                         She's been so touchy lately
                            anyway, even before this.
               But *he* called *me*. I couldn't say no.'

'Maybe he should have spoken
to her himself.'

'Tell me about it. He also asked me not to say anything to Alex's sister about it all – says she wouldn't agree.'

'I'm with her on that.'

'I get the point.'

I wanted to know more, but Rosie didn't give anything else away. They stayed a little while longer. I didn't follow what they said after they stopped talking about Bea – instead, I thought about her ranting about the impossibility of leaving me. I knew her. The more she said she couldn't, the more I knew she would be considering it, even though she hated herself for it.

Would I blame her for falling for someone else and carrying on with her life, without me? No. It was only natural. Rosie had done the right thing. I hoped Bea would come round to the idea.

Those thoughts came easily without another man actually on the scene.

7

'... shown no signs of awareness in more than eighteen months patients in a vegetative state are balancing between life and death they are somewhere between consciousness and nothingness so is he in a coma no we call it permanent vegetative state coma is slightly different the patient wouldn't be awake or aware but he is awake so he can hear us no we don't think so as I said no signs of awareness since the accident we have run tests but he is not aware of his surroundings at all he does not respond ...'

I woke up groggy, with a dry mouth and aching legs. I could hear voices – one I recognized. A doctor? Two others I did not. Three men, talking a few metres away from me. They sounded similar and I could barely make out when one stopped speaking and the other began. My eyes were open enough to make out shapes moving in the doorway to my right.

I tried to strain my neck muscles, desperate to lift my head and look in their direction.

'... what happens next there's the possibility of withdrawing treatment or nutrition effectively his life support this may have to be referred to the courts that changes things yes that would change any charges I'm sorry detective I'm not sure I follow we have new information we wanted to start by seeing how Mr Jackson is doing and then shall we step into my office ...'

My door clicked shut, and the volume of the noise from the ward behind it dropped.

What's going on?

My forehead itched and tickled. Sweat breaking out.

Who are you?

The police? What 'new information' were they talking about? I waited, but they didn't come back.

They must have been police. *Charges. Information. Detective.* And there was something in the way they spoke – not just the words they used.

Were they looking at my accident again? Perhaps the insurance company needed more from them. Something wasn't right. I couldn't think why the police would be interested in me now. Maybe someone else had been injured and one of the manufacturers of my equipment was being sued.

No – it couldn't be. I knew my kit. I knew it was safe. I trusted that kit more than I trusted these policemen – that was for sure. I was still sweating, agitated by old feelings of suspicion. I'd always respected the officers I dealt with for work. I would roll my eyes when a reader called in to complain about the 'pigs', and I automatically tended to believe the police's version of events over an alleged criminal's in court. That changed when I was working on one of my last big stories, a campaign to release a convicted murderer we believed was innocent. Not only did I discover that they had blatantly coerced a murder confession out of this guy – who was learning-disabled and vulnerable – but they also tried to stop me reporting on his family's attempts to appeal. 'It's not in the public interest,' the press office had told me. 'Stirring up the idea that someone else might be responsible will only scare people unnecessarily.'

I told them they should be more concerned with working out who the real killer was than keeping me quiet. Who had really murdered Holly King? Who had beaten her to death with a spade and left her to die in a cemetery? That man was still a risk to the public. Needless to say, they didn't like me telling them how to do their job – but if they were going to try and tell me how to do mine then I was going to give as good as I got.

Ten years. This poor guy had been in prison for a decade – missed the freedom of each and every year of his twenties. So far, I'd only lost, what? Eighteen months or so? Even before the police stopped by that day, I had thought a lot about him and our parallel custodial existences. I had been right in the middle of that case when I ended up in here. Was he still stuck in a cell? Or had they got him out? The letters his mother had shown me were full of his fears, full of the physical claustrophobia, the words dark and heavy with the lack of daylight he wrote about. Within weeks of reading them I was in my unique version of his prison: my own body.

For the rest of that day I itched more than normal, along my arms and down the insides of my legs, where the skin clung together in clammy dampness. I felt as though flies covered me, walking their shit-soaked feet all over me. And they wandered into my head, too. They circled in my mind, tormenting me with questions.

It seemed like days since Bea had last visited me. She hadn't mentioned having spoken to the police, and neither had anyone else. Were my family hiding it from me, or did they not know that something was going on?

Why did nobody ever tell me anything?

Back when I still had things to lose and the ability to lose them, it would drive me nuts. Once, I spent hours looking for a small deep red sandstone pebble that I'd found at Rhossili when I was a kid, walking along the beach with Mum. She turned it in her hands and said I should keep it, that it reminded her of Ayers Rock. 'You wouldn't believe that place, Alexander, it's magical.' I didn't know anything about Ayers Rock, but I looked it up in my encyclopaedia when I got home, and after that I kept it in my school pencil case alongside my pens, set square and Tipp-Ex. When I got older, I used to leave it in the toe of one of my climbing shoes at the bottom of my wardrobe as a kind of good-luck charm.

But this one time, it got lost. I took it out of my shoe but didn't leave it in its usual place in my wardrobe. I only realised a few days later that I didn't know where it had gone. I ransacked the place – Bea came home and thought we'd been burgled. It was the loss of control, I think, that got to me. When did I last have it? Where could it be? For hours, I couldn't get past it. Those thoughts rotated in my head, those same little insistent flies.

They were at it again now. Going round and round and round. Not because I had lost something, but because of those men and their words: their meaning just out of my reach, their implication far beyond my control.

Looking back, I can see that this was the point when things changed. From then on, it wasn't just me who was in trouble.

8

Federer to serve. I'm down two sets already, and three games to love in the third.

The crowd's chatter hushes.

He drops the ball on the bright green grass in front of his feet, bounces it a couple of times. He looks at me once. He thinks he's got this.

Bring it, Roger.

His left arm shoots the ball up, while his right swings back with the racket. A mirror image – both arms now outstretched. His knees bend, weight on his toes. The racket lifts as he watches the ball loop up and then he jumps, brings the racket onto the ball, sweeps it down to his hip. His foot lands on the baseline but I don't see it – I'm watching the fluorescent yellow bullet, dancing on my toes.

This is the moment. I've lulled him into believing he can win. But he can't win. I'm the next Wimbledon champion.

I fire back the strongest forehand known to man. The crowd goes wild. He only just returns it, throwing his body across the court to swipe a backhand straight back to my racket.

I tap a drop shot which he can't reach.

Love-fifteen.

I take off my cap, wipe my forehead, wave to my adoring fans. The good things about imaginary tennis: always winning, beating the best, the ability to return impossible shots, knowing exactly where the ball is going to go and regularly doing things that are brilliant and unexpected. The only downside: you're not actually playing tennis. I'm not dancing on my toes: my feet are stuck still. They are cold. I'm not whacking backhands across the court: my arms are deadweights at my side. They only move when the physio works my joints, or the nurses roll me over.

One of the doctors gave me the idea for these pretend sporting activities. Early on, when I was still emerging from what must have been a deep coma and still regularly slipping in and out of sleep, they rolled me into another room, trolley wheels squeaking. My eyes fell open a little when they moved me, and I watched bright white shapes fly past me on the ceiling, doctors' and nurses' heads bobbing into my view like black and grey balloons drifting overhead.

They told me I was going to have a scan of my brain. Occasionally they explain things to me, like this. But not always. Not when they first came at my mouth with their suction machine, for example. I've worked out that it has to do with removing mucus from my chest, and the spit I can't swallow from inside my mouth. But that first time? I honestly thought they wanted to kill me.

Before he scanned my brain, Dr Sharma gave me a few instructions, his blurry balloon head floating over my face. The scent of soap on his skin nearly masked the room's disinfected aroma. 'We're going to put you into the MRI scanner. It will let us take a look at that brain of yours.' He sounded young, I always thought. My age. And kind – I liked him. 'We're going to try something called a functional MRI – to look at where the blood goes in your brain when we ask you to do different things.' Specks of spit landed on my face. 'Alan, if you can hear me, here's what I want you to do.'

Did you call me Alan?

'I'll talk to you through these headphones we are putting on you. The machine will be quite noisy, but we'll play you music to drown that out. When you hear my voice, I'll be asking you to do two things. First, imagine playing tennis. Really think about swinging that arm of yours. Pretend you're Tim Henman.'

'Henman? Is that the best you can think of?' This female voice came from another person leaning over me, putting headphones over my ears. I smelled coffee on her breath. 'At least you'd want a chance of winning,' she said.

'Thank you, Caroline. I'm not sure winning is the objective here.' I had learned that you can hear a person roll their eyes.

She laughed. Her coffee breath didn't repulse me – instead it felt intimate. She moved close and the room suddenly felt very warm.

'We will watch your brain on the scans,' Dr Sharma said. 'Look for signs that you are responding. If you do, we could then try using this method to help you communicate with us. Cutting-edge stuff, Alan. Your family have agreed to let us give it a go as part of our research trials.'

At last. They were going to help me talk.

'After the tennis, I will ask you to imagine you're walking through the rooms of your house. Try and really see the rooms and the furniture. This will work a different part of your brain. Just do what I say and we'll see what happens.' I felt a sudden pressure around the side of my face and Dr Sharma said, 'I'm just putting your head in a brace to keep it still. We don't want you moving around in there.'

Not much chance of that.

I felt the bed moving underneath me. I could imagine what was happening – I'd seen pictures before of patients sliding backwards into the middle of a big doughnut-shaped machine. Then the music started in my ears. Rolling Stones, 'You Can't Always Get What You Want'. Excitement raced through me. In those days I was still hopeful, and they had given me a chance to show them I was conscious. To communicate with them!

I imagined knocking balls across the court. Lifting my racket high into the air. But as I did so, a familiar feeling swept over me. A sleepiness, a heaviness.

No. Stay awake.

I swung my racket, looked frantically for the ball on the court. I couldn't see it. The neat white lines on the grass court were fading away.

No.

Why was this happening now?

The last thing I remembered before I lost consciousness was my racket being snatched away. I felt the foamy grip of its handle slide against my fingertips as I fell backwards, and down.

I woke up back in my hospital room, with my eyes closed. I could feel the daylight from a window on my left, hear the chat and movement in the ward outside the open door to my right. The smell matched the rest of the hospital, of course – apart from my flowers (roses, this time?) and my sister's Chanel No. 5 perfume that Bea and I used to buy her for birthdays and Christmases, unable to think of anything more personal for a woman we hardly spoke to.

As I drifted into awareness I heard voices, mid-conversation.

'. . . didn't respond at all. I'm sorry, Mr Jackson. Miss Jackson.' Dr Sharma was speaking to Dad and Philippa. He was matter-of-fact but sympathetic.

I fell asleep – couldn't you tell that?

'If your son was conscious then we would have hoped to see activation in a region of his brain called the supplementary motor area when we asked him to play tennis.'

They had to give me another go. They would, wouldn't they?

'And when we asked him to navigate through his house there might have been activity in the parahippocampal—'

'The what?' Philippa sounded impatient, as usual. Her voice was quick, bitter, harsh: she spoke to the doctors with the same anger that she used with me.

'The ah, what I mean is, right in the centre of the brain. Basically, the area of the brain which he would use if he was physically playing tennis would light up in our scan. The part of his brain used for spatial navigation would light up when we asked him to imagine walking round his house. But we didn't see this happening. It may well be, in part, down to the reliability of the test – it is still in development.'

I had missed my chance. I screamed at them. *I'm awake! You've got to get me out.*

My tongue lay heavy in my mouth, mocking me. It tasted of bitter antiseptic.

'So we can't try and communicate with him that way? You said we might be able to communicate.' Philippa sounded choked up.

Dr Sharma continued. 'No. I'm sorry. If – and it was a long shot – he had responded to this test, we could have tried asking him yes/no questions, asking him to imagine tennis for yes and the house for no. But it hasn't worked.'

'That's okay, thank you for trying.' Dad remained as polite as ever, his voice low and quiet. I felt like a little boy. I wanted him to put his arms around me. But instead of reaching out to me, he comforted Philippa. 'It's all right, darling. Come here.' Clip, clip, clip – her heels were loud on the floor as she moved towards him. I heard her sniffling into his shoulder as he pulled her close. I wanted that. 'It's still early days,' he said.

'Exactly, Mr Jackson. No one knows what any patient in a vegetative state is experiencing. Alan could still turn things round.'

'Alex.'

'Sorry?'

'Alex. You said Alan.'

'Did I? Terribly sorry, there's so many patients but it's no excuse—'

'Don't worry about it. Easy mistake.' In the midst of my despair I thought how the doctors must have loved my dad. I had heard relatives of other patients shout them down, and once I listened as an emotional brother pinned Dr Sharma to the wall by his neck. But not good old Dad. My dad. Would I ever speak to him again? Had I told him that I loved him? How much I appreciated him? No. I'd bottled it on several occasions, because it would have been too corny. We didn't do emotions – not me and Dad, not before all of this. When I found out that he'd won his school's Teacher of the Year award, voted for by students, I didn't tell him how much I respected him. After he gave the eulogy at Mum's funeral, defying everyone who had told him it was a bad idea and he wouldn't be able to hold it together, I hadn't told him that I was proud of him. I had never told him that if I ended up as half the man he was, I would be pleased with myself.

Philippa interrupted my list of regrets. 'Can we try the tests again? Next week?' I was always surprised that my sister was so vociferous in her demands for doctors to do everything they could to help me. 'We need to keep trying. *You* need to keep trying.'

'I did explain to your father.' Dr Sharma hesitated.

'What? What exactly did you explain to my father? Dad?'

'It's a question of funding.'

'You've got to be kidding me,' she snapped.

'I'm sorry. This is a very new test.' Dr Sharma sounded terrified of her. Your father agreed to let us try with your brother as part of our research, but that's all we can do for now – just one round.' He paused. 'We may be able to try again in a few months, but it depends on whether we get the money to continue our trials.'

I'd missed my moment. What if they didn't run the tests again?

Shit. Shit. Shit.

Tiredness overcame me. Wafts of overpowering Chanel No. 5 sedated me.

I lost consciousness again.

That was what it was like, in those very early days, long before I decided I wanted to die. I haven't always been as awake as I am now. As well as the vast holes in my memory from before the accident, there are big gaps from the start of my time in hospital when I was slipping in and out of consciousness – like that day of the initial tennis test. I have no idea when I first came round. It began with vivid dreams, waking up for what felt like a few minutes, hearing voices, and then dozing again. This time is blurred. No one clicked their fingers and turned my mind on suddenly. Each time I woke up I felt groggy, as if emerging from a general anaesthetic. I didn't know where I was, or why.

As well as experiencing the slow process of coming round from my head injuries, I now know that I must have also been suffering from frequent bouts of pneumonia; there were spells when I hallucinated for days on end and woke up with no sense of how much time had passed. It still takes me down regularly, and is the reason for me being kept in hospital for so long since my accident. The doctors say I can't be transferred to a nursing home or to my family until I have been free of any lung issues for a while.

But in those early days and weeks, my inability to move hit me far harder than the gaps in my knowledge and time.

What is happening to me? I thought, over and over. I repeated it, like a chant – semi-delirious with the painkillers they must have been pumping me full of. *What is happening to me what is happening to me what is happening to me what is happening to me.*

I could hear Bea, Dad, Philippa. Tom and Rosie. Others, too – doctors and nurses. I desperately tried to lift my arm, turn my head, somehow let them know I could hear them. But nothing seemed to have any effect. I tried to make a noise, open my mouth, grunt. That didn't work either.

The big surprise for me came when I discovered the limits of my paralysis. That moment came during an early visit from Philippa. She sat next to me and dug her talons into my arm. Her hand conducted icy coldness to my skin.

'Seriously, Alex?' she spat. 'You're an idiot for not wearing a helmet. It's your own fault you're in this mess, why would . . .'

I let her voice disappear, and focused my attention on my arm. I could feel her nails, couldn't I? Although I couldn't move, I could still feel anything that came into contact with my skin. I felt the nurse touch my shoulder, I could feel the sheets above and below me. And I could feel pain: the stab of the injections, cramp in my legs and arms, headaches.

For so many years my mind and body had worked together. I took everything for granted, from simple things like opening a tin of baked beans and walking down the road, to solving complicated climbing problems. No matter how many pull-ups I did, I would never have been able to do any of it without my mind. Climbing is about puzzles. You have to think two, three, four moves ahead. If you put your foot on that ledge, and your fingers into that gap, will you be able to reach that flake with your other hand? But now I had become my own jailer. My mind roamed free: a raging, howling beast trapped inside the cage of my body.

Crying appeared to be the sole thing I *could* do: real tears rolled down my face when I was sad or in terrible pain. But they – the nurses, my family, Bea – would wipe them away, thinking my eyes were watering. They never spotted that there was a link between my tears and what they were saying or doing.

'It's amazing, isn't it?' one nurse said in those early months, after describing her busy weekend of socialising – the type of weekend I thought I would never have again. I was suddenly overwhelmed by the loss of everything I had valued in my life. 'He's completely out of it but here he is, crying like a baby. Isn't it amazing what the human body will do, all of its own accord?'

Why had everyone written me off like this? I couldn't understand. But then, I didn't know what the diagnosis should be, either. My symptoms didn't fit with any illness I had ever heard of. I remember the day I heard my official status for the first time. One of my nurses was briefing a new member of the team.

'. . . he was taken off the ventilator a while back now but still has his tracheostomy. He's been in a vegetative state for three months, so we need to keep an eye on the usual – pressure sores, phlegm build-up . . .'

Vegetative state?

My mouth went dry and my heart began to beat quicker. It couldn't be that. I could hear them. A vegetative state? Like a coma? What had happened to me?

The nurses kept talking but my ears filled with a high-pitched buzzing as they grew hotter and hotter.

What's happening to me?

It soon became pretty clear, from what I heard the doctors say, that I might never regain control of my body again. Not being able to walk, run, climb, have sex: that amounted to a life I could not bear to consider or accept. Before all of this, I never sat still. I got things done. Which gave me another reason to give up trying.

Could I hope for nothing better than communicating with them, one day? I didn't think that would satisfy me. If I had lost my body, I would lose my mind. I was done.

After the first tennis test I had hoped and hoped for another chance. Another go at the game. But it came too late. By the time it did, I didn't want to play. After Bea started going to grief counselling, Dr Sharma told my dad that they had more funding approved. Would he let them run more tests on me? Dad agreed, and the doctors wheeled me into the MRI machine again, stuck headphones on me and played the radio through them to dampen the noise of the scanner. New songs I had never heard filled my head. When they asked me to start a rally, I ignored them. I imagined myself in a white-walled room, and made my mind go blank. My heart cracked when the doctor gave my father the results – still no sign of life. He wept this time. I tried not to hear him, but I couldn't block it out.

It wasn't an easy decision to make – it meant giving up on the hope of ever speaking to Bea again, of ever climbing again. But once I made it, I refused to indulge myself in grief. Every time I had a weak moment and tried to speak when my dad came into the room, desperate for him to hug me, I repeated my mantra. *It's the right thing to do. It's the strong thing to do. Man up, Alex.* I told myself I wasn't giving up on life. Did this even count as life? I could breathe on my own. My heart beat freely. My brain functioned. But this didn't feel like being alive. It lacked, amongst other things, one huge and vital element: acknowledgement that I existed.

I found it easy to fall into step with other people's view of me. They all seemed so convinced of my brain's inactivity that I started to believe it myself.

What I hadn't understood yet, when I refused to participate in that second round of tennis tests, was that my body wouldn't let me give up so easily. In the weeks that followed that visit from the police – while they were busy unearthing evidence in a case that would turn out to be more complex than even they could have imagined – I had my own set of discoveries to make. I was about to find out that we all have an instinct to defend ourselves when we are put in danger. Even when there is very little we can do to fight, we will still try.

9

I kept waiting for Dad or Phil to mention why the detectives had been talking to my medical team, but neither of them did. They continued in the normal, yet unique, pattern of their interactions with me. Everyone's visits were different. In the early days Phil used to talk to me, even if most of what she said was borderline aggressive. 'Don't you dare die on us,' and 'You'd better be getting well in there.' Or, 'You can't leave me to look after Dad on my own. Don't even think about it.' But the underlying message was always that she wanted me to wake up. When she spoke to my doctors she insisted they try every new treatment possible, suggesting things they might have missed. It seemed that she did care about me, after all. She may have been pissed off with me, but she wanted the opportunity to say that to my face when I regained consciousness.

Now she had given up hectoring me. As time went on she visited less, spoke less, and stopped telling me to get better. The only explanation I could come up with was that she was losing hope for that face-to-face confrontation. Perhaps she was trying to wean herself off these hospital trips, in preparation for a time when there would be no one to visit any more.

I always knew when it was her – she was the only woman in high heels to come into the room on her own. There were clipped and elegant footsteps from a female doctor, too, but she was always with a colleague and made much more noise than Philippa. I had no other stiletto-wearing visitors – the thought of Bea in anything other than trainers was laughable. I used to tease Bea by saying her glamour had attracted me to her, and she'd respond by throwing a cushion or book at me with terrifying accuracy and force. She and Philippa were about as different as two women could be.

Philippa would stride in with quiet, businesslike purpose and a choking Chanel breeze. My little sister was the definition of a fiery redhead – something passed down the female line in Dad's family. I'd been blessed with the same hair, but thankfully not their special brand of blazing, angry oestrogen. Whatever was behind the decrease in frequency of her visits and words, I knew one thing: she was still angry. She may have been furious with me for getting myself into this situation, but I got the feeling she was even more annoyed that I wasn't getting myself out of it. Rage was the only way Philippa knew to handle difficult emotions. Once more, she was lashing out at the very person she was afraid to lose. Not that she would ever have admitted it.

These days she never stopped at the end of my bed, but walked straight round to my left-hand side, where there was a table with a vase on it. She always brought a new bunch of flowers, but none of them smelled like love; there was a whiff of guilt and duty about them. Once she'd replaced last week's bunch I heard the crackle and thud of the plastic rubbish bag as she chucked them into the bin in the corner. I never heard her sit down. She'd probably come straight from the office and didn't want to crease her designer clothes. She would stand still for several minutes at a time. Was she watching me? What was she thinking? I tried to understand what might be happening in her life, but she never told me, and Dad never filled me in. Bea had an even more difficult relationship with her than I did, and the accident hadn't brought them any closer. Did Philippa have a boyfriend waiting back home? Where was she working these days? Still in family law? I imagined her watching the clock, calculating when her duty was done and she could forget about how mad I made her for another week or so.

We used to be so close. One of the last memories I had of things being good between us was the day I told Philippa that Mum was ill, when I went to pick her up from school. She knew something was up as soon as she saw me – she usually walked home alone. She caught my eye from across the road as she came out of the school gates, cocked her head and looked at me curiously. She said goodbye to her friends distractedly, without looking away from me. 'Why are you here?' she mouthed. I just smiled, and started walking.

'What's going on?' Philippa asked, jogging along behind me.

My mouth was dry. Why had I offered to do this? 'She'll find it easier, coming from you,' Dad had said. He would be sitting at home with Mum, now, waiting nervously for us to get home – although he'd given me twenty quid to take Philippa for some food if she needed more time to get her head straight.

'Don't freak out.' Bad start. Why had I said that? She manoeuvred herself in front of me and reached out to my chest.

'Stop. Tell me.'

'There's a bench over there.' I pointed into the park we were passing. 'Let's sit down.'

'You're scaring me,' she said, following me.

When we sat down, she tried to make eye contact. I looked away. 'Mum isn't well,' I went on, and kept staring at my fingers twisting in my lap as I gave her the full explanation that Dad had given me after he'd asked for me to be sent home from school.

When I finished, she didn't say anything, so I looked sideways at her. She'd turned her face away and she was gripping the edge of the bench with both hands. 'It'll probably all be okay,' I said. 'She'll probably be fine.'

She pulled her sleeve down over her fist and used it to wipe her face. 'I knew something was up,' she said.

I squeezed her arm, but it felt inadequate.

'It was only a matter of time, I suppose,' she said, coughing, wiping at her face again, and turning towards me. 'Nearly everyone at school knows someone with cancer. It was just a matter of who it would get in our family.'

I smiled, despite myself. I should have known she would come out with something like that – Philippa never said quite what you expected her to, and had always been old for her years. She seemed to be taking it well; maybe we didn't need to go for dinner before we headed home. I put my arm around her.

'Don't let her die,' she whispered. 'Promise me you won't let her die. Not my mum.'

'I won't.'

It was a promise that I hadn't been able to keep.

Our relationship deteriorated after Mum's diagnosis, when Philippa started acting up. And then Mum's death – and my part in it – fractured any remaining bonds between us.

I tried to make it better. Every time I attempted to speak to her she shut me down. While I was in Canada and then at uni in London, she didn't reply to my emails. Whenever I called home she would get Dad to tell me she was too busy to speak to me, and she avoided me when I was back for the holidays. So then, I tried giving her space, but that didn't change anything, either. I wrote her a long letter in my second year of university, when she was a fresher in Newcastle, explaining why I had done what I had done, apologising for upsetting her, and saying that Mum wouldn't want us to still be fighting about it. She never even acknowledged that she had received it.

Then, finally, I tried pretending that everything was okay. That seemed to work for her. When we were both at home, I didn't mention Mum – we just chatted blandly about neutral topics. Dad looked pleased that we were talking, at last, but it was superficial. Eventually she moved back to Bristol too, wanting to be closer to him, and we would occasionally meet for lunch at a café halfway between our offices. I used to say to Bea that I thought she only did it to keep Dad happy. She had one soft spot that I was aware of, and that was him.

These lunches were only just civil – Philippa clearly still hated me. She usually found a way to take her simmering feelings out on me by criticising my hobbies ('You're not still climbing, are you? Aren't you getting too old?'), slagging off Bea ('She just doesn't seem your type, that's all'), telling me I didn't do enough to help Dad ('When was the last time you offered to mow the lawn?'), and – her favourite – picking out faults in my court reports. She would bring a copy of the paper along to our catch-ups, and my latest article would be covered in red pen. I did my best to bite my tongue, because the point of these lunch breaks was to keep things friendly between us, not to make things worse. But it was hard, because although she had never set foot in a criminal court, she always thought she knew better than me. Tactfully, I tried to suggest that things might be different in county court, where she spent her time dealing with things like custody battles, divorces and prenups.

How long would we have been able to keep those polite coffee shop conversations up? I was convinced that one of us would have cracked, eventually. Would our relationship ever have returned to how it had been before Mum's cancer?

Lying in my hospital bed as Philippa stood silently, watching me, I often wondered if she was thinking the same thing.

Then there was Dad – another type of visitor entirely. I listened over the months as his uneven tread worsened – the coins in his trouser pockets clinked in a jagged rhythm as he moved. Was there a problem with his leg, or his hip? I would feel my mattress sink as he put one hand on my bed to lower himself into the chair. He sometimes chatted, but I almost wished he wouldn't. He told me about his new students, the big news stories of the day, what was happening in the Premier League. He never mentioned having close contact with anyone other than Philippa. Through the mundane and lonely updates, the pain strained his voice, betraying what he was really thinking.

On most visits, he used to get his book out to read to me. I got snippets of good stories which succeeded in taking me into them and away from myself, but he clearly didn't think I could hear. He never started from the beginning or took me right through to the end. And he never told me the name of the book. I knew what happened in the middle of a spy thriller set in Amsterdam, the end of what seemed to be a wartime crime novel about a family hiding a German soldier, and only the opening chapter of a book he introduced as 'the one everyone was talking about'.

Very occasionally he brought his guitar to play to me, as I'd loved him to when I was a boy. 'They say it might help,' he would offer by way of an introduction. 'How about some Beatles?' It was always the Beatles; he knew most of their hits. Without fail, he played my favourite, 'Let It Be', a song that I once told him had taken on new meaning for me after Mum died. I read once that Paul McCartney was referring to his mother, not making a biblical allusion. She died of cancer when he was a teenager, and he wrote the song after having a dream about her where she said, 'It'll be all right. Let it be.' I wanted a dream like that with my mum in it.

I had other visitors. Rosie and Tom came in regularly, and always together, normally in the middle of an argument. Then there was Auntie Lisa – Philippa and I always used to call her Lisa Loudmouth when we were kids. She brought in muffins that smelled fresh and nutty for the nurses and doctors, and I would hear her laughing with them in the corridor. 'Got to keep you all well fed with all this hard work you have to do. Go on, take a second one for later . . .' Then she'd shut the door behind her and sit in complete silence by my side. She had words for every situation but this one, it seemed. There were a few more random familiar voices – other members of the climbing club, old work colleagues – but they became rarer as time went by. Most didn't come back after their first time. I lost count of the number of friends who came in the early days, took one look at me, said 'Oh my God' and then stood awkwardly at the end of the bed for the shortest amount of time possible before they could justify leaving. 'We brought you this, thought it would cheer you up . . .' they might say, leaving an unnamed and completely useless gift on my table. It was only when one of the nurses came in and said something along the lines of, 'Who left these CDs here?' or 'I'm not sure you really need this TV guide, do you, Alex?' that I would find out what I had been given.

My climbing partner Eleanor came in every now and then and told me things she wouldn't ordinarily say to anyone. She confessed to one-night stands; admitted when she had voted for UKIP (and then regretted it); she even told me once that sometimes she wished her father would die, because it was the only way she could see herself being able to get over their difficult relationship. Quite early on in my confinement, she also revealed why she had stopped climbing for a few months in the year before my accident. At the time she'd said she had tendonitis in her elbow. Looking back, I could see that she had gone to great lengths to convince me that this was the case. When I went round to her flat to see how she was doing, she would bring out an ice pack or do a series of stretches. But I only saw her a handful of times – whenever I called she was seeing other friends and when I tried to suggest she come round for dinner with me and Bea, or out for a pint with me and Tom, we could never find a time when she was free. I didn't think much of it at the time, but it all fell into place when she came into my hospital room one day and made another confession.

She had been sitting, without saying anything, in the chair next to me for several minutes. I knew it was her from the small noises she had made, her sniffs and sighs. Several times she had seemed about ready to say something – and then stopped. When she did speak, it came out in a rush.

'I don't know why I feel the need to tell you this,' she said. 'But I had a massive crush on you last year. I thought I loved you.'

She was joking. She had to be joking. Me?

'I guess I always thought I would tell you one day, and we could have laughed about it. I guess that's why I want to tell you, get it out in the open. I never told anyone else.' She stood up and walked a few steps away from me.

How had I known nothing about this? I had never had any indication from her that she wanted to be anything more than friends.

'That's why I stopped climbing.' She sniffed. 'There was no tendonitis. I just couldn't be around you every weekend. It was driving me crazy. I thought I'd be better off without you in my life. If I couldn't be with you like that, then—'

This is madness, Eleanor. What were you thinking?

'It took me those few months to sort my head out. When I started again I thought I was over you, and I really missed going climbing – I thought it would be okay.'

I never led you on, did I? I didn't make you think something could have happened between us.

'I wouldn't have done anything to try to split you and Bea up. If you'd been single, then maybe, but I couldn't say anything.' She walked back towards my bed, and put a hand on my arm.

It felt strange, her touching me, after she'd said this. I didn't like it. I didn't feel the same way about her, and it felt somehow like I was being dishonest to Bea. It was the kind of thing that I would have told Bea about if it had happened in 'normal' life. It would have felt wrong to keep it from her, even if it had made things difficult with Eleanor.

'I wish I could talk to you about it and we could have a laugh, you'd tell me I was an idiot and we could move on,' she said, without taking her fingers away.

'That day. I can't stop thinking about the noise you made, when you hit the rock. It isn't getting any better; I dream about it, I hear that sound whenever someone drops something on the floor, when a car door slams.' This was to become a theme in her visits – she went over it nearly every time. 'How could you have slipped so badly?'

The way she spoke about it naturally led me to assume I had fallen because of a terrible mistake I couldn't remember making. And, in some twisted way, I had.

10

It was possible that Dad and Philippa would not mention this 'new information' the police had about my accident. But I thought I could rely on Bea to tell me.

If Eleanor's visits were among some of the worst after her revelation about her feelings for me, Bea's had always been the best. She would come in about three times a week, and I hated it when she left. I wished she would crawl her little body into my bed and fall asleep with me. She talked and talked – more than she ever did before. When I got home from work she would often still be sitting at her desk, working on a magazine illustration or a logo design for a new restaurant. She would raise her green eyes to me behind her glasses, just for a moment to say hello, but I knew not to speak to her until she finished. And even when we did discuss our days, it was always me that did most of the talking. Since I found myself in hospital, she'd spared no details. She let me into her mind, told me how she felt and what she saw and re-enacted whole conversations, leaving me exhausted after the onslaught of life-lived detail. This new version of her made me fall in love with her a second time.

The first time was not long after we first met, but still a good two years before anything happened between us. Her prettiness hadn't escaped my attention in the first couple of weeks in

Canada – but I first really noticed her when we took a group of kids hiking up to the Grassi Lakes. The trail took us up through forests to look down over two small, spectacular pools of bright blue. We sat above the upper lake, sorting out a picnic lunch for the group, and as I jealously watched other hikers setting up their kit to take on steep climbs on the grey cliffs towering over us I promised myself I would come back on my next day off. Bea came over to sit next to me.

'You're the climber, aren't you?' she asked, through a mouthful of ham sandwich. 'I don't think we've properly met yet.'

'That's me. And you're the Spanish girl.'

She rolled her eyes.

'What?' I asked. 'Aren't you Beatriz? Beatriz R—'. I stumbled on the surname.

'Romero.' She shook her head, swallowing her food. 'Spanish name. Doesn't make me Spanish, as such.'

'But your first name is Spanish too, right?'

'Dad got all sentimental when I arrived, you know? Named me after his great-grandmother. He can't pronounce it, though – he can order a beer in Spanish and ask for the bill but that's as far as it goes. He says *Beatrice*, like you just did.' She raised an eyebrow.

'So, it's not Beatrice?'

She shook her head.

'What's the right way of saying it?'

'Bay. Uh. Trees.' She laughed at the concentrated expression on my face, my lips silently repeating her pronunciation. 'But don't worry about it. Just call me Bea. As in bumble bee. You should be able to manage that.'

I nodded slowly. 'Okay, so you're the girl with the Spanish name, who isn't actually Spanish, who smokes outside the back of the counsellors' dorm when she thinks everyone else is in bed.'

Her eyes widened behind her black-rimmed glasses. 'You're thinking of someone else.'

'Maybe.' I laughed.

'Anyway,' she waved her hand. 'You want to go and see the pictographs? I'm taking the older ones up there.' She pointed her thumb over her shoulder.

'Pictographs?'

'Rock paintings. Cave art.'

'I know what they are, but how – I mean, how did you find out about them?'

'I read about it. I love this kind of stuff.'

'Right, okay.'

'You coming?' She got up, and walked away. I followed. Out of everyone at camp, I expected to have the least in common with her. But I was my father's son: a geography geek obsessed with rocks and anything to do with them.

I joined the group of kids heading off to see the pictographs. At the far end of the lake we found a set of steps that led us through the canyon. Soon we came to a huge boulder and gathered round the drawings. I moved past a couple of bored-looking teenage girls to stand beside Bea.

I touched the rock next to the painted figure, which seemed to be holding a hoop or a drum. 'Wow.'

'Amazing, isn't it?' She turned to me and smiled. The kids next to us were posing for photos, replicating the stance of the figure in the paintings. She laughed and turned back to the rock. 'It's hundreds of years old. They reckon this is red ochre. Apparently painted by the Hopi people, which means this is probably a medicine man.' She pointed to the figure with a hoop.

She leaned in to study it more closely, shifting her glasses up onto her forehead and then back down in front of her eyes.

'They reckon it was painted with their fingers because, look . . .'

As much as I wanted to look at the paintings, I couldn't take my eyes off her.

But there was a point when the nature of Bea's visits shifted – not long after I'd overheard the detective. Although the change occurred almost imperceptibly, with little else to concentrate on I noticed it clearly. Perhaps it became apparent in the way she paused more often as she spoke, or the way she started sentences but didn't finish them. I felt like, from that moment, I only ever got half the story from her. Could it have something to do with the police? I listened carefully every time she visited, waiting for any hint or unintended slip.

The day after her second round of counselling, she walked in, kissed my forehead as usual – with minty lips – and explained that she had been nervous about going back.

'I tried to keep my mouth shut this time,' she said, stroking my hand. The nurses had rolled me onto my right side and as Bea shifted in the chair in front of me, I listened, urging my eyes to open so I might get a hazy glimpse of her.

'It was all right, but then afterwards . . .' She sighed. 'I decided not to go back. So at the end, I went to tell the woman running it.'

She sat quietly for a moment. I heard a scrape and a twist and then a chemical smell hit me.

'I can't remember if I described her before. She's about my age, always looks angry about something. She has this really unsettling manner, the way she looks at you and stares . . .'

What have you got there?

'. . . she was a big part of why I didn't want to go back. For a grief counsellor she was incredibly unfriendly . . .'

What is that smell?

'Daniella – that's this woman – took it really personally. "You can't expect results after two sessions," she says to me . . .'

The fumes got stronger and I saw a flash of Philippa as a teenage girl with her ginger bobbed hair, sitting at the kitchen table admiring her nails.

'. . . I apologised over and over, but still said I couldn't . . .'

Was Bea painting her nails? She never did that.

'Then this guy comes over – one of the others. He gave me a cup of tea, and she just walked off.'

The smell made me feel queasy, suddenly aware that my cheek burned where it squashed against the pillow and conscious of the way my scalp itched around the edges of my face.

'. . . looked like I needed rescuing. But then I got stuck with him.'

This caught my attention. A knight in shining armour. He liked the look of her, clearly. Why did Bea never see through these acts of apparent kindness? I was always the one to break it to her when she came home and said she'd met a 'lovely man' who she had a 'nice conversation with'. She was oblivious to chat-up techniques. I'd always found it endearing, but then I'd never felt threatened before.

'We started chatting and he told me how his wife died about six years ago, how he had been to counselling before, but this was his first session with us.'

Tell me you know he was trying to pick you up.

'After his wife died, he eventually met this other woman and they were planning to start a family, but she left him.'

A proper sob story.

'It was a bit full on. I was trying to find a way to get out of there but he wouldn't stop talking.'

Sleazebag. I supposed some blokes would see this kind of group as a hunting ground full of vulnerable women looking for some comfort. Maybe his wife wasn't even dead. Maybe he'd never been married. At least Bea didn't seem too interested in him.

'He asked where I'd met you. He's travelled round the Rockies too. He's been all over the place, Europe, Asia . . .'

A man of the world. How sophisticated.

'He's a bit older than us – maybe early forties? A tall guy, kind of strong-looking.'

She paused again and I felt a change in the room. Every other noise faded away. The smell lost its significance.

Why do you care about what he looked like?

In my mind I saw her blushing as this man stood next to her. I saw her looking at his muscular arms.

'I guess you have to be strong in his line of work – he's a builder or something. But get this. He wears his hair in a pony-tail. Not like a long, lanky thing down his back or anything – it's a more of a hipster kind of look, you know? He has a beard too. You'd have a field day taking the piss.'

I didn't feel like laughing. This wasn't the kind of man I was hoping she'd find.

She put her fingers against my exposed cheek. Her skin felt cool and soft, and I let myself enjoy it. I could smell that chemical scent on her – I was right, it was definitely nail polish – and her favourite lavender hand cream. But then I caught something else too.

Is that caramel? Vanilla? Perfume?

She never wore perfume. She used to say that she didn't need any – her citrusy shampoo and 'Eau de Bea' were enough.

'When I told Cameron I wasn't coming again, he said that it was sometimes more helpful to meet people one-to-one.' She took her hand away. 'He said it helps in a different way.'

I'm sure.

'He asked me if I wanted to meet up for a coffee. I tried to say I was busy and stuff, but we ended up swapping numbers. It was too awkward not to.'

Nice move. Dickhead.

'I'm definitely not going back,' she said. 'God, I hope he doesn't call.'

My heart punched against my ribs.

You want him to call.

She had enjoyed the attention. She overplayed the line about this guy being 'full on', and about not wanting to meet up with him. She liked him. Maybe she hadn't worked it out yet, but it was clear to me. She liked him.

My head filled with unwanted images. Bea in the arms of another man. Him kissing her. Holding her. More.

I'd never had any reason to feel jealous before. Sure, there had been times when a guy would approach her in a bar, or I'd see her getting on really well with someone at a party. But she always made it so clear that she was only interested in me that I never felt the need to worry. It was only now, hearing about her encounter with this Cameron guy, that I got a taste of what I had put her through in the first year of our relationship while I was in London, when I'd found myself in that girl Josie's bed. It was a rare example of me not putting a difficult conversation off: after waking up that morning, being reassured by Josie that we hadn't actually gone all the way, and sobering up a bit, I skipped my lectures and drove straight back to Bristol to confess.

It hadn't gone well. I grovelled, I promised never to do it again, I cried and begged her to forgive me. After showing me the door, she ignored my texts and calls for two days, and when she did eventually pick up, she made it very clear that I only had one more chance, which she was only giving me because I had been honest about what had happened. We didn't speak about Josie again and things started to go back to normal. But a couple of weeks later Bea phoned me. 'I just can't stop thinking about you with her. That's the worst thing – how you must have looked at her. What you must have been thinking.'

Bea had always been unwaveringly loyal. She had never put

me in the kind of position I'd put her in. What I didn't know then was that, despite being confined to a hospital bed, I was about to put her through much worse, all over again.

So was this encounter with Cameron part of my payback? My turn to be tormented with thoughts of her with someone else?

Since hearing about her conversation with Rosie about moving on, I had filled my head with noble wishes. What is it that they say? Loving someone means knowing when to let them go. That was my sentiment. I thought that equated to bravery. Martyring myself.

But hearing her talk about him, I saw my mistake. Even though I wanted to die, I wanted to do so as her boyfriend. Yes, it sounded selfish. But she would have all the time in the world to find a new guy, later, when I didn't have to know about it.

Loving someone means knowing when to let them go? Bullshit.

You don't let them go. You fight for them. Let them be the ones to choose whether or not they want you.

11

I'm painting a bleak picture of my existence here, but that's not entirely fair. No matter how much bad news I get in one day, no matter how uncomfortable I am, I have learned that life has its ways of sending something small your way to provide the relief you need to make it through another twenty-four hours. It's something I'll take away from here with me, if I ever get out. At any given moment, within a certain undefinable radius of your sorry body or soul, there will be something that can lift you. The trick is knowing where to look.

I'm in no position to go hunting out one of these small comforts when I need it, but if I were able to walk out of my hospital room I know who I would look for: Pauline. At times my favourite nurse feels like the closest friend I have, these days. That's not to say I don't appreciate visits from Tom and Bea and Dad, but there's something in the sheer amount of time she spends with me, the way she talks to me, and the experiences she has shared with me, that makes me feel connected to her in a different way.

She only has to walk into my room and I feel a little bit better. For a start, she smells motherly and comforting, like marzipan – I love it when she leans over me, and I let myself imagine sitting down to a slice of Battenberg. In those days after Bea told me about the guy hitting on her, it was Pauline who cheered me up.

'There's a right to-do down the corridor, I'm telling you,' she said one morning as she gently brushed my hair. She was the only one of them who bothered to do this. It felt good: as close to a head massage as I ever got.

'I don't know why I find it so funny,' she laughed. She wasn't usually one for gossip, but this had clearly entertained her too much for her not to share with someone. 'One of the older men down the corridor – well, I say older, but he must be about the same age as me. Sixty going on sixteen, he is. Keeps proposing to all the nurses.' She smoothed my eyebrows with her fingers, and laughed again, quietly. 'A regular Romeo. We don't get many folk who are so well as him in this ward, I can tell you. No offence, my love.'

None taken.

'And such a joker. It's the way he wraps himself in that bed sheet that gets me. Top to toe, like a mummy.' She was almost crying with laughter now. 'We have to peel it back to check on him, and he's always pulling a silly face when you get the sheet down past his chin.'

I wasn't convinced it was that funny, but maybe you had to see it to get the full comic effect. Nonetheless, I let Pauline's amusement seep into me and allow a little light into my dark.

Something as small as this – not even finding something particularly funny myself, but being around someone who did. It's a trite thing to say, but laughter really is infectious.

'Now, that's better, isn't it?' she asked. 'We need to have you looking your best for when you're ready to start proposing to us yourself.'

Still got it, have I, Pauline?

'Let's have a look at the rest of you,' Pauline said, running a hand down the stubble of my cheeks towards my jaw, and stopping by my mouth. 'Collecting some dust there, are we, my love? Saving a snack for later?' She swept a finger over my lips, and I permitted myself the fantasy of imagining she could feel me trying to move them, to say thank you.

For a long time I didn't know what exactly had put me on this ward with its changing cast of patients and under the care of my consultant Mr Lomax, Dr Sharma and the less distinguishable team of more junior doctors like Quiet Doc. From comments people made, I knew that I'd fallen in a climbing accident – but other than that I had no idea. My memory was blank. What route did we climb that day? The Crum? Gronk? How had I managed to have such a serious fall that I ended up like this? Now I knew that something had happened that meant that the police were involved again, a year and a half after the event. It had to be an insurance issue, didn't it?

Eleanor finally filled in a few of the details for me. She stopped by around the time of Bea's second counselling session, sniffling away with hay fever. Yet again, I assumed my role as a priest behind a metal grate, hearing confession. 'Forgive me, Alex, for I have sinned. It has been five weeks since I last came here to offload my problems on you.' She was talking about her ex, Jimmy. I wondered if things hadn't worked out between them because of how she felt about me.

I listened to her bunged-up voice behind me as I lay on my right side. 'I know I should be over him . . .' she said, shuffling around the room.

'It's hard, though, when you don't meet anyone else . . .'

I let my attention drift. Had I just not seen this side to her before – or had she changed since I had been hospitalised? We'd climbed together for about five years, ever since my previous partner moved away. I'd known her for a while before that, climbing indoors over the winter with her as part of a bigger group of friends. She was tiny and not particularly muscular, but she had such great technique that she was able to get up most of the same climbs as me. While I looked for a new partner I tried climbing with a few different people, and the reason I enjoyed partnering up with her the best was because she was solid, trustworthy, and didn't make a fuss. Tom, for all his good qualities, could get really wound up when he was struggling with a particular climb. Eleanor just got on with it. Alberto – who ended up becoming Tom's climbing buddy – would get pissed off with me for being late (I often was). Eleanor never seemed to care. Another girl I tried climbing with spent the entire car journey to and from South Wales talking at me. She was fun to be around in small doses or when diluted by other people – but one-on-one it was too much. When Eleanor got in my car the first time we went out together, she stuck a CD in the player and only spoke to talk about a new route she'd heard of and wanted to try. And that was what she had been like ever since: constant, calm, no big dramas. So what had changed? Maybe she had been bottling all these thoughts up over the years, and now, finally, she had found a way to let it all out.

'Sometimes I think I should have just . . .'

I should have been more sympathetic, but I couldn't find the strength. Here she stood: perfectly healthy. She was still able to have a relationship with someone, hold them, kiss them . . . Just because she couldn't have Jimmy any more didn't make me feel sorry for her. She was still walking, talking. Still climbing. I could see her in my mind – skinny-limbed, her long blonde hair tied back, moving lightly up the rock face. Still moving, still climbing. Every self-absorbed word she said made me angrier and amplified the throbbing ache in my feet and hands. I'd never noticed that her voice was so nasal before – and not just because of her allergies. It was so whining. I couldn't bear to listen to it.

'And I know he isn't seeing anyone either . . .'

I used to think I had things to be unhappy about. I had no idea how fortunate I was. 'Glass half-empty?' I wanted to yell at my old self, and Eleanor. 'Fucking fill it up then! It's half-empty because you've already drunk a load of it!' I couldn't find any reserves of compassion to draw on.

I felt her touch my shoulder. I really wished she wouldn't touch me.

'. . . need to go over what happened to you, remember exactly what I saw . . .'

She squeezed at the material covering my collarbone.

What? What are you talking about now?

'. . . ready to go back over my statement . . .'

Statement?

Her hand moved away. I heard a creak behind me as she sat down, and the sound of skin smoothing over paper.

She started reading, '"A Bristol journalist is fighting for his life in hospital after a rock-climbing accident in the Avon Gorge."'

An intro. A news article, about me? Was this from the papers after I fell?

'"Alex Jackson, twenty-seven, is believed to have fallen nearly twenty metres when he was out climbing with friends on Saturday morning, on the cliff face above the Portway."'

Twenty? How had I managed to fall twenty metres?

'"Members of the Avon Fire and Rescue Service rope rescue team and the Great Western Ambulance Service hazardous area response team were lowered to Mr Jackson. They safely lowered him the rest of the way down the cliffs to the Portway. He was then taken to hospital by ambulance. Police closed the Clifton Suspension Bridge for approximately three hours."'

Images skidded through my mind. I had seen the rescue teams at work before, I could imagine them lowering me down carefully, people watching from above and below.

' "It is not known how he came to fall. Mr Jackson is a reporter at the *Bristol Post*, where he has worked for four years." '

Eleanor shook the cutting next to my ear and I felt the tiny breeze it generated.

' "A spokesperson for Great Western Ambulance Service said: 'We were called at about midday to the Portway, where a man in his twenties had fallen as he was rock-climbing. He was taken by ambulance to Southmead Hospital.' His condition is described as life-threatening at this time." '

I wondered who they'd got to write this. How they had all reacted in the office. When did they find out?

She sniffed, then read on. ' "His immediate next of kin have been informed." '

Dad. Who had told Dad? How had I never thought about all of this before? Had someone called him? Poor Dad. He would have been a mess.

' "A spokesman for Bristol Climbing Association spoke last night on behalf of Mr Jackson's family. He said Mr Jackson was in a serious condition in hospital, having broken five ribs, his left arm, and sustained head injuries in the fall." '

I cringed. Who had written this crap? Head injuries should come at the start of the list. Most serious first. Had they let a trainee write about me?

' "The spokesman said: 'Alex is currently in a coma. Friends and family are keeping vigil at his bedside and are hopeful about his recovery.' Police also attended the scene of the incident." '

How have I never heard any of this before?

'The sound you made.' She was straying away from the article, back into the information I already knew. 'No matter how many times I go over it I can't understand what happened. Tom says there's nothing I could have done differently even if I had led the climb that day, instead of you.'

I was leading?

This was news to me. I'd assumed I probably was – I led most of our climbs. But this was another small piece in the puzzle of that day, and it helped me imagine it better.

'It was an awful time,' Eleanor said, with a sigh. 'I was a mess. And then Jimmy said he was moving out . . .'

Whine, whine, whine.

With that final burst of rage, cramp kicked in, gripping my left calf first, then the right. It's bad enough when you can stretch it out, or hobble around the room. But lying there, forced to let it do its worst, unchallenged – the agony mauled me.

I must have passed out with the pain. The next thing I knew, a nurse was moving me roughly on my bed.

'Come on, you fucking ugly ginger donkey,' she muttered, pulling me by my arm so I fell violently onto my back. I recognised my nickname, and the prawn cocktail flavouring on her breath was a giveaway too. This was Connie – my least favourite member of staff on the ward. I guessed she must be in her thirties or forties, based on the sound of her voice and some of the things she said. She didn't talk about going clubbing or the difficulties of still living at home with her parents, like some of the younger nurses did. But she also didn't mention how many years she had until retirement, like some of the more mature ones. Mostly, she moaned and gossiped, and talked about TV shows she had been watching. She always smelled of her latest snack and had – how can I put this? – a special bedside manner. It would be so easy for her to put me out of my misery by holding a pillow over my face. I often wondered why she didn't.

She yanked at my arm again. My whole body tensed in pain: my hips were still twisted to the right and my head felt unsupported by the new positioning of my neck.

All I could hear other than Connie's laboured breathing was the tapping of rain at the window. I tried to listen for any sign of Eleanor. She must have already gone.

'Why they keep you alive I do not know.' Connie moved to the foot of the bed, grabbed my legs and straightened them out with a sharp tug. 'Shitting hell.' The door slammed.

Trying to distract myself from the discomfort she had induced, I replayed Eleanor's visit. She had said she was giving another statement, hadn't she? Piecing together the police investigation now, I realise that at this point they were still fishing around. At the time I guessed they must be wanting to gather everything there was to know about the climb – but now I see that wouldn't have been their primary concern. What they wanted from Eleanor were the other things she might let slip.

And then there was the article Eleanor had been looking at.

Had anyone read it to me all that time ago? Would they have bothered?

I didn't remember the quotes about my condition, or the details of my other injuries. Had I even known that I broke ribs and my arm? Maybe not – I didn't know how long I had been here before I started to become aware of what was going on. I remembered it had felt like weeks and weeks after I did start to come to before I knew what the hell had happened to me. It would become clear that I didn't really understand it, even at this point. The newspaper report couldn't tell me the most important part of the story.

'This weather,' Bea said when she visited, not long after Eleanor. She paused every few words to chew her gum noisily – a horrible habit, but she said it helped her resist smoking too many roll-ups. 'It's creeping me out,' chew, chew, chew, 'it feels like a bad omen.'

I heard the sound of a zip and felt a sudden shower of tiny, cold drops of water on my left arm. I imagined her sliding her arms awkwardly out of the sleeves of her mac. The water felt good – refreshing.

'Look at that sky – it's like night-time in the middle of the day. It's unnatural.'

Her tone changed as she turned away from me, perhaps looking out of the window at the sky she described. It became too much for me. Thirst ravaged me: my tongue shrivelled in my mouth and my throat screamed with rawness. Before she arrived I had entertained fantasies of an ice-cold bottle of Corona with a neat wedge of lime shoved into its neck. I felt the bubbles on my tongue, the sourness of the fruit. But now, with all this talk of rain, I saw myself walking out of the room – escaping under the nurses' noses. Running down the hospital corridors and out onto the road outside. I turn my head up to the deep purple sky and open my mouth wide, letting it fill with rainwater, gulping it down. My hospital gown is soaked, clinging to my skin, but I don't care. The water overflows from my mouth and runs down my chin, my cheeks, down my neck. I look at the ground and see puddles forming in the bright green grass at the edge of the pavement; I walk towards them to dip my feet.

Bea leaned over me, breathing spearmint across my face, rearranged the pillows under my head, then kissed my forehead. I caught that vanilla scent on her again. Like a freshly baked cake, or one of those posh candles she used to burn in our bedroom.

Who are you wearing that for?

I felt her sit on the bed next to me – the gentle pressure of her flesh against mine.

Has he called you?

'I wish I could stay here,' she said, still chewing nervously. 'Maybe I'd feel safer.'

A huge clap of thunder drowned out whatever she said next, and rain began drumming against the window again. I only caught a few of her words.

'. . . nervous . . . don't know who . . .'

She shifted her weight against me, put a hand on my thigh and squeezed my leg. She must have leaned closer because when she spoke again I could hear her more clearly.

'I leave the flat and I'm looking over my shoulder constantly. I double-check the door is locked at night. Triple-check. I jump every time my phone rings.'

What was she worried about? An uneasy feeling spread through me.

'I mean, I must be imagining it, mustn't I? Who would follow me? I'm being paranoid.'

She let out a half-laugh, half-sigh. 'I know what you'd say.'

She knew better than me, then. I had no clue what I would have said, because I didn't know what had been going on.

'But I'm sure there was a woman walking a few metres behind me, on the other side of the road, for ages. And the guy watching me from that parked car yesterday.'

That half-laugh noise again. 'There must be another explanation. I must be imagining things. I am, aren't I?'

It did sound like a possibility. What did she think I would have told her, if I could? Well, first of all, she was forgetting that in the real world – the world before my accident – she probably wouldn't have told me any of this. It would have left her vulnerable to me taking the piss out of her, even though I would only have done it to reassure her and cheer her up. But let's say she had let some of it slip. I would have said, 'Forget about it – why would anyone be following you? It wouldn't make any sense.'

And then I probably would have held her face firmly under the jaw, and kissed her Cupid's bow scar, before saying, 'You think you're special, do you, Honey Bea?'

Feigning dismay at the nickname, she would have screwed up her nose, and when I kissed the bridge of it I would have felt the skin wrinkling beneath my lips. 'Think you're important?'

I'd have traced my mouth upwards towards her brow, and

kissed her eyelids as she closed each one for me. 'Worth MI5 sending their best spies out for?'

Then I'd have pulled her close, drawing her body towards mine so that my chin rested on top of her head and I could smell the orange scent of her hair. 'Don't worry,' I would have said. 'Why would anyone be watching you?'

12

I can't see my body, but I can feel how little there is to it these days. The hollowness of my stomach – as if my belly button has sunk to touch my backbone. Not an ounce of food or drink has passed my lips for months. My breakfasts, lunches, suppers, late-night kebabs, Christmas dinners, birthday cakes, charred burgers, lemon and sugar pancakes: all of these have been replaced by this tube running directly into my stomach. There's no pleasure in it. Whichever nurse is on duty sits me up at a forty-five-degree angle to prepare me for what will be a fourteen-hour overnight feed. She presses a few buttons on a machine next to my head. A whirring noise begins – my lullaby for the night, unless the tube gets kinked and the machine starts beeping until a nurse notices it.

I didn't appreciate how much I enjoyed my food until I didn't have the chance to eat it any more. Bitchnurse Connie likes to put cookery programmes on my TV, and then she leaves me listening to the torture of dish after dish being described and tasted. The saliva glands in my mouth work overtime, thinking they are about to get a piece of that chocolate cake or a spoonful of that beef stew. They can forget it. These days, liquid food is pumped into me to keep me alive, but only just. I can still sense my weakness, my skin-and-bone limbs, and I imagine my starved face – all cheekbones and eye sockets.

I remember a conversation I once had with serial-dieter Rosie. 'Have you ever thought about where your weight goes when you lose it?' I asked her. I can't remember important things, like the day of my accident, or the last time I kissed Bea. But I can remember reading about weight loss in a magazine, and then boring Rosie with it. All that fat you are losing quite literally disappears into thin air. You breathe it out. A little leaves your body as sweat and piss but you puff most of it out through your mouth as carbon dioxide.

Those images have stuck in my brain. When I get a sniff of the stink of my sour sweat on the days the nurses miss a bit of me with their soapy water, I can't help but think of my body expelling my fat. When my catheter somehow breaks free and I lie in bed, soaked and unable to call for help, I think of the weight I have lost. And when I rasp air out of my lungs I imagine myself losing a few more ounces, ready to be filled up by more flavourless, liquid calories. Philippa used to say to me, 'You're so lucky to be alive.' She has more sense these days.

I never used to think I had much of an imagination when I was younger. I didn't get into journalism because of my love of storytelling. I saw an ad for a job going on the UCL student newspaper, and something made me go for it. So I ended up on the university newspaper and then on a journalism master's before my first proper job back in Bristol at the *Post*.

But even then, I didn't see myself as creative. At work I enjoyed meeting people, getting their stories, digging for the information that officials wanted to bury. Writing the article only involved getting the words typed up quickly – and even that got in the way of me finding the next story. I didn't waste time crafting an elegant piece of prose, and as a result my copy often appeared heavily rewritten by my news editor when I saw it in the next day's paper. No one would ever have called me a raconteur, or said I wrote beautifully. And I was never tempted to write anything fictional – even writing a first-person opinion piece felt a bit too inventive and took me well out of my comfort zone. I preferred cold, hard facts. I wasn't one for daydreams. I never saw much point in imagining my life any other way. But now? Now I can see the advantage of it.

So, while slightly-too-cold liquid pumps into my stomach, I pretend I am sitting down for a steak dinner with a bottle of deep crimson Merlot. Blood oozes out of the medium-rare meat. On the side, there are golden triple-cooked chips (I never understood what that meant and now will probably never know, but they sound good). A pile of bright green runner beans. Fucking hell, vegetables. Who knew you could miss them this much? The waiter is friendly, and brings out extra portions of whatever I want.

On other days I might have an imaginary takeaway with Bea – unnaturally red crispy shredded beef, duck pancakes with spring onions, egg fried rice and sweet and sour pork. The reek of garlic and ginger fills the flat so that when we go to bed I will be able to smell it on the pillow as I lie at her side, kissing her neck, running a hand over her hips. There are prawn crackers that remind me of the shoulder pads Mum used to stick into her jackets when I was little. Sweet chilli sauce. I lap up the salt and fat and decadence of it – no need to watch what I eat in the restaurant of my mind.

Clearly oblivious to the fact that the police had asked Eleanor to go over her statement, Bea spent a lot of her time with me worrying about what Rosie had said to her, about moving on. On one visit she sat next to my bed, her feet tapping nervously on the floor.

'I can't do that to you.' Tap, tap.

'Even if—'

Tap, tap. Through my half-open eyes I saw the shape of her head dip down. She kissed my knuckles.

'I had so many plans for us.' Tap, tap, tap. I was facing her, and I could make out the agitated jiggle of her legs. She leaned down to her bag on the floor, and when she sat up again I could see another movement – her hands fidgeting in her lap? There was the rustle of paper. A rich, moist aroma wafted up to me. She was rolling a cigarette.

'There were places I wanted to travel with you,' she said. I tried to ignore the fact that she was talking in the past tense. She stopped talking; there was only the sound of paper between her fingers as she finished rolling the cigarette, and the tap, tap, tap of her feet. Where did she want to go with me? I wondered. We didn't have any holidays planned when I'd had my accident – not that I could remember. The only thing in my calendar – pencilled in for the Easter holiday break – had been a trip to France with my dad.

It was his idea – he wanted to take me to see the Gouffre de Padirac, a huge sinkhole near the Dordogne. It was once thought that the chasm had been created by Satan but, actually, he explained, it was down to the formation of a massive underground cavity, whose roof had collapsed. As a kid I'd been enthralled by his description of the stalactites that looked like the peculiar pairing of cauliflowers and fireworks, hanging from the ceiling of the network of caves.

One weekend before my accident I had been over to his. We were going to have a takeaway and plan the finer details of the trip. It may have been seven months away but Dad wanted to make sure we had everything covered.

I found him bent over his desk and navigating his way through a series of open windows on his computer screen to find the website he was looking for. 'I think we ought to camp in Carennac – it's this village – oh, where is it—'

He kept clicking away on his mouse, sliding it across the desk dramatically, far beyond the confines of the mousemat.

'Here it is! Here it is, look – Carennac.' He was still standing, apparently too excited by it all to sit down. 'It says here that "Carennac is one of the most beautiful villages in France, along with one hundred and forty-eight others".'

'Where are you reading this?'

'Wikipedia. It's a very useful webpage. "The summer months are notably warm and dry, temperatures averaging 30 degrees".'

'But we're going in April, aren't we?' I sat down on the edge of the desk and started flicking through some of the test papers piled up by his computer.

'And then I thought we could go to Collonges-la-Rouge. Heard of that?'

'Don't think so.' I couldn't help but smile. I hadn't seen him this happy in a long time.

'It's a village built entirely with red sandstone,' he said, turning to look at me. 'Can you imagine? Your mum loved red sandstone. I should have taken her there, but I only just found out about it.'

I got up and put an arm around his shoulders. 'Shall we talk about this over some dinner?'

'I'm sorry,' he said, taking his glasses off and rubbing them clean on the bottom of his jumper. 'I'm going off on one, as your sister would say.'

'It's fine, I'm just thinking the food will be getting—'

'I'm just so looking forward to a road trip with you. A real lads' holiday, isn't it?'

It felt cruel to laugh at him but he was being so funny, and so sweet. I couldn't help it. It was hardly the kind of lads' holiday people usually meant when they used those words. I— Something touched my face.

My mind had completely wandered into another world. That trip to the Gouffre de Padirac had never happened. I doubted Dad went on his own.

Tap, tap, tap. Dad's study faded away and I was back again in my hospital bed. Bea's legs were still jiggling up and down, and she was rubbing a tissue against my face, wiping away a stray tear that had rolled down my cheek.

I couldn't remember what she had been saying before I drifted off. I tried to work backwards. Travel. Plans. That was it – she was talking about Rosie wanting her to find a new boyfriend.

'Are you going to come back to us?' I could feel her eyes on me, looking for an answer.

The foot-tapping was somehow worsening an itch in my arm, which had been irritating me all day.

'What if I do meet someone?'

Like that tosser at counselling?

'I can't believe everyone would see it the same way as Rosie, you know? People would say I was cheating on you. I'm surprised at your dad. I'm sure Mum and Dad wouldn't like it.' She paused. 'I wonder where they've got to? I'm sure they said they'd be here by now.'

I didn't get many visits from Rick and Megan – Brighton was a long drive and even before my accident they normally left it for Bea to go and see them. 'She's less likely to have accidents, with those young eyes of hers,' Rick would say, but Bea and I suspected the real reason was that they just didn't like leaving the cats at home, being looked after by their neighbours.

'They'd say I should stick with you. They've been together through thick and thin.'

She squeezed my shoulder.

'But.'

You're thinking about him.

'I'm lonely.' She moved onto the bed, behind my turned back, and put her head against me. Her glasses dug into my flesh as she kissed my pyjamas. 'And all this weird stuff going on. There was another one of those calls last night – I could hear someone breathing at the other end. If you were around, I'd feel safer.'

What calls?

She hugged my body to hers. 'I would have married you, you know that? You must have known that.'

Leave me. Go.

Frustration flooded me. I wanted to push her away.

I can't protect you. Find a man who can.

'If we'd got married we would have said those words – "In sickness and in health". "Till death us do part."'

But we never did.

'Last night, I googled "when to move on when your boyfriend is in a coma".' She hugged me closer and the itch in my arm intensified again.

She was hardly going to find a sensible answer on the internet. But that was typical Bea – she asked the web everything from 'how to tell your best friend you don't like her fringe without hurting her feelings' to 'will music ever be good again?' (after listening to the top forty countdown on the radio, one Sunday afternoon in my hospital room).

'There are forums full of this stuff,' she said. 'People like Rosie saying it's all right, no one should judge you for finding someone else. And then all these angry people quoting marriage vows.'

They don't apply to you.

'I want someone to – well.'

She sat up, and her tone shifted into a false brightness. 'Anyway, you should hear the other things they said.'

She got up and walked back round the bed, past my face, then disappeared from view as she bent down and rummaged in her bag. I saw her sit down in the chair next to me, and again I could see her hands moving in front of her. There was a muted rip and the air filled with the smell of an orange being peeled. Bittersweet. She talked with her mouth full.

'One woman said, if she was in a coma, she wouldn't want

her partner to waste his life waiting for her. There was a man who said that in certain societies, someone in a coma is already dead.'

She paused to swallow and I saw her arm move up towards her face. 'Another person said, if you really love your husband, why would you leave him? And then this woman said – this made me laugh.'

I liked hearing the smile in her voice for a change.

'They said: "Some loveless marriages are not much different to having your husband in a permanent coma. And what do people do then? Cheat." I shouldn't laugh.' But she did. A beautiful, breathless sound.

She sat in silence for a few minutes, finishing her orange, before walking across the room. I heard her pump alcohol gel out of the dispenser, and when she returned to the chair she started digging around in her bag again. Eventually, when she sat up, there was a rapid clicking sound, unmistakable as the end of a pen being pressed in and out. She was holding something large and white against the darkness of her clothes – a notebook?

'She reckons I should keep a diary of everything,' she said.

Bea always used to hate it when I did this to her. I had a bad habit of assuming that she knew exactly what I was talking about. She would punch me on the arm and say, 'I'm not a mind reader!' And now she did it all the time, although I'll admit she had a pretty good excuse. But who said she ought to keep a diary, and why? Was it one of the women on the forums she had been looking at? I hated not being able to ask questions.

'Okay, so I've got the date,' she said. 'And I've listed the previous days.'

She clicked the end of the pen a few more times.

'It's what the stalking advice websites say to do.'

It's that bad? You think you're being stalked?

'She said I should probably keep a list of the times of the phone calls too, and how long it was before they hung up.' She paused. 'Tom thinks it's a good idea too, so . . .'

Was it Rosie telling her to do this stuff? Good. She'd look out for her.

She leaned her notebook on the side of the bed and I heard the scratch of her pen on the paper.

'If I put the dates here . . . and keep adding to this page . . .'

She kept scribbling, and I watched the blurry movement out of the lower corner of my eye.

'Should I say other things? The effect it's having on me? Not . . . sleeping . . .' she said slowly, as she wrote the words. 'No appetite . . . Weight loss . . .'

She sighed, put her head down on top of the pad of paper, and slipped her hand into mine, curling my fingers around hers.

It felt good to rest there with her, as she kept muttering under her breath.

'. . . something about the way they breathe down the line . . .'

My eyelids responded to my feeling of contentedness and comfort, decided it was nap time, and closed out the light of the room.

'. . . seems familiar . . .'

13

We must have dozed like that for a several minutes before a voice jolted us awake.

'Bea?'

Her head lifted quickly off the bed and she pulled her hand away from me.

'Huh?' She sounded groggy, confused.

'Sorry, love, I didn't know you were sleeping.' I recognised Megan's voice, always slightly hoarse. 'Come here, love. Come and give your mum a cuddle.'

'Hi, Mum.' The chair creaked as Bea stood up and walked to the other end of the room. 'Where's Dad?'

'Just behind me,' Megan said. 'He was sorting out the parking ticket.' There were muffled noises – embraces and greetings. 'You've lost weight,' Megan fussed. 'And your highlights need doing.'

'Mum.'

'What? If I can't tell you, who can?'

Rick blustered in, the door banging against the wall as he pushed it open. 'Where's my little girl?' he asked. 'Get over here, you.' He growled affectionately as Bea made some indistinct noises, muted by his hug.

My nostrils filled with a floral scent and I guessed that Megan had moved towards me. 'How is he?' she asked. Her voice sounded very close, but she didn't touch me.

'The same, no change,' Bea replied. 'Do you want to go out for some food, or stay here for a bit, or—'

'We'll stay here. Good to stretch my legs. It's a long old drive, isn't it?'

Rick always spoke loudly – he possessed no volume control. Even without seeing him I could tell he was moving around the room energetically; I knew what he would be like, looking at everything, inspecting all the furniture closely, running a hand along the walls. He was a professional artist – an oil painter – and his flamboyance on the canvas translated into a certain showiness in his behaviour. He was always slightly over the top.

'And Graham?' he asked. 'How's the old boy? I still say, don't I, Megs, I simply cannot imagine having a child in this condition, I just can't put myself in his boots.'

I heard a gentle click and sensed the light in the room change – then there was another click as the room brightened again on the other side of my closed eyelids.

'Dad,' Bea scolded. 'Leave those alone. Chill out, would you?'

I heard the air wheeze out of the cushions in the chair to my right and Megan's knees click as she sat down. It was always difficult following all the sounds and movements when there were so many people: it was sensory overload, and I didn't know where to concentrate my focus.

'Your dad asked you about Graham, darling – how is he?' Megan asked.

'He's okay,' Bea said, hesitating. 'The usual.'

'Wait a minute, what's up? Come on, you can't hide from your dad. What's wrong?'

'Nothing's wrong, I—'

'I don't believe you.'

I was hit by the smell of stale cigarette smoke – the stench that always came with Rick and his tobacco-soaked clothes. He had moved closer to me. He put a rough-skinned palm to my cheek and said, 'What's up with this girlfriend of yours, Alex?'

'Dad,' Bea said. 'Don't do that. Don't make a joke out of him.'

Rick pulled his hand away. 'I'm not. Come on, tell me what's bothering you.'

Bea sighed. 'It's just that Graham and I have had a bit of a disagreement. He thinks I should be getting out more. Maybe even be looking to meet someone else.'

'Ah.' Rick clicked his tongue.

'What?' Bea asked. 'Why did you look at Mum like that?'

'It's funny that Graham has been saying that, love. That's all,' Megan said.

'That doesn't answer my question. Dad?' Bea was already getting wound up by their presence. It didn't bode well for the rest of their stay.

'What it is, see, we also think you should be getting out a bit more. Not necessarily to meet someone,' Rick said, perching on the edge of my bed. The mattress sank to the right-hand side, making me feel like I was going to roll over backwards. 'But to just get out. Then see what happens. If you do meet someone, you meet someone.'

'Your dad's right, love,' Megan chipped in. 'To be honest, we're mostly worried about you being here all the time.'

Bea was standing by the windowsill in front of me. I heard fingers drumming on the wood. Thrr-ud, thrr-ud, thrr-ud.

'I'm not here all the time,' she said quietly.

Thrr-ud, thrr-ud, thrr-ud.

'Whenever we call you, you're either here or on your way here,' Rick said. 'Or you've just left.' He got up, off the bed, and walked round to where she was standing. 'When did you last go out with your friends?'

'I see Rosie.' Bea sounded defensive. Thrr-ud, thrr-ud, thrr-ud.

'Other than Rosie?' Rick asked, sitting down on the other side of my bed, making me feel as if I'd roll forward into him. 'You used to go out with – what were their names? I can't even remember their names, that's how long it's been. Polly, was it? Poppy?'

Bea laughed, sadly. 'That's just your memory going.'

'Nice try, Beatriz,' he said. 'Okay then – what about your work? How's that coming along?'

'Fine.'

'Really? How come you needed money for rent again last month?'

Thrr-ud, thrr-ud, thrr-ud.

'I've been finding it hard to get my head in gear, that's all,' Bea said.

I didn't know about this.

'How is that comic book project progressing?'

'It was a stupid idea,' Bea said.

Thrr-ud, thrr-ud, thrr-ud.

'It wasn't a stupid idea, darling.' Rick was exasperated. He was right – Bea had always dreamed of working on a graphic novel. She described to me once how, as a little girl, she would spend hours crouched on the floor of Rick's art studio, drawing cartoons on sheets of paper stolen from his sketchbooks. 'You were meant to be putting out feelers for someone to collaborate with. What happened? You can't put your dreams on ho—'

'Leave it, will you?' Bea snapped. She slapped her hand down on the windowsill to make her point clear. 'Couldn't you even wait five minutes before you laid into me about everything I'm failing at?'

'Oh, darling. You're not failing,' Megan said.

'I should have known you would say all of this. Stupidly, I thought you might be on my side. I don't want to "get out more". I'm happy where I am.' She spat the words out.

'We *are* on your bloody side!' Rick stood up and slammed a fist down onto the mattress. 'The fact of the matter is that you are our priority. Alex is not. You need to look after yourself better and stop putting your life on hold for him. You know I'm right.'

'No, Dad, actually – all I know is that you never liked him,' she said, her voice rising.

This was news to me.

'When you asked me, "Is he for the long term?" what you really meant was, you didn't think he should be.' She was nearly shouting now.

'Of course I liked him,' Rick shouted back. 'We more than liked him. We loved him. But I didn't always think he was good enough for you.'

Bea laughed bitterly. 'You're glad this has happened. You think I've got a chance to find someone better.'

'That's not fair,' Megan said from her spot on my right-hand side.

Bea laughed again. 'Interesting you should choose those words, Mum. You don't say it's not *true*, do you?'

They don't like me? Why didn't you tell me?

'I thought he shouldn't leave you alone so much, yes,' Rick said, his voice returning to a more normal level. Still loud, but not shouting. 'Did you really see yourself being with him for the rest of your life? He neglected you. The number of times I spoke to you on a Saturday afternoon and he was out climbing in some—'

'You know what? I don't need this.' Bea sounded close to tears.

'And what about that other stuff you used to say, about—'

'Excuse me. I think it's time for a cigarette.' I heard the door slam shut.

What other stuff did she use to say?

A sudden draught from the corridor fluttered over my face.

'That went well,' Megan said, with a sniff. 'Well done.'

'Don't start.' Rick sat down on my bed again. 'She's my little girl.'

They both sat in silence for a moment.

'You'd better go after her, darling.' Megan spoke more softly now.

He stood up and patted my hand a few times. 'No hard feelings, old boy,' he said, and I listened as he walked out of the room.

No hard feelings?

I waited for Megan to speak, but when it became clear that she wasn't going to say anything, I began to process this new shift in my world. I had always thought I'd been a pretty good – and welcome – addition to the Romero family. I thought Rick had liked me. I'd taken him out for a pint or two on the odd occasion when they visited us. He'd enjoyed the Exhibition cider at the Corrie Tap, even though I'd had to pretty much carry him back to his bed and breakfast. I'd endured a round of golf with him at Ashton Court, taken him to a Rovers home game, been to all of his exhibitions and even written a story for the paper about a show he was involved with in Bristol.

What could I do about it? I was unlikely to ever get the chance to defend myself. I would probably never get the opportunity to change his mind.

Every memory I had of time with them needed reassessment; when I replayed each one I started to see the hints of dissatisfaction, the barbed comments, the way Bea would put a hand on Rick's arm – to stop him laying into me, I now realised, not just to stop him hogging the conversation, as I'd always assumed.

That first time I met them, when we drove up to Brighton for a weekend – Rick had made his mind up about me even then, hadn't he?

We'd left 'the girls' catching up in the house and walked down through the garden to his studio. As I chatted nervously about my work – I'd covered my first major court case that week – Rick ripped a piece of thick A2 paper out of a huge sketchbook and used bulldog clips to attach it to a board on his easel.

'It's so interesting watching the jury,' I said, looking around the messy room at the bold sketches of seascapes and lighthouses, the piles of art catalogues, the radio covered in paint and grubby scraps of masking tape. 'Watching their faces, working out which way they might go.'

Rick nodded, but seemed unimpressed. 'Done much painting?' he asked, smoothing the paper down. He picked up a palette and started squeezing some paint onto it from the pile of tubes on the floor.

'Painting?' What was the right answer? 'I did some at school.'

'School painting is different to real art,' he said, giving me the palette. He wiped his hands down the front of his crumpled denim shirt. 'You'll need a brush,' he said.

'I mean, I—'

'This one will do.' He pulled a long-handled brush out of a jar, thrust it at me, then left me standing by the easel as he walked away, dragging a paint-spattered stepladder across the floor with him.

'You don't want me to waste your paper,' I said, panicking.

Rick struck a pose next to the ladder, one hand on his hip. 'I think you'll find I'm quite easy to paint, old boy.'

How had I got myself into this situation? I couldn't draw a circle without making a mess of it. I suddenly felt very lightheaded – it must have been the paint fumes.

'I find that you can tell a lot about a man from the way he paints,' Rick said, looking me in the eye from across the room.

Shit. He was really going to make me do this.

'Beatriz is our only child, you know,' Rick said.

I nodded at his non sequitur. Instead of working out how to reply, I painted an egg shape for his head, in the middle of the page. He had only given me blue and yellow paint, which put me at an immediate disadvantage in creating a realistic portrait.

'She's talented,' he went on. 'She should really be focusing on more creative projects. Not this newspaper illustration work.'

I used yellow for the A-shaped frame of the ladder next to Rick's floating egg-head.

'Do you think she should make a go of her own stuff – look into that graphic novel idea?' he asked, casually.

There was clearly only one answer, but I didn't want to give it just to impress him.

I painted in the rungs of the ladder as I spoke, slowly. 'I think she should work on it, yes. But she is really good at the newspaper commissions.' The ladder now had about twenty rungs – at least three times too many. 'Perhaps she could do both.'

I risked a glance up at him: he was still staring right at me. He changed tack. 'Could your salary support her?'

Christ alive. No, was the short answer. Before I could reply, Rick started to say something else, but stopped himself. 'Hmm.'

And then I got it: I was being sized up for an entire future with Bea. We'd been together for a year, but this was a serious man-to-man chat. I stood there holding my dripping paint-brush, like an idiot.

At that moment, Megan and Bea walked in, laughing at Rick's efforts to wind me up by insisting on a portrait, and saving me from what had rapidly descended into a very awkward conversation. At the time, it seemed odd. But when I told Tom about it later that week, I couldn't help but crack up as I recounted my embarrassment. The rest of the weekend had been fine, Rick was perfectly pleasant and didn't mention Bea's career again or that she was their only, precious child. He'd just been having a

bit of fun making me paint him, putting me on the spot –
father's prerogative and all that. Hadn't he?

Now I saw it all differently. I remembered his stance by the
ladder, hand on his hip, shoulders square to me. Trying to make
me look ridiculous at the easel.

He had never liked me. Not even back then.

14

Bea had got truly angry with me only twice before in our relationship. Of course, we'd had our shouting matches, and plenty of bickering. But those two times, when her furiousness peaked, it was different. The control she exerted over her rage terrified me. The first time was when I told her about my night with Josie. The second was on the anniversary of Mum's death, about three years ago.

I had made the last-minute decision to take the day off work. Bea had meetings all day and was going for a drink with Tom in the evening to advise on some kind of graphic he needed for work. Did I want her to cancel so I wouldn't be on my own? No, I told her – I planned to go for a walk, maybe put pink lilies on Mum's grave. Her favourites.

But after she went out, I suddenly had a better idea. There was a cluster of bouldering problems I'd never tried at Oxwich Bay in the Gower, where we used to go camping when I was a kid. I remembered watching a woman ride a horse along the water's edge on that beach when I went for a walk with Mum. Building sand castles with Philippa, and burying Dad up to the neck of his 'Geology Rocks' T-shirt that we'd bought him for his birthday. I checked the tides: they would be at their lowest around one o'clock – perfect for me to spend a few hours scaling the large rocks at the foot of the cliffs. I got in my car and set off for a day of climbing, in a place Mum had loved.

The day's beauty stunned me: a salty winter breeze blew in off the sea, the sun shone and the skies glowed blue. When I arrived at the beach, I went to check my phone in my rucksack, but couldn't find it. I must have left it at home. It didn't matter, I thought. I would make sure I arrived back in the flat before Bea missed me.

It didn't work out quite like that. On the drive home, my car broke down. I sat on the hard shoulder of the M4 near Cardiff for ages, waiting to be rescued – it was a busy afternoon, the call handler explained, when I'd walked half a mile to the nearest emergency phone. At seven o'clock I finally managed to get hold of Bea, by borrowing the recovery driver's mobile. She burst into tears when she picked up and heard me. 'Where have you been? I've tried calling you about twenty times.' Her voice was shaky. 'I saw you'd taken your climbing shoes. I was starting to think something awful had happened.'

Another couple of hours later when I walked in the door she took one look at me and walked out of the living room into our bedroom, closing the door gently. No slam. I left her there for a few minutes, unsure what tactics to employ. Then I knocked softly, and went in. She was sitting cross-legged on the floor by the radiator, reading her book, looking quite content. I was bewildered. She looked beautiful. I wanted to pick her up, hold her, kiss her. But something told me I wasn't welcome. She put her book down, took her glasses off and tilted her head up towards me.

'You didn't need to change your plans,' I said.

'For some reason I didn't feel like it after two hours going out of my mind with worry.'

'Look, I'm really sorry. I didn't mean to leave my phone. I thought I would be back.'

'Couldn't you have left a note?'

'I should have done. I'm sorry.'

'I called Eleanor, I called everyone. No one knew where you'd gone.'

I bit my lip. She was overreacting, but now wasn't the time to say so.

'You know I hate it when you go climbing on your own,' she said. Rage was boiling underneath the calm surface.

'I was only bouldering – you know I don't need to go with anyone else to do that. I wasn't going high. A few metres at most. It wasn't dangerous. I took my crash pad.'

'Did you take a helmet?'

'I don't need a helmet.'

'You know what your problem is? You think you're indestructible. You think nothing can hurt you. It's pure selfishness.'

'I'll always make sure I take my phone with me, from now on. I'll make sure it's the first thing I pick up.'

'Your dinner's in the bin, if you're hungry.' She put her glasses back on, returned to her book, and refused to talk to me for two days.

The next time I found myself on the receiving end of a similar level of carefully measured rage was here, in this room – a few days after the visit with her parents. She hadn't been in for a while, presumably because she was busy entertaining them. I should have expected it earlier, but I'd forgotten all about the letter.

I hardly had time to notice her presence before she slapped the side of my face. Hard.

It hurt – but like any touch from her, I wanted more, to make me feel alive. I inhaled the scent of the lavender hand cream that had transferred from her skin to mine.

'That,' she whispered into my ear, 'is for cheating on me again.'

Again?

Chair legs scraped to my left. I had no idea where this was going. Blood pumped in my ears, so loud I feared I wouldn't be able to hear her explain. The lavender smell crawled down from my nose to my tongue and I felt like throwing up.

'How could you do this to me?' she hissed. I heard the rattle of keys, pens, her purse, as she looked through her bag.

'It's a good job, isn't it? A good job that I haven't been sat here like a mug, day in, day out, for a year and a half. Waiting for my loving, faithful boyfriend to wake up. Because that would be tragic, wouldn't it?' She laughed.

I don't understand.

'How long did it go on for?'

The chair scraped again and I listened to her footsteps as she walked away from me.

'And a baby? Christ.'

A baby.

'And here I am, refusing to even think about anyone else.'

Her hand smacked the wall.

A baby.

Her words triggered a half-formed memory in my mind.

'I need explanations and I'm never going to get them.'

I heard paper rustling.

The letter.

You found the letter.

'Let's have a look what she says, shall we?'

As she read, I saw the typewritten words before my eyes, just as I had when I opened that envelope, so many months earlier.

Dear Alex,
You will pay for breaking my heart twice over.
We deserved better than you.

I hadn't thought of those words for so long. Had I even remembered the letter since being in hospital?

'And then this photo with it,' Bea spat. 'A baby. I—'

I know it looks bad.

It wasn't what it seemed, but how could she know that? I felt nearly delirious with the desire to break free and hold her.

'Here are my questions. One. Who sent this to you? Two. How long were you seeing her for? Three. Was it one of the girls at work? Do I know her? Four. The baby. How old is it? I can't tell when this was taken.'

She breathed heavily and jaggedly.

'I bet it's that girl – Josie, wasn't it? You told me you didn't sleep with her. Was that a lie?'

She paused, leaned forward again, and spoke in a slow, deliberate whisper into my ear: her lips so close that I could feel the moistness of her breath, her glasses butting up against the side of my head. 'How. Could. You. Do. This. To. Me?'

I had received the letter and photo not long before my accident. It was posted to our flat. The idea that someone was telling me I was a dad had sent me into shock. It was all I could think about. Did I really have a kid? What was I supposed to do with that information? And who was the mother? Since I had been with Bea, I had barely looked at another woman. Could it be Josie, like Bea said? I couldn't remember my night with her, but she'd told me we hadn't had sex – and there was no reason for her to lie. Or was it one of my girlfriends or one-night stands from the first couple of years of uni, before Bea and I started seeing each other? It didn't make any sense. Why wait so long to contact me, in such a strange way? I tried to piece the memories together as I lay in my bed and Bea sat next to me, silent.

The problem was, I couldn't remember all of them. I'd probably been with about ten, maybe fifteen girls in that time. It could have been any one of them. Although I had always been careful, there had definitely been a few girls who told me I didn't need to worry about a condom. I couldn't remember which ones they were. I'd been so stupid. There were some pretty girls at the university climbing club, and others who came to the inter-university events. But I wasn't interested in anything more serious than a few nights of fun, maybe a couple of dates here and there.

When the letter came, the one name that kept coming back to me was Clare, the barmaid at the Union with the dark fringe and big eyes. I'd been on more dates with her than with most of the others. She was clingy, and she'd flipped out when I stopped returning her calls – she'd turned up my flat. I'd come home from lectures one day to find my flatmate John sitting with her on the sofa, comforting her while she cried and said she had been sure I was different to the other arseholes she had dated. She'd found out that I'd been texting another girl who worked behind the bar – I definitely wasn't the model gentleman back then. Looking back, I think I was in love with Bea all that time, and probably overcompensating for not being with her by bedding any girl I could get to talk to me for more than ten minutes. It was my way of saying to myself, I don't care about her, it doesn't matter that I'm not with her, I can have whoever I want. I pretended to myself that she was just a friend. And she didn't like climbing. It would never work. Now, I wished I hadn't been so stubborn and cowardly. If I'd been with Bea, I would never have been with all those girls, and there would be no letter.

I remembered that when I received it, I had planned to contact old uni friends, see if anyone knew any of my exes, any of the girls we used to hang out with at the climbing walls, and whether they had children.

I had wanted to talk to Tom about it – *did* I talk to him? I couldn't remember. Had he told anyone? I tried to bring to mind his reaction. I thought I could remember a look of disapproval, but I could have been confusing it with when I had told him about my past recklessness with Josie – he was very fond of Bea. Maybe I had never got round to finding the right moment to show him the letter. Those weeks before I fell remained hazy.

I definitely remembered that I was going to try and track Clare down, if John could help me remember something more about her. I was going to see what had happened to Josie.

'I've been holed up in the flat since Mum and Dad left. I'm trying to avoid going out more than I absolutely have to. So I decided to tidy through your stuff, your paperwork in the cupboard.'

I could see the pile. I had slipped the letter into the middle to hide it.

'The envelope is postmarked 1st August. You had weeks to say something. If you'd explained right then, maybe . . .'

I hadn't wanted to worry her, not until I knew what it meant. Had I really got someone pregnant? How was I going to break that to her? Would she believe that it must've happened before we were together? She'd made it very clear to me after Josie: one more chance. I should have shown her straight away. If it was Clare, then perhaps Bea wouldn't have been too angry – but if it were Josie . . . Maybe, if I'd had just a couple more days before my accident, I would have summoned the courage.

Since the slap, Bea hadn't touched me. Her voice stiffened into a distant coldness. How could this be happening?

'Maybe you got back together with her, whoever she is – after you got the letter. Has she been visiting you, too?'

No, that's not what it's like.

'God, my dad would hit the roof if I told him about this.'

So don't tell him.

'I don't know what I would have done, if you'd told me when you had the chance. Would I have stayed? Probably not. So where does that leave me?'

I heard Bea pick up her bag. 'Where the fuck does it leave me?' She hissed the words and let them hang as she stood there. The door closed with a click. No slam.

I honestly didn't know if she would ever come back.

She didn't visit the next day, but Dad did.

'What's all this about?' he asked, after I heard him limp in and awkwardly lower himself into the chair next to me. 'Bea came over last night, interrupted me and Philippa having dinner. This letter.'

Bea, Dad, Philippa – everyone was going to think I was a lying philanderer at this rate. It was killing me not to be able to explain myself.

'I told her it would be a mistake. You can't have a child. I would know. It's probably a prank. One of your friends.'

I don't know.

'Bea was asking if we knew anything, and if I had any other paperwork of yours still in the loft. I tried to tell her to stop, but she says she's going to start contacting all your old friends.'

He sniffed. Blew his nose.

'I'm worried about her. She looks ill. Tired. She was jumpy – not herself at all. When she left she asked if I'd walk her to her car.'

As I listened, I felt liquid dripping from my nose, running down my skin to my lips.

'Philippa said—'

The door clicked open. 'Cuppa, Graham?' I heard Pauline ask.

'No, no. I don't think so. Not right now. Thank you.'

'If you're sure, my love.'

'Don't want to trouble you,' Dad said quietly as the door clicked shut again.

He wiped at my nose with his handkerchief. For a moment I

could smell him intensely. His soap, the strong alcohol of his aftershave. Leather.

He cleared his throat.

'We talked about other things, too.' He paused. 'We talked about how you wouldn't want . . . this.'

Another sniff. The jingle of coins in his pocket, and then the flick of him flipping one with his thumb, the slap as he clasped it against the back of his hand when it landed.

'You wouldn't want to be kept alive like this.' Flick, slap. Flick, slap.

My whole body strained. *What are you saying?*

'Diane would know the right thing to do,' he said. 'I can't have quite the same conversations with your sister. It would just be nice, sometimes, to have someone to talk to about it.' A couple more flicks and slaps. Then the jingle of his pocket, as he presumably deposited his coin back with the others.

'Bea still thinks it's too early. She said, not until she finds out the truth about this letter.'

Let me go, Bea.

'I told her, that's not reason enough to keep you alive.'

You're going to do it? Thank you. Thank you, Dad.

Elation flooded my body, like a drug.

'It's the only thing she and your sister have ever agreed on, I think,' he said. 'Philippa refuses to talk to me about it, she says I'm giving up on you.'

Perhaps I shouldn't have been surprised that Philippa wanted to keep me alive, after the way I had heard her talking to the doctors about doing their utmost to make me better. But for some reason I'd assumed it would be the other way round. Given how distant our relationship now was, I thought Philippa would be the practical one, trying to persuade my dad that the time had come to let me go. I could imagine her putting on her stern lawyer voice to convince him, maybe even bringing up other cases to show precedent for the best thing to do. I couldn't envisage the scenario of Dad trying to talk her round.

'Obviously I'm not going to rush things. I want the girls onside first.' He cleared his throat again, and put a hand on my shoulder. Squeezed it. Then he leaned his face against the side of mine, his rough beard scratching at my jaw and the plastic arms of his glasses feeling greasy as they slid on my cheek. 'I hope I'm doing the right thing, Son,' he said, into my ear.

He was a good guy, my old man. I knew he'd come through for me.

I had never told my family what I would want to happen if I became a vegetable. I had to hope my dad knew me well enough, and this showed that he did. It had taken a long time but, finally, death was coming for me.

I exhausted myself after Dad left, trying to reconcile myself to the idea that I might die with Bea thinking I had cheated on her again. Surely she'd believe Tom when he told her I hadn't? Eventually I was unable to defy the lulling whir of machinery from the building work outside my window and fell into a fitful sleep. There were no drills today, just the sound of trucks moving around, rubble being scooped up, dropped into piles elsewhere. The occasional unintelligible shout from one man to another. I imagined them, several floors below me, in their hard hats and heavy boots. They crept into my dreams when they yelled at each other: I dreamed they were talking to me and I asked them to repeat their muffled words. *What? What did you say?* Except they weren't workmen in my dream. They were my climbing buddies. One of them was my belayer, controlling my rope, standing at the foot of the limestone face of the Gorge, fifteen metres below me as I climbed – up, up, up. They shouted to me: 'Hhgbsh, mate. Tfshjd kishbro hey, Deano?' *What was that? I didn't quite catch what you said.* I was on my favourite route. The Crum. I had dreamed about this intimidating, but hugely satisfying, climb almost every day and night since my arrival in hospital. I could, quite literally, do it in my sleep. I knew all the holds, all the sketchy sections. I knew precisely where I'd have a chance to lean back and shake the lactic acid out of my pumped arms.

The machinery hum outside the hospital morphed into the rush of traffic in my dream landscape – the traffic on the busy road behind and below me. I watched the cars race past: overtaking, undertaking. Then CRASH. A rock smashed noisily to the ground. I hadn't noticed it drop from above me, but when I looked down I saw that it had narrowly missed one of my friends, and lay in two halves on the grass below. As soon as I saw it, and thought how lucky I was that I hadn't been hit myself, the scenery started to fade away. The voices became the workmen's once more; the noise of the traffic returned to its original owners – the trucks and lorries outside. As I came round, the smashing noise of the rock nagged at me. It had sounded familiar, unlike a rock cracking in two, more like –

More like –

The slam of the door.

Is someone here?

There were no other noises. I strained to listen. Nothing.

No noises. But there was a smell.

Spice. Smokiness. Aniseed. Very faint, but there all the same. And something stronger, burning in my nostrils – paint, and maybe something like white spirit.

Quiet Doc.

What do you want? You going to tell me how disillusioned you are with modern medicine again? Try and freak me out again by pretending to give me drugs?

Nothing. He must have been looking at my charts.

Go on, then. I'm ready for you. Do your worst.

He still didn't make a sound.

No check-up this time?

Nothing. The door slammed again, and I was alone.

15

I drove myself mad trying to work out who the letter could be from. It had been bad enough when I'd received it – at least then I could do something about it, or distract myself. Now I had no escape and no way of solving the mystery other than using what I had in my memory.

What else had Clare said to John that time she came over? He'd said it was difficult to understand most of it, because she was crying so hard. And when I'd arrived she'd just screamed abuse at me, most of which I had deserved. Had she said anything that could have implied she was pregnant? Maybe that was why she had been so upset.

It didn't add up. She wouldn't have held back from telling me. She would have come out with it. But I couldn't be sure of that – I barely knew her. I couldn't even remember her surname.

Even if I could work it out, it wouldn't do me much good. I couldn't tell anyone. And I was going to die soon, if I had my own way. I tried to tell myself to stop going over and over it. There was no point.

But sometimes, even the self-torture of trying to make sense of it all was a better option than the reality of my hospital room. A few days after Bea had found the letter, I felt a slight shift in my bed. I had my suspicions that I knew what it was – which were confirmed when an alarm began to sound.

Bleep. Bleep. Bleep.

No. Not again.

My mattress was deflating.

I knew there wasn't anything I could do – I just had to wait until someone noticed the noise. So I started on another element of the letter mystery – the baby in the photo. Did it look like anyone I knew? It was all made much more difficult by the fact that I couldn't actually remember what the baby looked like. It was tiny, and it looked like it was still in hospital, in a plastic-looking cot. But beyond that, I couldn't remember any facial features. Or hair colour. They all looked the same at that age, didn't they? At least my attempts to remember took my mind off the imminent danger I knew was the other side of a flat mattress.

My hi-tech airbed didn't feel much different to a normal mattress, but by all accounts it stopped me getting the sores that some of the nurses were so worried about me developing. I once heard Pauline explaining to a new nurse. 'See this plug here? Hmm?' She rattled something. 'If this comes out then the whole thing'll deflate. As soon as the pump comes out, it starts beeping.' She pulled at something and a noise started up. Bleep. Bleep. Bleep. She rattled it again and the noise stopped. 'Listen out for that. If we don't realise in time, Alex here will end up right down on the metal. It's like lying on concrete. It won't take long for him to get a pressure sore.'

'Shit,' the new nurse said.

'Exactly. We don't want that.'

I had never had pressure sores, but I knew enough about them to understand they would make my already poor existence considerably worse. I didn't want to end up on the cold, hard bed frame, as I had when the cleaner dislodged the pump once before; that was bad enough, even though it had only been a few minutes before Pauline came in to fix it. The baby photo was going to have to keep my mind off that scenario.

Bleep. Bleep. Bleep.

I compared it to my memory of Clare, trying to remember if it had her dark hair and brown eyes. Did it look like any of the baby photos Dad had at home of me, or— I heard the door open, and a draught of vanilla hit my nostrils.

Bea?

She hadn't visited for days.

You've come back. Thank you. I'm sorry. That letter isn't what you think.

No kiss on the forehead. But no slap, either. Silence. I listened for the sound of her sitting down in the chair next to me, but it didn't come.

Say something.

Bleep. Bleep. Bleep.

She didn't seem to notice the sound. If she did, she didn't say anything. I could feel the bed slowly falling away beneath me.

Can't you hear that? Bea?

'I don't want you thinking you've got away with this,' she said. She sounded tired, frayed.

The chair legs scraped, but more than they usually did when she sat down. They grated on the floor for several seconds, moving away from me, down towards the foot of the bed.

You don't need to sit so far away. Please.

She sighed again and I heard her body collapse into the chair. 'Just because I'm here doesn't mean I've forgiven you.'

Bleep. Bleep. Bleep.

I thought I could hear the telltale rhythmic rustle of her rolling a cigarette.

You need to call one of the nurses.

Her phone buzzed against the floor and I listened as she fished it out of her bag, paused, dropped it back in.

Who was that?

Bleep. Bleep. Bleep.

Make it stop.

How could she not hear the alarm? Maybe she didn't know what it was.

Another possibility suggested itself, but I couldn't believe it was true. She wouldn't, would she? Even if she was angry with me?

Please tell me you're not deliberately ignoring this.

Her phone vibrated again, more insistently this time. Bzzzzz. Bzzzzzz. Bzzzzz.

She did something with her bag, and the buzzing noise disappeared. 'Hi,' she said. No, it's okay. I can talk.'

Who was it? She never took calls in my room.

'I'm at home. Doing – doing work.'

Why was she lying?

'I did. They were useless. I ended up speaking to the same one who dealt with things after the accident. PC Halliwell.'

Halliwell?

'No, he was nice enough, just—'

You've been to the police?

'Recognised me, weirdly. Considering it's been so long.'

Halliwell. Wasn't he on the Holly King murder investigation? I was surprised he'd wanted anything to do with my case – we hadn't exactly hit it off when I'd questioned his methods.

Bleep. Bleep. Bleep. She'd have to notice my body sinking lower soon.

'He took me into one of the interview rooms, and I showed him my diary.'

Is that Rosie on the phone? Your parents? Or him?

'No . . . he said not to worry. Like I was imagining it all.' Her voice rose. The more she talked, the angrier and more tearful she became.

Sounds like the arsehole I remember.

Bleep. Bleep. Bleep.

'He looked uncomfortable, like he was embarrassed on my

behalf.' She wobbled on the final word. 'He didn't believe me. Just told me to keep writing it all down.'

She paused, took a deep breath. Sniffed.

'Okay, okay. I'm trying.' Another breath. 'He said to go back if anything more happens or if I get a better idea of who it might be.'

Footsteps. She must have stood up. She walked round the room as she kept talking.

'Before I left he said he needed to talk to me again soon, bring me in for a chat, because they – what were the words he used?'

Her footsteps stopped, and she continued to speak more slowly, as she tried to remember what he had said.

'Because they have concerns about Alex's accident.'

Concerns?

'No, that's all he would say.'

What kind of concerns?

'The only thing I can think of is that they're looking at the equipment again. I thought they'd ruled all that out.'

My face grew hot as my mind raced, trying to work out what this meant. First, the visit from the police here in hospital several days ago. Then Eleanor, preparing to go over her statement. Now this. Then I felt coldness cutting into my back, in bars across my spine, arse, legs. I'd hit the bed frame.

Bleep. Bleep. Bleep.

Bea, I need a nurse. Now.

'Okay. I know, I'm trying.' She took another deep breath. 'Something good. It's hard – I can't think of anything.'

My mind flickered through a series of time-lapse images as I imagined bedsores waiting to form along the lines of the frame beneath me. I knew from what the nurses said that the damage could be done surprisingly quickly – an hour was all it took, they had said. I saw redness, deepening, eating into my flesh. I'd managed to avoid them so far. I didn't want this added pain.

'The only thing is my work. That's the only good thing in my life, you know?'

She sniffed.

'Seriously? You'll find it boring.'

Bleep. Bleep. Bleep.

'Okay. I've had this big commission for the *Wall Street Journal*. I can't believe they want me. They want watercolour illustrations of five different kinds of burger.' Bit by bit, her voice calmed down. Her breathing returned to normal. 'They've sent me the copy for the article and there's loads to go on. They're talking about all the salads you can have – so there's the reds, greens, purples . . . lettuce, tomatoes and red cabbage in coleslaw. It's bright. Then cheeses, bacon, pulled pork . . .'

I listened as she went on, letting her words take me away from my discomfort as I lay on the unforgiving bed frame. Her descriptions made me feel hungry and brought my grey world to life. I loved it when she did this – talked about what she saw. The colours and the patterns in her work. The way a street looked when she walked down it. The sunset she'd seen when she drove home from a hospital visit. She somehow knew what I needed. I clung to her descriptions and fleshed them out.

I imagined her sitting at the desk in our flat. She had a spot-light lamp bent over her workspace, a little plate smeared with paints to one side, a jam jar of water, sketches everywhere, a laptop open with images or words to work from.

Colours layered upon colours. I imagined running my fingertips over the texture of the thick watercolour paper she used. I saw her, with faint smudges of paint on her face. But her face, when I saw it, was not clear. I couldn't completely remember it or its features. When Mum died, the same thing happened. After a couple of years I couldn't bring her face into my mind. That was easy to fix – I pulled out a photo of her. I couldn't do that now – not for Mum, not for Bea.

In my imagination I could make out Bea's expression, though. She was sad. Tense. Scared. My imagined world fell away and I returned to the present moment.

Bea? I wish I could be there for you. Keep you safe.

'. . . okay. Tomorrow?' She was still on the phone.

'Bye.'

Bleep. Bleep. Bleep. The machine hadn't given up.

I heard Bea, at last, moving towards the foot of the bed. Rattling the box that controlled the mattress. 'That's not normal.'

She must have noticed the bed, then, and she said, 'Oh God, that's not right. I'll get a nurse. Wait there.'

At least she still cared enough about me to not want me to be in pain. Maybe all was not lost between us.

A squeak as the door opened, and a click as it shut.

I lay there, left alone with my thoughts for a minute. What concerns could the police have? Maybe it didn't matter. I was still here, still unable to speak to the people I loved. Unable to move. Unable to wash myself, go to the toilet. Nothing could change that.

But the news had shaken me. I lay waiting for a nurse to come and re-inflate my bed, listening to the ambulance sirens outside on the road ringing out like warning alarms.

Feet squeaked in – rubber soles against lino.

'Oh, great. How did this happen?' Bitchnurse Connie sounded as chirpy as usual.

'I've no idea,' Bea said. 'I'm sorry, I didn't touch it.'

'Don't worry, dear.' Connie had her 'friends and family' voice on. The profanity-free, less-abusive one that I didn't qualify for. 'We'll sort it out.' She huffed and rattled the pump. The beeping stopped, and a soft whirring noise started up again as the mattress began to inflate. 'There we go.'

'Actually, while you're here, I wanted to ask a few questions, about who visits him.' Bea sounded brisk, businesslike.

'You as well? A lot of interest all of a sudden in who comes and goes.'

'What do you mean?'

'The police were in the other day, asking the same thing. Don't ask me why. God knows, I tried my hardest to find out.'

What have my visitors got to do with their investigation?

'I wonder why that was.'

'If I knew, I'd be the first person to tell you.' I didn't doubt it. Connie wouldn't pass up an opportunity to spread a juicy bit of news. 'Now, I don't think I could tell you every single—'

'No, of course. I just want a rough idea. Anything you could tell me would be helpful.'

'Well, I'll do what I can, dear. Of course I will.'

I could have retched. This woman disgusted me. Could no one see through it?

'Do any other women visit him?' Bea asked.

'Let's see. Vis-it-ors.' Connie drew out her last word, exaggerating the effort it took her to think of an answer. 'There's his sister, and the aunt. The one with the cakes. Sometimes she brings a friend.'

'Anyone else?' Bea was impatient. She started picking at her nails. Tck. Tck. Tck.

'There's the friend, with the boyfriend – Rosie, is it? And the skinny blonde girl.'

'Eleanor. No other women?'

'No, I don't think so.'

'What about children?' Tck. Tck.

'Children? No, never seen any kiddies. Why do you ask?' The sniff of more gossip perked Connie up.

'You can't think of anyone else that you've not mentioned? It's important.'

'Only men – his dad, and that good-looking chap—'

'Tom. Yes, know about him. It's women I'm interested in.' Bea sighed. 'Never mind. Thank you.' Tck. Tck. Tck.

'Any time, dear.' A few squeaky steps and the door opened.

'Wait – one more thing,' Bea said. 'You wouldn't want to hazard a guess at why the police were sniffing around? Even if it's just a hunch?'

'Maybe it's the same reason as you? You didn't say why you were asking.'

Bea didn't take the bait. 'Maybe.' She sounded dubious, and I could tell what she was thinking. The police didn't know about the letter. Whatever they were up to, it wasn't trying to find out if I had a bit on the side.

Connie must have realised she wasn't going to get any more out of her. The door shut.

I heard Bea sink back down into the chair in its new position at the end of the room.

'You've covered your tracks well,' she said. Tck. Tck. Tck. 'I've asked everyone. Your dad. Tom. I've emailed everyone who got in touch after the accident. No one knows anything.'

Neither do I.

'I've been going through all of your stuff. Everything I can find. Nothing.'

Because there's nothing to hide. You've got to believe me.

She didn't stay long, and I was distracted thinking about why the police would be asking about my visitors.

When was I going to find out what they were up to?

It's been interesting revisiting the events from earlier this spring. Remembering, re-telling. It's difficult to remember conversations word for word. I guess part of all this is me trying to keep myself alert, prevent the onset of boredom-induced madness.

But I am trying to be accurate, as far as I can. It is difficult to remember what happened on what day and how much time passed between certain events. But I am doing my best. The problem is that when this all started, I wasn't well. Another round of pneumonia, my nemesis. My opponent in the ring. We circle each other constantly, size each other up, then close in and throw a few punches before the referee tears us apart. The odds are always on him winning – I'm always the underdog.

The last time was rough, the worst I can remember since the first few months after my accident. Back in those early days they batted me back and forth between the neuro ward and intensive care, which I recognised because it had a different sound – lots more machines, more beeping, more whispered voices. More last rites being read. 'May the Lord who frees you from sin save you and raise you up.' Death seemed inevitable, each time I went through the disorientating fevers, that terrifying gurgling feeling of liquid filling my lungs, and the all-over body aches. But each time, I pulled through. Antibiotics dragged me out. I have no idea how many rounds I've done with the fucker. Too many to count. But the latest bout was one of the worst. So when all of this strangeness – Bea's phone calls and thinking she was being followed, the police at my door – started, I still hadn't recovered. I slept a lot, and my waking hours blurred with haziness. I know *what* I remember, but timing is difficult.

My efforts to remember get interrupted a fair bit, too. For one, there's the daily ablutions, as they call them. Except I don't think that's the right word. I haven't been able to consult a dictionary, for obvious reasons, but I think that means 'washing oneself'. It's the nurses who wash me. For a long time, when I sank to my lowest ebb, I wished they would leave me alone. I would have lain there and festered in my own stink. What I really wanted was a proper shower. Deep green body wash in my hands, in my hair. Sometimes Quiet Doc smelled like my favourite shower gel and I felt physically sick with envy. I imagined the steaming hot water running down my face into little rivers on my body. Standing there until my neck burned and the smoke alarm went off in the hallway because of all the steam escaping from the bathroom, and Bea having to leave her desk to bat a tea towel at the ceiling to stop the noise. Emerging, dripping onto the bath mat, drying myself off, and sniffing the eucalyptus and pine oils still on my skin.

It's not quite the same experience, getting a bed bath.

But the worst thing is the suctioning – once every few hours, day and night.

Occasionally I notice one of the nurses walking round to the wall behind me and to the right, and I have a few seconds to work out what they're about to do.

No. Not again, not so soon.

They switch it on. It sounds like a slurping blender, a Hoover, a dentist's drill, all mixed into one devil machine.

Please. Not again. Give me a break.

They stick it into my mouth for starters, then they shove it down my tracheostomy tube and into my windpipe, wiggling it around. It's as if my throat is the drain under a plug hole and the devil sucker is a wire coat hanger being used to scrape out hair and gunk.

Fuck off. Take it out.

It's like having flaming sambuca poured directly into your lungs.

No more.

Like having razor blades casually dropped into your throat as if they are nothing but drops of honey.

I've had a lot of opportunities to experience it. A lot of time to think about ways to describe it.

16

I always thought there could be nothing worse than losing your sight. People crossing the road with a guide dog made me feel uncomfortable – a mixture of pity for their dark or distorted world, and relief that light filled mine. I used to think: what would life be like if I couldn't see?

But when I was younger, as a boy, I found blindness intriguing. One Christmas morning when I was seven or eight, I made what Mum called 'creative use' of a boring tie Auntie Lisa gave me, by tying it round my head in a blindfold and opening the rest of my presents without looking. I tried to work out what was hiding under the wrapping paper, then tore it off and felt the shapes, materials and weight in my hands, identifying a remote control car, a Discman, and the new dinosaur encyclopaedia I'd asked for. I walked, arms outstretched like a sleepwalker, across the room to find Dad, Mum and Philippa, to give them the traditional Jackson family Happy Christmas kisses. Philippa giggled with delight as I tripped over her present on the floor, and begged me to let her have a go with the blindfold. Up in my bedroom I manoeuvred myself by running my hand along the wall, fingers tripping on the edges of Blu-Tacked posters of my Liverpool heroes – John Barnes, Ian Rush, Robbie Fowler. But after an hour or so I got a bit scared by my own game. I panicked, ripped off the tie, opened my eyes again and looked around.

Because I could.

Now, I knew what it was like to be blind – even if it was only for some of the time. I still got that sense of claustrophobic panic, like I did as a kid with the tie around my head. Many of my hours were spent in total darkness, with my eyelids shuttering out the view, but there was the rare day when I woke up to find those shutters slightly lifted for a while.

Exhilaration pounded through me at those precious times and I would try to ignore the dry burning – only relieved when a nurse put drops in – desperate for Bea to walk in so I could see the shape of her for once. I could make out her rough outline when her visits coincided with those moments. I saw her body, the movement of her light-coloured limbs and the tilt, turn and dip of her featureless face. But not the perfect line of her nose, the brown-flecked green of her irises, or the small scar above her lip. Never the soft white blonde of her cropped hair dropping into a kiss-inviting V on the back of her neck. No. As much as I treasured my infrequent glimpses of her, they were cruelly incomplete. My eyes only let in distorted visions – and all in shades of grey. Blurred shapes and hues of black and white swayed in front of me, totally out of focus.

To my left: I could make out the bright whiteness of the window, the glow shooting off from it in shards;

straight ahead of me
the drab darkness of the walls,
beyond the grey lumpiness of my body
underneath the sheets;

a subtle change in the light to my right,
where I knew there was a door, after
hearing countless people walk in and out of it.

But still, no matter how imperfect my vision was, I wished Bea would realise that I had some sight. If she lifted my eyelids when she visited, I would have seen a version of her more often. As it was, only nurses and doctors opened them – people whose faces I had little interest in.

They did this when they wanted to run a few tests on me, check that nothing had changed. Around the time of Bea finding the letter, my consultant Mr Lomax brought a team of medical students to gawp.

Get them out of here.

'First, we lower the lights in the room,' Mr Lomax said, standing to my left. The overhead brightness dimmed like a cloud passing between my closed eyes and the sun. 'We want to make sure Patient isn't dazzled.'

I know what you're going to do to me. Get out.

'As part of our assessments, we will now test how the eyes react to certain situations. Eyelid, please, nurse.'

The warm pressure of a finger on my right eyelid stretched it up, holding it in place next to my eyebrow. I could smell Pauline's marzipan scent close to me. Cool air teased my eyeball, and the brightness struck me even with the lights lowered. My hands prickled with the desire to rub the blurriness from my eyes.

I could make out the black-rimmed circle on the wall ahead of me which I had decided must be a clock, and a row of white-coated bodies standing below it. The window let in the daylight, but I knew the futility of trying to turn my eyes in their sockets to look out of it – they would refuse. What kind of day was it out there? They kept the hospital stiflingly hot year-round, but I was sure I felt the presence of summer outside. When Dad had been here the day before, the skin of his copper-smelling hand had been clammy and hot against my cheek; I had heard the slap of flip-flops the last few times Tom visited. So maybe the sun shone outside – people would be walking along the streets in brightly coloured shorts and T-shirts, sunglasses on. The trees would be full of green leaves.

'Now, we use a torch to take a look at the pupil,' Mr Lomax said. A mass of white hair; bushy black shapes which must have been his eyebrows. A sweet whiff of last night's drink on his breath. Whisky? Brandy?

Get away from me.

'Let's take a look.' He shone a torch in. I couldn't blink away the discomfort as I was forced to stare right into the dazzling silver circle. My eyelashes appeared, illuminated, as two rows of tiny white stars. They would almost have been pretty if I wasn't so distracted by the intense itching of my unlubricated eyeball.

Do you have any idea how much this hurts?

'The pupil is constricting. Now, left –' he flicked off the torch. One of the bodies at the end of my bed coughed.

Pauline closed my right eye, and as soon as she had opened the other Mr Lomax shone the torch into it.

'Again, constricting nicely. Can anyone tell me what we would expect to see in a brain-dead patient?' The change in his voice told me he had turned away to address his students. In my left eye, still open, the burning white afterglow from the torch obscured the room.

'No response?' a girl said.

'Correct!' he bellowed. 'But how would we know if there was no response? What would we see?'

I'm not your toy to prod and experiment on.

'The pupils wouldn't change size,' the girl ventured, stumbling over her words. 'They wouldn't – they wouldn't react to the light.'

'Yes.' He paused. 'Both eyes, please.'

Pauline obeyed the instruction, and lifted my right eyelid again so that both were now open.

'Now we will check the oculocephalic reflex. Can anyone tell me another name for this?' Mr Lomax leaned in. Silence met his question.

'What do they teach you in your lectures these days? Too many multiple-choice exam papers, if you ask me.'

'Is it . . .'

'Yes?' he barked.

'Is it the doll's eye reflex?' A male student, sounding more nervous than the girl.

'Bingo. The doll's eye reflex. What we do is turn Patient's head from side to side.' He placed a hand under my chin and turned my face towards the window, back to the middle, and to the other side. 'The eyes stay looking ahead, where they are looking when the head is centred. If Patient was brain-dead, we would see the eyes fixed mid-orbit – what we call negative doll's eyes. Finally, for now, we will do the caloric reflex test.'

I knew this one.

Piss off.

'Cold water please,' he said.

The clap of a solid object being placed in his hand. He grunted.

'We put cold water into Patient's ear, like so.'

Cool liquid dribbled into my left ear, and simultaneously my view of the room shifted to the right – more shapes in grey, black and white.

'See how his eyes slowly deviate away from the left ear, where I put the water? That tells us the brainstem is intact.'

'Is he definitely unconscious?' This came from another male voice among the students.

'Did I say you could ask questions?' Mr Lomax barked.

The student didn't take the hint. 'It's just that I was reading about a case where the patient didn't respond to eye tests like these but then they discovered that he—'

'That's enough, thank you,' Mr Lomax interrupted.

They discovered what?

'But he could be aware, couldn't he? Just unable to move and talk. It's this rare condition called L—'

'Will you please be quiet!' Some of Mr Lomax's spit landed on my face. 'Funnily enough, I am aware of what it is called, but thank you for the lesson, young man.'

Why wouldn't he let the guy finish what he was saying? This condition, what was it called? 'L' something. Is that what I had?

'I'm sorry, I didn't mean to offend . . .' the student stammered.

Mr Lomax muttered to Pauline, 'One is reminded why one doesn't like having students tagging along. Thank you, nurse.'

Pauline, bless her soul, blotted at my ears with a tissue, but didn't close my dry eyes. 'There you go, my love.'

Thank you.

I listened to the students shuffle out, none of them daring to speak as Mr Lomax herded them to their next destination.

I wanted to know who my letter was from and what the police were up to, but that couldn't change my mind. Encounters like this only served to reinforce my belief that I wanted a way out of this dead-end existence. The doctors had written me off. Even if I got well enough to get out of bed, would my eyesight ever improve? Did I want a life without colour? A life where I wouldn't be able to see well enough to climb?

No. I was doing the right thing.

'. . . worried about her.'

Rosie and Tom walked in later that day, mid-conversation as usual.

'But she looks seriously ill. It's this whole stalker thing. Did I tell you she thought someone had been in her flat?'

'No.' Tom walked around to the right-hand side of my bed, his flip-flops slapping on the floor. By now I was lying on my side, facing the door. I saw his body pass my cracked-open eyes.

'Because it *smelled* funny,' Rosie continued. 'She isn't sleeping. Or eating.'

'Huh.' Tom rearranged my pillows, gently lifting my head as he did so, the sweetness of the ever-present balm on his fingers.

I saw Rosie's slim shape drop into the chair next to him and caught a draught of her coconut scent. It made me think of holidays – cocktails on the beach.

'He looks weaker,' Tom said.

He prodded my arm where my biceps should have been. 'They should rig up a pull-up bar, and strap his hands to it. Lift him up and down.'

'What are you talking about?'

'I could make it,' he said. 'We've got that bit of pipe at home. I'd just need to . . .' I heard him rattling at fittings in the room, tapping on the wall.

'Tom? What are you on about?'

'Trigger his muscle memory. Good as anything else they've tried.'

'They're not going to get him doing pull-ups.'

Tom squeezed my lower arm. 'We were working towards little finger, one-arm pull-ups. Before.' He lifted my little finger, flexed it.

'Tom.'

He cleared his throat, holding his hand over mine. 'What's the latest on the letter?' he asked, with forced brightness.

'T.' I could just make out part of Rosie's body reaching out for him.

'Tell me about Bea,' he said.

'Okay.' She sounded reluctant. 'Are you sure you're all right?'

'Tell me about Bea.'

Rosie exhaled. 'She says she can't abandon Alex, not until she knows exactly what the letter means. Which makes sense. I suppose.'

'But what?'

'I don't think I would keep coming back here, in her position. What other way is there to read it? He screwed someone else.'

That's not true.

Tom's fingers squeezed mine. 'We don't know that for sure.'

He let go of me and I felt his weight on the edge of the mattress as he sat down on my bed. My body tipped forward.

'It makes me angry, imagining being her, imagining if you'd done this to me. It makes me furious. With you.'

'Me? But I haven't done anything.'

'Are you sure?'

'Bloody hell, Rose.'

He stood up and walked away from me, out of my field of vision. The flow of air around me, caused by his movement, irritated my eyes.

'Maybe she comes back out of habit,' Rosie said.

'Or guilt.'

'What do you mean by that?' She was cross again.

'Only that—'

'She hasn't done anything to him. He's the one who's messed around.'

'We don't know that. Stop saying it. Maybe she feels guilty for being the one who's still healthy, when he's like this.'

'How can you say that when she's done nothing wrong? Typical.' I heard her push the chair back, and her greyness moved in front of me.

'Where are you going?'

136

'I can't stay in this room with you right now. I need a coffee.'

'Rose.'

'How can you say that? How can you say that she should feel guilty?' There were rushed footsteps and the door slammed.

In the silence that followed, I could swear Tom said, 'Because that's how I feel.'

17

After months of boredom, my mind suddenly had a lot of material to turn over. I kept coming back to the same questions.

What were the police looking for? Why were they interviewing Eleanor again? Little did I know then that they had several more 'fact-finding' conversations ahead. There were floorboards to pull up and search under. People to intimidate.

And then there was the letter. Who had sent it? Was I really a dad? Did my child know about me?

Was someone following Bea? I couldn't shake the feeling that she was hiding something from me.

What about the plans to let me die? Had Dad persuaded Philippa yet? Had he spoken to Bea again?

And that day a new question crept up on me: *What if I don't want to?*

But I talked myself down. *Have to. Have to. Have to.*

I forced myself to remember my reasons. My old reporter-self sat my new bedridden-self down for an interview.

Every so often, I would have these conversations with myself and they always made me remember what I'd called my 'radio interview series'. I'd liked asking questions as a kid, so I suppose I didn't become a journalist just because of my mum; maybe it was in me all along. I would use tape interviews I did with family members and neighbours to make a radio show, with Philippa and I as the only two listeners. I called it 'The Al and Phil Super Radio Show' – I must have been about nine at the time; Philippa could only have been seven. In fact, the first 'show' – featuring an interview with my best friend American Paul about his baseball card collection – was just called 'The Alex Jackson Super Radio Show,' but Philippa begged and begged to be involved and I finally gave in. It would have been a long summer holiday of tears and tantrums if she hadn't got her own way.

The interview with Dad was my favourite to listen back to when I found the tapes in the loft, many years later. I thought about calling Philippa to tell her to come over and listen with me. She probably would have done – but I envisioned her making disparaging remarks and spoiling the memories for me, so I didn't bother. We made Dad our main interview of the week, and I asked him about how he learned to play guitar ('from my brother'), why he liked rocks so much ('they hold so many secrets') and how he met Mum. That was always one of our favourite stories, and you could hear Philippa squeaking happily in the background of the recording when I asked that question.

'I was playing in a band at a small festival somewhere in Somerset,' Dad said.

'What instrument were you playing?' I asked. My interview style left something to be desired – I hadn't learned the art of letting someone answer as fully as possible before interrupting them. I thought the thing to do was ask as many questions as possible.

'You know the answer to that,' Dad replied.

'Yeah, but, Dad, come on. For the rest of our listeners. What instrument?'

'Guitar.'

'And what was Mum doing?'

Philippa squealed again, and you could hear me shushing her on the tape.

'Mum was a bit of a hippy chick back then, and she was at the festival with some friends, making daisy chains or something.'

You could hear Mum shouting from the next room at that point. 'I heard that, Graham!'

The questioning continued, painfully, as I extracted every tiny detail from him. Eventually he ran out of patience and excused himself.

I couldn't help but remember that summer holiday with fondness, so it felt reassuring to go back to that activity from my childhood. It also helped to clarify my thinking.

So, Alex, reporter-me asked hospital-me. *Talk me through the emotions you experienced in the lead-up to you making the decision to die.*

The main thing (hospital-me answered) is that I spend a lot of time remembering what it felt like to *do* things. I miss *doing.* Everyone uses that word all the time – just another verb. Do this, do that. But I had never fully appreciated the joy that *doing* brings. Especially physical things. I was always running, climbing, playing five-a-side. I miss the feeling of tired muscles. My body used to be strong and now I'm just a bundle of feeble limbs.

And when did you decide? I asked myself.

It was Christmas Day, last year. My first Christmas had been hazy, because I wasn't properly awake yet. The day I decided was my second Christmas in hospital. They had carol singers come round to each bed on the ward. I got 'Silent Night'.

Bea didn't visit, because she was in Brighton seeing Megan and Rick. But Dad and Philippa came by. It was miserable. Dad sounded on the edge of tears the whole time, and Philippa wanted to leave almost as soon as they walked in. 'I told you we shouldn't have come here,' she said. 'It's only going to upset you.' It wasn't what I remembered of Christmases, growing up. No Jackson family Happy Christmas kisses. No gifts, no joy.

From that day, I knew that by staying alive I was ruining their lives. That's the day I stopped trying.

It's a huge decision. Are you sure about it?

My accident was fate. A punishment, for everything I'd ever done wrong. I should have kept Mum alive. I never doubted that I was doing the right thing when I took her side – she was so convincing. She was so sure of what she wanted. I never doubted it, not even at the funeral, not when Philippa stopped talking to me, not in all those years afterwards. It was only after I woke up here that I started thinking about it differently. What if that treatment could have saved her? They wanted to cut away more of her tongue – maybe that would have got rid of the rest of the cancer.

Confined to this bed, wishing for another chance at my own life, I started to get the horrible feeling that I had misread the situation. What if Mum had wanted me to persuade her the other way? When she wrote that note to me had she actually wanted me to talk her out of it?

I should have made her have the treatment. I should have made more effort to fix things between me and Philippa, I should have paid closer attention to those kids, I should have been more careful about who I slept with, I should have spent more time with my dad, I should never have gone home with Josie, I shouldn't have been so arrogant at work. I should have been there for Bea more. I should have left my ego at home when I went climbing and worn a fucking helmet. Stupid, stupid Alex. Careless. Asking for trouble.

Everyone's done things they regret.

I can't speak for anyone else. All I know is that it was fate. And I have to pay for what I've done.

*

After finishing up on an interview, you always think of things you should have asked. If it's within a few hours, you can call the person back, see if they'll spare you a few more minutes. But there are times when new information comes to light, weeks after the piece goes to print, which makes you wish you'd had the foresight to ask the one question which could have really stirred things up.

The question I would have asked myself back then, if I'd known what I know now, was: *But what if it wasn't fate that made you fall?*

18

I remember that day.

My memory is a panelled door frame made up of panes of distorting glass, each revealing a different twenty-four hours – but one of them has been kicked through to reveal what's behind it in sharp definition. That particular day – the day after Tom and Rosie were here – is strong in my mind.

I woke up with cold feet – the kind I wouldn't have been allowed to join Bea in bed with. 'Don't touch me!' she would've shrieked, curling herself into a defensive ball on the edge of the mattress. I wanted a nurse to rub them for me, get the blood going. I woke up with cold feet and the sound of television, which must have been on since the night before. An American sitcom – canned laughter. Laughing at me? I woke up with cold feet, the television on, and the smell of dying flowers. Philippa's latest bouquet had decayed quickly. What were these ones? Carnations? Daisies? Daffodils? I never knew. Identifying flowers wasn't a skill of mine – not even when I could see them properly. I woke up with cold feet, the sound of the television, the smell of decay, and a coil of apprehension in my stomach.

It was a normal morning, apart from my nervousness. A huge storm raged outside my window, dulling the sound of ambulances coming and going. Rain drove in at the glass – waves of pitter-patters blown in by the wind, as if someone was turning the volume dial up and down every few seconds. It was only interrupted by several minutes' worth of hail so noisy that I entertained the possibility that we were, in fact, under machine gun fire.

When Connie and Pauline came in, they had plenty to say about the weather.

'Alex, I'm going to roll you onto your side now so that we can give you a wipe down,' Pauline said loudly into my ear as she turned me away from the window. 'I've never seen hailstones the size of these, Con. Honest to God. They were like golf balls. No – tennis balls.'

One of them pulled up my pyjama top and wiped a warm wet cloth over my back. 'The *Daily Mail* is calling it the zombie apocalypse, according to Dan in the kitchen,' said Connie.

'They never are!' Pauline said. The cloth moved around to my chest and rubbed my stomach, underarms, neck.

'Zombie apocalypse,' repeated Connie. 'That's what they said. I don't know where the zombies come into it but I'm not looking forward to driving home tonight.'

At that moment a huge clap of thunder shook the building like an explosion beneath us. I felt the pair of them jump.

'Shitting hell,' said Connie.

In the middle of another deafening hail shower I missed the sound of footsteps. With my eyes closed, I only noticed I had a visitor when a wet hand landed on mine. I felt the edge of a sopping sleeve on my fingers. When it lifted away, the sheet was still damp – a cold, wet patch spreading towards my left hip.

'I'm so sorry.' It was Bea, sounding upset.

What for?

She unzipped her coat and took it off noisily, shaking drops of water onto my skin. As she moved I thought I could just about smell the remnants of her orangey shampoo. No vanilla perfume today? I tried to detect it – but no, it wasn't there.

'Who did this to you?'

She sat down on the edge of the bed and cupped a cool, moist hand under my chin, holding my jaw.

You're touching me again.

'All this time,' she said. 'We've assumed it was an accident.'

Her fingers slid from my face, down onto my chest. My heart beat insistently against her, reaching out for more.

'Why would anyone want to kill you?'

What are you talking about?

'Why won't they tell me anything?'

Slow down –

'Why tell me they think it was deliberate, if they can't tell me how it happened?' She tutted and then put on a deep, mimicking voice. ' "New information has come to light, Miss Romero." '

Was she saying what I thought she was saying?

'They must have tampered with your kit.'

In my mind's eye, I saw the walls of the room pushing in on me.

It's all right – I'm dreaming. This is just a dream.

'It has to be linked to the letter,' she muttered to herself.

Wake up, Alex. Bad dream, just a bad dream. Wake up.

She tapped her fingers on my collarbone. She felt too real to be a dream version of herself.

'What did you do to that woman that was so bad she wanted to kill you?'

This can't be happening to me.

'I can't imagine how you've hurt someone that badly. You're a good guy. Even I think that, even after this letter.' She sighed heavily. 'A cheat, maybe. But you don't deserve to die for that. All you've ever done is try to help people. Jesus, listen to me. You've had a kid with some other woman and here I am sticking up for you.'

My mind split in two. On one side, I rejected the whole idea. This was the kind of thing that happened to other people – not to someone like me. No one would want me dead. On the other side, I knew the police wouldn't open a case from more than eighteen months ago on a whim. Not the Avon and Somerset Constabulary that I had dealt with as a reporter. What did they know that we didn't?

'She must have tampered with your rope, or your harness.'

I'd have noticed if my kit was dodgy. There must be another explanation.

I shivered.

Eleanor?

No.

She was the only person who would have been close enough to make me fall.

No.

What are you thinking? There's no way she would do that to you. She told you she loved you, remember?

But what if it was some kind of jealous thing? What if she was angry because she couldn't have me?

No, Alex. This is Eleanor you're talking about. She wouldn't do that.

I was sweating. My pyjamas stuck to the insides of my arms and liquid trickled down the back of my neck.

Bea kept tapping.

'I've looked at home. There's no matches on the handwriting from the envelope. I've been through birthday cards, letters, everything.'

'You will pay.' That's what the letter said. You think this is what it meant?

Her hand stopped tapping on my chest.

I thought of Clare. The letter could be her. But this? Even with her shrieking and tears and fists flailing against me, I couldn't see her wanting to kill me, let alone trying.

'Christ, Alex. Who is she? Is this why the police were asking about who visits you?'

Another trickle of sweat rolled down the back of my neck. Other girls' faces flashed through my mind: half-memories, blurred and hazy. It still didn't make any sense. Was it really one of them? Again, I asked – why wait so long?

Someone tried to kill me.

The hairs on my arms stood on end and a horrible shiver passed along my sweat-damp body. What if we'd both been thinking along the wrong tracks with the letter? What if it was someone else entirely – not the mother of my supposedly illegitimate child?

Because if that was the case, I could think of one person who might have wanted me dead on that September day.

I thought again about my parallel prisoner, William Ormond. Jailed more than ten years ago for the brutal murder of Holly King – a murder I didn't think he was guilty of. Whoever had really done it had walked away free. I thought of how that man might feel if he knew a journalist was digging into the case again, and supporting the campaign for an appeal. How he might feel about my paper asking for anybody with information to come forward. I couldn't imagine Clare trying to kill anyone, but here was somebody who was definitely capable – he'd done it once, he could do it again, couldn't he? A murderer, someone who had beaten a woman to death with a spade in broad daylight, clearly wouldn't need much of a reason to decide to take another person's life. And I'd given him plenty of reason to focus on me.

'You will pay.'

Was that what the letter meant? That I had to pay for attempting to expose the truth? But then, what did the baby in the photo have to do with any of it? Why did whoever sent it 'deserve better' than me?

Bea's weight shifted on the mattress as she stood up. The sound of a zip, and something smooth against fabric. I heard the air escape from the cushion in the chair by my side as she sat back down, and a beep and whir I recognised as a laptop being switched on.

She took a deep breath. 'Right. I need to –'

This was her practical, let's-get-things-done voice.

Tell me more. You must know more. What exactly made them suddenly reopen the case?

Tap, tap, tap. Her fingers on the laptop keys.

'They said to make sure I could remember everything that happened that day.'

Tap, tap, tap: strangely soothing.

'Ready for my new witness statement.'

Tap, tap, tap. Her fingers on the keys mingled with the backdrop of the rain on the window, now that the hail had stopped. It was a calming white noise. My head rattled with thoughts. Someone tried to kill me. It wasn't an accident.

Could it really have been Holly King's murderer? 'New document.' There was the knock of metal against wood as Bea patted her ringed hand on the arm of the chair.

'September – the – eighth,' she said, keying in the words as she went. Tap, tap, tap. 'The day of Alex's accid—'

Taptaptaptaptap – a word being deleted.

'Attempted murder.'

She talked as she typed, and for the first time I heard a full account of what she had been doing on that day. I had images in my head of uniformed police in our flat, Bea grabbing her things to take to hospital. Of her, breaking down in tears by my side in intensive care. The hours of waiting, her draining polystyrene cups of tea while I was in theatre. But these details must have been created by my imagination. The events she described were different.

September 8: The day of Alex's attempted murder

It was a Saturday. I left the flat first. Alex would have been close behind me, going to meet Eleanor, Tom and Alberto and head down to the Gorge for a day's climbing.

I wanted to make the most of the last warm days of the year.

Drove into Somerset for a walk in the Quantocks, parked at Cothelstone. I took a bottle of water, and ham and coleslaw sandwiches. I remember because I threw them back up later.

I walked for a couple of hours – a seven-mile loop including Lydeard Hill. My phone was switched off to save the battery. I forgot to switch it back on when I got back to my car.

If I had turned it on, I would have seen the text and voicemails. Tom, Rosie, Eleanor. Dad and Philippa. Even my parents. According to what the police later told me, about two miles into my walk, Alex had fallen.

How our days unfolded:

Time	Alex	Me
Eleven o'clock	He fell.	Two miles into my walk.
Midday	He was in hospital.	Four miles in, I was stopping for lunch.
One o'clock	They were taking Alex in for emergency surgery. They set his broken arm. Did something to help reduce the swelling in his brain.	Six miles in, I remember crouching for at least five minutes on the path, watching a bold field mouse scurrying around on the bank, looking for food.
Two o'clock	Alex was still in theatre. His dad and Philippa waited in the hospital café for news.	I was finishing my walk, coming back to the car.
Three o'clock	Alex was coming out of surgery, but being kept in a coma to help reduce swelling and pressure on his brain.	I was nearly home. The traffic was good on the M5, for once. I felt happy – it had been a good day.

When I arrived back at the flat, expecting to walk in the door and see Alex on the sofa, I saw Rosie's car parked outside. She jumped out as soon as she saw me. She was crying.

She told me what had happened, and told me to prepare myself for the worst.

Rosie drove me to the hospital. I couldn't talk. I was in shock.

When I saw Alex, he was in intensive care. He was hooked up to machines, a ventilator breathing for him. I threw up.

The doctors gave me a sedative, and I slept on a chair in the family room until the next morning.

I saw it all with her. Watching myself being wheeled in and out of theatre, I realised that looked different, now that I was the victim of a crime. Anger flushed my face with heat.

Bea stopped tapping on the keys. The rain had stopped too now, leaving behind it a series of persistent drips outside my window.

'I showed the letter to the police.' She spoke louder, addressing me. 'I told them it must be her.'

Was it PC Halliwell again?

'They were so patronising. I thought they'd be interested. They said they would look into it, but . . .'

Wankers.

It sounded like Halliwell's style. This was him all over. He was dismissing Bea just like he and his buddies had dismissed Ormond's family. Like they'd tried to dismiss me as a trouble-maker. Were they treating her like this because of her link to me? She'd had nothing to do with my reporting of the Holly King case.

The pillow behind my head felt wet with my sweat and my mouth was dry. It was all too much – the new information, the uncertainty, my inability to do anything about it all.

Bea dropped her head onto my bed and it nudged against the

sheet covering my thigh, still damp from her wet coat. The only good thing to come of this news was that she seemed to have returned to me. She hadn't pulled the chair to the end of the bed. She wasn't as angry with me now. She was touching me again. I felt a flash of hope drive through me, from my thigh, where I felt her contact, up through my abdomen, chest and heart.

Had she forgiven me for my 'affair'? Or was it simply that this turn of events made it pale into insignificance?

It was good to be close to her again.

Let me win you back.

'I don't know why they want me to bother giving another witness statement – they don't value anything I say,' Bea murmured into the bed. 'My stalker. The letter.'

In all the drama of the last hour or so, I'd forgotten about Bea's stalker. The truth about my fall – and my theories about who might have had it in for me – made this significantly more sinister.

What if it's the same person?

Images of Holly King forced themselves into my mind. Her battered semi-naked body lying by a gravestone. All that blood.

That can't happen to Bea.

The police would take more notice of her being followed, now that they were investigating my attempted murder. They would see the link, and protect her. Wouldn't they?

Be careful. Please be careful.

It was a busy afternoon – Bea stayed for the whole of it, as I willed her to stay close to me and not leave the safety of my room. After a couple of hours, Dad showed up with Philippa.

'Hi, Graham. Philippa.' Bea sounded formal.

'Bea,' Dad said. There were muffled noises of him hugging her, coins jangling in his pockets. 'The police came to see you, too?'

'Yes,' said Bea. 'They didn't explain much. Did they tell you what this new information they have is?'

'Nothing.' Philippa's voice, curt and unfriendly. She never managed to hide her dislike of my girlfriend.

'What're we going to do?' Bea asked, her voice coming from my left-hand side.

'Not a lot we can do,' Dad said. 'Let the police do their job. Answer their questions.' His words were weary.

'Did they tell you who they thought . . .' Bea trailed off.

'No,' Dad said. He started stroking my face, his hands smelling of copper and leather, and a hint of the alcohol in his aftershave. 'They must be talking to Eleanor, I suppose. Tom, Alberto, maybe? But I can't believe they would know anything.'

It couldn't have been Tom or Alberto. They were climbing a different route when I fell, I was sure Tom had told me that on one of his visits.

But Eleanor?

Would the police really look at her?

Why would she want to hurt me, if she had feelings for me?

She couldn't've done it. She had no reason to want me dead.

'Just goes to show, you can't trust anyone,' said Philippa, coldly.

Can I really trust you, Eleanor?

What if we'd had an argument while we were climbing, that I couldn't remember? Could she have done something to make me fall, in the heat of the moment? Distracted me, or startled me somehow? Made me lose my footing? It seemed so unlikely. We never argued; certainly not while climbing.

Philippa's clipped steps moved towards the left-hand side of my bed. 'These flowers are dead.' The familiar scrunching thump, as she tossed them into the bin. 'I won't bring any more until my next visit now,' she said to no one in particular. 'He'll have to do without.'

'I showed the police Alex's letter – the one I found,' Bea said.

'The . . . ?' Dad sounded confused for a moment. 'Oh, yes. I suppose they need to see it. You never got to the bottom of it?'

'No.'

Dad's hand disappeared from my face. He blew his nose loudly.

'It felt like the right thing to do, to come down here and be with him.' He was on the verge of tears. 'Do you think he – who knows.'

'Think he what?' Bea asked.

'Do you think he knew what was happening, when he fell?'

No one answered.

'I didn't think it could get worse than it already was.' Dad swallowed his last words and Philippa clipped round to his side.

'Hey, now. Dad,' she soothed. All her affection was reserved for him. Daddy's girl.

'Nothing changes with his condition as a result of this, I suppose,' Bea said. 'It doesn't make it better. Or worse.'

'Of course it's worse,' Philippa snapped. 'There's a murderer out there.'

In the middle of that night, I woke up as I often did, disorientated and sweating.

Where am I?

You'd think I'd know by now.

I'd been dreaming, vividly, about Bea walking on Lydeard Hill. It didn't feel like I was with her, but more like I was in her body. I saw the mouse on the bank, felt the sun on my skin. But in my version, her phone wasn't turned off. It rang in her pocket, and when I pulled it out to answer, I saw that it was attached to a portable charging pack. I tried to take the call but the ringing wouldn't stop – and the noise forced me out of the dream.

There was an alarm faintly sounding in the ward, I realised, once I worked out where I was. I couldn't get back to sleep. The dream had bothered me, but why?

It wasn't until I began to drift back off, what felt like hours later, that I jolted awake again with the answer. Bea never switched her phone off – she made a point of it, especially after that incident where I had forgotten mine when I went to the Gower. She had bought us each one of those charging packs, so we would always have enough battery if we went out for the day. We should never have a reason to be out of contact, unless we had no signal. Why had she turned it off when she went up Lydeard Hill?

It was also unusual for her to have gone hiking on her own. Running, yes. But a long walk like that? Never. What had been going on with her that day? There had been too many moments like this in recent weeks, when I felt like I didn't understand her. When I felt a distance growing between us.

She wasn't telling me something.

19

Waking up? No.
Getting dressed? No.
Saying goodbye to Bea? No.
Meeting Eleanor? No.
Climbing? No.
Falling? No.

I couldn't remember a single thing from the day my life changed, which made it hard for me to believe, at times, that any of this ever happened. There had to be a picture in my mind somewhere. I tried to retrace my steps, to trigger a memory of what went wrong.

It was almost as impossible to order my memories of the week leading up to it, but at least I had scraps to play with. I went climbing on Saturday – I knew that much. My memories seemed to go back to Wednesday, although even those gaped with holes. On Wednesday night I played five-a-side with the boys from work, as we did every week. I remembered jogging over to the pitches at Clifton College – it stuck in my mind because I was halfway there before I discovered I'd forgotten the single pair of putrid goalkeeping gloves that we all shared. It was a hot night – which probably contributed to the fight that broke out between the court reporter Michael and our newest trainee, Jacob. Two of the most placid men in the office disagreed over the legality of a tackle and ended up rolling around on the ground in a blur of punches, and I had to pull them apart.

On Thursday we'd run the first of our series of articles about William Ormond. My editor, Louise, had decided to go big on it: she stuck it on the front, gave me four pages inside to fill, wrote that day's leader about it. I'd used the space to go over the details of the murder – how, while I was still young enough to be at school, twenty-year-old Holly was attacked in the grounds of Arnos Vale Cemetery in her lunch break. How police believed she had been sexually assaulted. How she had been bludgeoned to death with a heavy object, believed to be a spade – but which had never been found. How nineteen-year-old Ormond was the prime suspect, because he worked as a gardener at the cemetery and was found covered in her blood, cradling her head in his lap. Even though he told the officers who found him – one of them being Halliwell – that he had been trying to resuscitate her. Even though he had learning difficulties and no record, he was arrested and questioned without a lawyer present and made to sign a confession. At trial he pleaded not guilty, but the jury didn't buy it.

A few days before – Monday? Tuesday? – one of the newsdesk secretaries had taken a call from a man who refused to give his name, instead repeating four words over and over. 'Drop the Ormond story. Drop the Ormond story.'

Bill was on newsdesk that day, and had laughed it off. 'What's the best way to guarantee that we run a story? Tell us not to.'

I agreed. I was fired up, ready to fight the injustice of Ormond's incarceration, ready to expose the failure of the police. I had assumed – I think we all had – that it was one of the detectives or a police press officer who had called, trying to scare us. They'd really been putting the heat on, talking to Louise when I wouldn't back down. It hadn't occurred to me that the real murderer might know we were running the piece; not before anything had been in the paper. How could he have known? It never crossed my mind that the call might have been from him. I didn't remember having spoken to Bea much about the case, though that was strange as I would normally talk to her about important things at work. Had Bill asked me to keep quiet about it? Possibly. Would he remember the call now and realise it could have been the real killer? Would that help put the police on the right track?

On the Friday, I went to a care home in Downend and interviewed a man who was about to celebrate his one hundredth birthday. Larry Thomson. God knows how his name has stuck in my head. It was small fry compared to the Holly King investigation, and I was knee-deep in that, but Bill liked to make sure everyone knew they weren't above the bread-and-butter stories. It was the kind of interview that never made the front page, never won you any prizes, but, despite my reluctance, I knew readers would like it. Larry had flown with the RAF in the Second World War, outlived three wives, had five children and twenty-one grandchildren. He'd worked as a milkman, a car salesman and then bought a corner shop. 'What's your secret?' I'd asked him. 'How do you know about that?' he'd replied, aghast. 'No,' I assured him (although I wanted to know more), 'what I meant was, what's your secret for living to such a ripe old age?' He laughed. 'Whisky,' he said. 'And a decent steak, every now and then.' Ignoring calls from the office wondering where I was, I stayed for a few hours chatting to him, helped him change a dud light bulb, and made us both some lunch from what I could find in his cupboards (beans on toast was the best I could do). He had grabbed my hand as I got up to leave. 'Send me a copy of the paper, will you, lad?' I promised I would. But I never got the chance. I never saw the story in print. Good old Larry Thomson – he probably wasn't around any more. One hundred was one thing – he looked fit and healthy, with massive ears and cheeky eyes. But one hundred and two? I didn't think he would've made it that far.

I must have filed a page lead on Larry, but I couldn't recall the rest of that afternoon, no matter how hard I tried. Presumably I just sat at my desk, working? But I couldn't be sure about anything. Had something happened in those lost hours to make someone want to hurt me?

At the end of the day I would've caught the number eight bus. I didn't remember the journey, but I remembered getting home to Bea. I walked into the flat desperate for a shower, and kissed her on the head. I definitely remembered feeling unhappy – or perhaps uneasy? – about something. I didn't breeze in; I didn't remember feeling excited about the arrival of another weekend. Bea was bent over her desk, sketching. The windows gaped open, and the blind tapped against the wooden frame every so often when a breeze caught it.

She had said hello without looking up. Engrossed in her work. There was nothing particularly unusual about that, but it troubled me now. I couldn't pin down the cause of my disquiet.

Later that evening, less than twenty-four hours away from the moment that everything fell apart, I went to a barbecue at Tom and Rosie's place in Redland. Bea wasn't with me, but I couldn't remember why not. It was a clear night, and as darkness fell and Tom and I finished off the last overcooked burgers and sausages, I looked up and was surprised to see so many stars. Now, I wondered, was my attacker looking up at those same stars and planning to kill me the next day?

20

'Let's lift your chin a little, hmm?' Pauline said loudly into my ear. She pulled my jaw up and away from my chest. I felt the blade drag down against the skin and stubble on my neck; breathed in the cheap lemony scent of the foam. Once I got over the fear of her holding a sharp piece of metal to my throat, I had found that I quite enjoyed this occasional treat. Thankfully Connie never bothered with the added extras like this. 'I'm not a fucking beautician,' she told me once.

'My husband, God rest his soul, he used to say you should go with the grain.' Pauline swilled the blade in water with a slosh, before bringing it back to my neck.

I didn't know your husband was dead.

This small piece of news struck me. I didn't like to think of Pauline having sadness in her life.

'A bit more here and here. And we're done.'

Gently under her breath she hummed a tune I didn't recognise as she moved around me.

'Now let's cream your skin a bit.' She spoke loudly again, with the usual exaggeration for my benefit. There was the sound of a cap being unscrewed, and the undeniable, though faint, smell of lard reached my nostrils – the charming fragrance of the moisturiser they used all over me. Very carefully – even tenderly – she rubbed the cool cream into my face and neck. 'That's better, isn't it, my love?'

Much better. Human contact felt remarkable, when I spent so much of my life untouched. I looked forward to these moments with Pauline, and the regular visits from my physio, Sarah. Her job was to keep my joints moving and stop me seizing up. Carefully, she'd lift each arm, each leg. She'd move them side to side, up and down. Bend them at the knee, the hip. The wrist, elbow, shoulder. Each movement made my hairs stand on end. She never spoke to me; she was in the camp of people who didn't think I was listening. But I didn't care. The time she spent with me – half an hour? an hour? – was the most intense human contact I ever got.

When Pauline had time to shave and pamper me like this it was a luxurious and heavenly bonus. It wasn't a sexual thing. When I talk about being 'touched', I'm not saying it with a raised eyebrow and an elbow nudge. It was much more basic than that. My skin came alive under her hands. The slightest stroke of my face equated in satisfaction to a full-body massage in my previous life.

What would I do without you?

'Now. I have five minutes, I reckon. Shall I take a look at those fingers of yours?'

I heard the clatter of metal next to me. Like cutlery. Instruments, or tools.

'Think I could have a new career as a manicurist, hmm?' She chuckled, and took hold of my left hand. I felt a tug and then heard a clip as she cut my nails, finger by finger.

The squeak of the door hinges in the corner of the room interrupted her.

'Sorry, I can come back.' Bea's voice.

'No, you're all right, my love. We're nearly done here, aren't we, Alex?'

I heard the rattle of her nail scissors, creams, razor blades as she collected them up.

'Thank you,' Bea said. The door clicked shut.

She stayed down the far end of the bed, near my feet.

'Al,' she said. But before she could continue, the door slammed open again and immediately more voices filled the room.

'How dare you.'

'Eleanor.'

'Why are you defending her?'

Rosie and Eleanor were talking over each other. Would Eleanor keep visiting me if she had been the one who put me here? Wouldn't she be more likely to stay away?

'What's going on?' I smelled cigarette smoke as Bea moved towards me, and vanilla.

'What's going on?' Eleanor mimicked, then dropped to an angry hiss. 'You want to pretend that nothing is happening here?'

A feeling of dread washed through me.

'Rosie? What's she talking about?' Bea seemed genuinely confused.

'We saw you,' Rosie said. 'Downstairs.'

I felt Bea place a hand lightly on my chest, and the hairs on my arms stood on end in response to her unexpected touch. I was even more confused.

'You're sick,' Eleanor spat.

Rosie stepped in. 'Keep it down, Eleanor. They'll throw you out.'

Bea still didn't speak.

'No, Rosie. I want to know what the hell she's up to.'

What's going on?

I was disoriented. Only Bea's hand on my chest grounded me.

After a pause, Bea said, 'Can we talk about this outside? Alex—'

'You don't want him to hear what you've been up to?'

What's she talking about, Bea?

'Please,' Bea repeated.

Eleanor ignored her. 'We saw you in the café. Who was he?'

He.

'She isn't doing anything wrong, Eleanor,' Rosie said.

'Apart from cheating on Alex? You can't go off and shag around just because your boyfriend's in a coma.'

Cameron.

'You can't pick and choose when you're his girlfriend,' Eleanor continued.

I felt sick. My stomach muscles clenched. I'd been so caught up in the news from the police that I'd briefly forgotten about Bea's smarmy admirer.

'And with everything that's going on,' Eleanor said. 'How could you? You find out someone tried to kill Alex and then you jump into bed with another man?'

'It isn't what you think,' Bea said.

'Maybe you should go, Eleanor,' Rosie stepped in again. 'Cool off a bit.'

'I don't know why you aren't angry too,' Eleanor fired back at her. 'I didn't think you would stoop so low, Bea. You don't deserve him.' She spat her final words in Bea's direction and the door slammed.

The room went quiet.

It's him, isn't it?

Rosie spoke first. 'Why didn't you tell me? I knew something was up.'

'I know.'

'So why didn't you tell me?'

'It doesn't feel right to talk about this here.'

Because of me?

'He can't hear us.'

'We don't know that for sure.'

'Come on, I'm not pissed off with you, and Eleanor will come round. I think you're doing the right thing. Seriously.'

Bea said nothing. My stomach twisted more.

'Who is he?'

Nothing.

'Give me something, a name, or how long it's been going on. Come on. I'm supposed to be your best friend.'

Bea took her hand away from my chest, and said, 'He makes me feel safe.'

Because I can't.

'That's good. Have I met him before?'

'Cameron? I don't think so. Not with me.'

So it was him.

'Cameron? That's his name?'

Bea whistled out a long breath. 'Yes.'

'Is it serious?'

Silence.

'I need a smoke,' Bea said. 'Let's get a coffee.'

'Come here, you,' Rosie said.

The rush of fabric against fabric. Bea's muffled words in her friend's shoulder. 'I'm sorry I didn't tell you.'

'No problem, Romero.'

The pain in my stomach continued to twist and grab, and I sweated through the skin cream.

I'm not ready for you to give up on me.

Their footsteps approached the door.

'And don't worry about Eleanor,' said Rosie, as they left. 'She didn't mean it. All of this – the police stuff – it's been a shock . . .'

Eleanor . . .

I tried to forget Bea's new boyfriend after they left and focused on Eleanor, going over everything she had said. The way she had reacted to seeing Bea with someone else – she was far more protective of me than I would have guessed. Could someone who cared that much about me being emotionally hurt bring themselves to physically injure me? It didn't add up. It couldn't have been her.

Distracting myself only worked for so long.

Someone wanted me dead and now Bea was leaving me. What had Rosie and Eleanor seen them doing? A bit of hand-holding? A kiss?

I obsessed like this for about two days. What did he look like? Was he attractive? How had Bea described him? Would he treat her well? Part of me hoped he would. But the devil on my shoulder felt competitive. I wanted to die but I wanted to do so with her as my girlfriend. With her still loving me.

I imagined romantic picnics on the Downs, with Prosecco and strawberries. The kind of thing I never did for her, though I knew she wanted me to. They were laughing. Kissing. I saw this faceless form of a man linking fingers with the woman I loved as they walked down the road, his hand slipping from hers to brush the small of her back, lower . . .

I tormented myself with these images. No wonder she had fallen for him, of course he would be treating her better than I had. He would be spoiling her, far more than I ever did in the early days of our relationship. It had all finally happened for us on my twenty-first birthday, at the end of my second year at UCL. Bea came up to London for the weekend to celebrate with me and some uni friends. We went for a curry at Blue Raj, and moved on to the Earl of Essex – all within a few minutes' walk of the second-floor flat I shared in Angel with Dom and John, two other members of the UCL climbing club. The others went out clubbing but Bea and I walked back to the flat and stayed up half the night talking, sharing headphones to listen to Vampire Weekend and Arcade Fire on my iPod, and drinking cans of Grolsch – sitting side by side against the worn green sofa with our legs pulled up to our chests, like old times outside the counsellors' dorms. She tried to pull her flimsy summer dress down over her knees, complaining that they were wonky. We opened the living-room window wide to let the muggy air flow in and out, and listened to the night buses and taxis, ambulance sirens, people shouting out on the streets. We watched the thin blue-striped curtains blow inwards with the breeze, and I told her I still thought about Abigail, the little girl who died at camp in Alberta.

'I can't get her out of my head.'

She put an arm around me. 'Neither can I.'

'The thought of her . . . in the water . . .' I was crying now.

'Shhh.' Bea kissed my head. 'Shhh. It's okay.'

And then, slowly, I tilted my head to look at her, our noses almost touching. And I kissed her.

'I can't talk to anyone else like this,' I whispered.

'Me neither,' Bea said, lifting her glasses off her head to push against her hair, before leaning in to kiss me back.

I ran a hand up her leg, squeezing her thigh. 'I just can't resist a good pair of wonky knees,' I murmured into her hair. She giggled, thumped me on my arm. And kissed me again.

I don't know why it took us so long to reach this point. But it marked the start of everything, of us.

Did Cameron mark the end?

With all of this going through my mind, I was glad, one night not long after, when my favourite cleaner came in. Bart was there most evenings, cheerfully introducing himself in a thick Eastern European accent. 'Hello, my friend. Bart is here to clean room.'

Then, without fail, he would sing. As a strong smell of disinfectant weaved through the air towards my face, jolly folk tunes danced in my ears. I didn't understand the words – he sang in

Polish. But once every now and then he would explain the story behind it in his stilted English and sometimes I thought I recognised a tune. The slap-slop of his mop held the rhythm, helped along by the occasional stamp he allowed himself. Usually, I enjoyed these performances.

But on this evening, he didn't choose a very helpful song. He greeted me as usual, as he moved around the few pieces of furniture to clean. Then he said, 'Tonight Bart is singing popular song from soldiers in the war. Is about Cossack – you know Cossack?' I didn't know how much he understood of my condition, but sometimes he seemed to look for a response from me. 'Cossack, he falls in love with beautiful girl.'

Oh great. A love song.

He started singing slowly, in a deep, sad voice, 'Hey tam jishna char ne vody, char dar nar carn corzak mwody . . .'

He stopped, and the chair screeched against the floor.

'But then Cossack must say goodbye to beautiful girl for last time. He go away for ever. Very sad. What other Cossack does she meet? Does she fall into love again?'

You're not helping, Bart.

He cleared his throat and clapped once, then set off at double the speed of his introductory lines. 'Hey tam jishna char ne vody, char dar nar carn corzak mwody, chew lay shev no sense yuh shweena, yesh chew lay zoo cra eena . . .'

He began clapping his hands on every beat for what must have been the chorus.

I tried to let his enthusiasm buoy me up but my mind kept bringing me back to Bea. When he had finished mopping the floor he left me alone once more in the horrible silence, surrounded by images of her with her new man – as if I was watching a non-stop stream of trailers for soon-to-be-released romcoms.

21

I didn't know what to expect when Bea next visited. Would she talk about him? Did I want her to?

When she did finally come back, it felt like several days had passed since the confrontation with Eleanor. I was facing the window and listening to the building work outside: lorries beeping as they reversed, the whir back and forth of diggers, the clatter of scaffolding poles, the ring of drills. I was lost in the noise and my thoughts as I tried to remember every small detail of the Holly King case, and anything at all about the day I fell. Between Holly's murderer, Clare and Eleanor, I knew who my money was on as the prime suspect. But as far as I could remember, I hadn't got anywhere with finding out who the real killer could be when I'd put together the campaign for Ormond's appeal. Neither had his lawyers, from what they told me. If I couldn't work it out while I was out in the world with piles of notes and witness statements at my disposal, how would I stand a chance of piecing it together now?

I didn't hear Bea come in – my door must have been propped open. I only discovered that she was there when she walked past my face. My eyes had been open – a slit – since I woke up that morning. I saw her white, ghostly shape. I smelled that perfume which I now knew she definitely wore for him. That vanilla scent. It brought a wave of nausea with it.

The first thing she did was drag the chair from my side down to the end of the bed, leaving me looking again at the dreary wall where it met the brighter greyness of the window. Just like she had on her first visit after finding the letter. Maybe it had been too much to hope that the investigation would bring her back to me. She sat in silence for several minutes, and when she did speak, all she could manage was one word.

'I –'

Then more silence, and she started picking at her nails. Tck. Tck. Tck.

'What am I –'

That sentence took her nowhere, either.

Will you ever talk to me like you used to?

'The police want to come and take away your stuff.' Her speech was cold with awkwardness, the absence of emotion. 'Whatever they don't take I'm going to box up and give to your dad.'

Tck. Tck. Tck.

'I can't afford the rent on the flat any more. I'm going to have to move out soon, so I might as well sort it all out. Graham will look after it.'

No. Don't give up on us. This is because of him, isn't it? Does he want you to get rid of any memories of me?

Tck. Tck. Tck.

'I've started sifting through some of it, getting all your things into boxes for when the police come round.'

There was something on her mind, more than boxes and rent.

Why can't you talk to me like you used to? I promise I didn't lie to you. There was no other woman.

'Christ. After that letter I wasn't going to come back. Do you know what you've done to me?' She nearly shouted her last question.

'But then there is this big what-if hanging over the whole thing. What if that letter means something else, something different to what I think it does?'

I don't know the answer. But you've got to believe that I wouldn't hurt you. Not again.

'And then everything with the police. Even if I want to forget I ever met you, forget how much you've hurt me, how can I do that now?'

Tck. Tck. Tck.

'It's like you keep pulling me back. I'm trapped. I can't leave you.'

Did this mean she was going to ditch Cameron?

She sniffed. 'I was getting everything ready for the police, pulling everything out of your wardrobe, and I found this one shoebox, pushed right to the back. I nearly didn't find it. I was so ready to find photos, notes, anything to explain that letter.'

I knew that box.

Her voice softened. 'I had no idea you'd kept all these things.' The final word cracked with her effort not to cry. I listened as she riffled through bits of paper and card – she'd brought it with her.

'Cinema ticket from our first date.' She allowed herself a small laugh. 'The first Valentine's card I sent you. These – notes I stuck to the fridge when we moved in together. Sketches I did of you when we went to Portugal.'

There was a thud as she dropped the box on the floor. 'Why would you keep all this if you didn't love me?'

Had this box given me another chance with her?

She took a couple of deep breaths in and out.

Bea. I didn't cheat on you, I swear. I learned my lesson after Josie.

She groaned. 'But how can I believe anything you ever told me?' She began picking her nails again. Tck. Tck. Tck. Slowly, rhythmically.

'I'm a sucker.'

Tck. Tck. Tck.

'They want to give up on you, you know that? Your dad and Philippa?'

Tck. Tck.

'And even after everything, I'm the one standing there saying they shouldn't, it's too soon.'

You've got to let them. I want it all to be over.

'After I found that box, I had to run it all off,' she said. The chair legs scraped slowly as she stood up, and immediately I saw her in my mind. Walking down the steps outside our front door. Checking her watch. Then: running. Running. A sheen of sweat on her brow. Elbows pumping at her side. 'Running it off' was what she did when problems were bouncing around in her mind. When things got too much, she ran. When things weren't enough, she ran.

'I went up to the Downs,' she said. 'I needed – I don't know. I needed the greenness. The clean air. I did laps up there, Upper Belgrave Road, Stoke Road, the Circular, Ladies Mile . . .'

Pictures came into my mind. These were roads I hadn't thought of for many months, and they led me up to the vast grassy expanse of the Downs: I saw myself as a little boy flying a cheap diamond kite with Dad, Saturday afternoon football league games, the brave lone saxophonist practising his blues licks in a clearing. At the far edge I saw the ice-cream van parked up by the viewing point overlooking the Avon Gorge. I looked up, at peregrine falcons soaring overhead, their fledglings leaving their nests and shrieking in the sky through June and July. I looked down, leaning over the green-painted railings, to the wide, muddy river banks far below: the Avon meandering between steep limestone cliffs and dense woodland, flowing into the distance underneath the magnificent suspension bridge and on towards the rest of the city. I heard the hum of cars on the Portway, its four lanes hugging the nearside bank of the river.

The Gorge: where I had fallen. It was mostly a trad climbing location, meaning that you had to ram pieces of protection into cracks in the rock as you went, which you then clipped your rope into to stop you hitting the deck if you fell. But there were also some sport climbs – where there were permanent bolts in the rock to clip into. They were faster and a challenge in a different way. I liked doing a bit of both. Standing at these railings, my two favourites would be just over the edge of the clifftop. Was I doing one of them? Morpheus, a classic trad route taking you diagonally across the sea walls. Gronk, just to its left – difficult but stunning, full of hidden holds. Another trad route, Transgression, with its risky 'wall of blocks' to negotiate before the final easy section of scrambling to the top. Then, my favourite: The Crum. The one that appeared nightly in my dreams. I always loved the stories behind the names, and The Crum had one of the best. Routes were named by the first person to get up them – often there was a pun involved (I'd always wanted to attempt A Steep Climb Named Desire in California), or reference to the features of the rock itself, or a connection to a historical event. The Crum was named in honour of a group of prisoners who escaped from Belfast's Crumlin Road Gaol, during the Troubles. They escaped using rope ladders thrown over the wall and became known as the Crumlin Kangaroos . . .

Thrr-ud, thrr-ud, thrr-ud.

Bea started drumming her fingers on the windowsill to my left, pulling my attention back to her. She slowed to a rhythmic tap. 'My iPod ran out of battery, so I had words going through my mind instead. I was pacing myself with the beat of them. Breathing in and out in time.' She kept tapping and spoke on the beat. 'BREATH by BREATH. STEP by STEP. WORD by WORD. KEEP RUNNing. WORK it OUT.'

Her fingers stopped tapping.

'Everywhere I looked I felt like someone was watching me. People sitting on benches, other runners.'

Everywhere? It can't be more than one person.

'I'm telling myself, it's nothing, you're being paranoid.'

I let myself hope that she was just imagining it, after all. Maybe there was no stalker. Maybe.

'And as if this isn't enough, I got another call from Daniella while I was running.'

I knew the name, but couldn't remember how.

'She left another one of her messages. "You must consider coming back again," she says. "You shouldn't tackle grief alone." Even when she's trying to be persuasive she sounds unfriendly, for fuck's sake.'

That was it. She was the grief counsellor, wasn't she?

'Three messages, and I've not been back. You'd think she'd give up . . .'

With that, she moved away from the windowsill and I felt her take up the beat of her tapping again by hitting my leg, with increasing force, as she stood by my side.

'It feels like my mind doesn't ever get a chance to rest at the moment. There's always something . . .'

She kept hitting my leg, a few inches above my knee. It felt like she wanted to hurt me, but I couldn't help but enjoy the contact – especially when a shiver ran through me, ending at my groin.

Touch me more.

'. . . but the run helped . . .'

Touch me more, please.

'BREATH by BREATH. STEP by STEP. WORK it OUT.'

With her touching my leg like that, I couldn't focus on her words. Images stole me. Bea, naked, on all fours over bright blue bedsheets. Peach and strawberry evening sunlight slipping through the blinds and gilding strips across her shoulder. Her bare white back arching, the small bumps of her vertebrae nudging out from under goose-pimpled skin as I reached one hand around to hold her heavy left breast, my other sliding between her legs.

My head spun with lightness.

Stop, Alex. Concentrate. You need to listen to her. She's stressed. Think of other things. Distract yourself.

Her nipple forming between my fingers.

Do some maths. Thirteen times sixteen. Come on, think.

Turning her head for me to kiss her ear. A small green stud in the lobe tasting metallic as I licked it.

One hundred and thirty, plus thirteen times six.

Bea, getting up to walk out of the room, without turning to show me her face. I never saw her face.

Thirteen times six. Seventy-eight.

The door closed behind her.

Two hundred and eight.

Bea on the blue bed had gone. I tuned back into the voice of the real version of her.

'. . . I just kept running. My legs were burning.'

My heart hammered. My body felt alive after our imaginary encounter.

'I went so far.' She coughed to disguise her voice breaking. 'I wanted to feel strong again. In control.'

I realised after she went that Bea hadn't mentioned Cameron at all. Did she feel too embarrassed? Whatever her reason, her decision didn't extend to other people. I heard plenty about the guy from Rosie and Tom.

They came in later that day. Or maybe it was the day after, I can't be sure. They sat in the chairs either side of me, each holding one of my hands. The most recent rearrangement by Connie meant my head was turned and tilted towards where Rosie sat. My neck was stretched on one side and the muscle, bones and skin crumpled up uncomfortably on the other.

Tom, on my left, asked about Cameron.
'I don't know if I'd have stuck around if I started seeing a girl and she told me she had a boyfriend in a coma.'

Exactly. What kind of guy would be okay with that?

Rosie leaped to Bea's defence. 'But she's lovely.'
She squeezed my hand.

'Not the point.'

'So what are you saying?'

'It's a messy situation.
I'm surprised he didn't run a mile.'

That's what I've been thinking. But then he is the type of guy who picks up vulnerable women by offering them a shoulder to cry on.

'Well, from what she said, she
didn't tell him straight away.'

'Ouch.'

'What's that supposed to mean?'

'Shouldn't she have told him straight off?'
Tom slid his hand off mine, and the chair's upholstery made a scrunching noise as he leaned back in it.

'He thought Alex was dead, at first.'

Oh yes. The grief counselling . . .

'What?'
I heard the click of cartilage in
Tom's knee as he stood up.

'Long story.' Rosie was flustered.
'She told him at first her boyfriend
had died, then only recently
broke it to him that he – well, that he hadn't.'

'And you're telling me this guy is still with her?'
Tom laughed.

'Yes.'

'He must be getting something *really* good
out of the relationship to have swallowed that.'

Don't, Tom.

'Tom! Everything isn't always about sex.'

'And he doesn't mind about the investigation?'

'No. He's really helping, especially
after what the police said.'

'They know what they're doing.'

'Do they?'

'They deal with stuff like this all the time. If they
say they haven't got enough evidence she's being
stalked, what are they supposed to do?'

So Bea had spoken to the police about her stalker again. Why
weren't they seeing a connection between this and my case?

'Well, whatever.
Cameron's good for her – he's settled.
Knows what he wants. Having him around makes her feel safer,
with everything that's been happening.'

Tom leaned his weight onto my
mattress as he spoke across me.
'She doesn't need a guy to feel safe.
She could come and stay with us.'

'Ah. So that's what this is about.'

'What?'

'You're jealous.' She laughed.

'Piss off.'

'I'm only kidding. But what's with all this,
"She doesn't need a guy to feel safe"?
You just don't think she should be seeing anyone, do you?'

'She can do what she wants.'

'But you still think she should be the
good, dutiful girlfriend to Alex.'

'It just seems weird to me, that's all.
She was always the possessive one.
You know what she was like, hated him
talking to other girls in bars.'

                              'She's not doing anything wrong.'

'But Alex can't fight for her when he's like this.'

        I imagined him waving a hand dismissively at me
                    as he said those words.
                        'Like this.'
        He was right. I could do fuck all about any of it.

22

' . . . it's not looking great for the poor chap.' Mr Lomax's voice gradually grew louder as he walked in.

'No.' A new doctor? I didn't recognise this voice. Whoever he was, he was standing by my side, checking the pulse in my right wrist. 'What do they think?'

'It's looking as if he will have to have both legs amputated,' Mr Lomax boomed from the end of the bed. 'There's no feeling in them and the damage is too bad.'

What? But my legs are fine, I can feel when you touch them.

'It's so sad for such a young man,' the other doctor said, taking his hand away from my wrist. He sounded young.

They couldn't amputate my legs. Somehow, for those few moments I forgot that I wanted to die. I guess an instinctive reaction kicked in and overrode everything else – all I could think was that I didn't want to lose my legs.

'And it was a car accident, Caroline told me?' the younger doctor asked. 'I wasn't working here when he was admitted.'

A car accident?

'No. Motorbike, I believe,' said Mr Lomax. 'Head-on collision with a bus when he was overtaking another car.'

I'd never ridden a motorbike. There must have been a mistake.

'And what about this one?' the new doctor asked, fiddling with the cover on my tracheostomy. 'How long will he carry on?'

This one? Me?

My legs were safe. I felt light-headed.

'He's a tricky one,' said Mr Lomax. 'On the one hand, his injuries have healed remarkably well, I must say. I was just reminding myself what a state he came to us in, looking through his admittance records. You heard those obnoxious detectives were asking for exact timings and the injuries he presented with and so on?'

'Dr Sharma did say something—'

'On the one hand, he's done very well. But obviously, the biggest risks now are infections. Pneumonia. As you know, one day it might be too severe for us to save him.'

His colleague murmured assent.

I listened carefully as they discussed my prognosis.

'That could happen in the next few weeks,' Mr Lomax continued. 'Or he could survive for many years. Patient hasn't shown any signs of improvement since we admitted him from ICU.'

I *had* improved. They just couldn't see.

'Wouldn't a fatal infection be one of the best options for him? For the family?'

'You could look at it like that, Dr Carmichael, yes.' Mr Lomax spoke sternly. 'They wouldn't have to make any decisions for him. Difficult decisions.'

'And you've discussed all of the options with them?' Dr Carmichael asked.

'Yes, of course. After the twelve-month period for diagnosing a permanent vegetative state, we told them we doubted there would be any improvement. Families generally hang on until then, hoping for some glimmer. But even after we pass that point, it isn't as simple as the cases you might have seen in ICU. It's not a case of switching off life support.'

'Indeed,' said Dr Carmichael, sticking something into my ear. I strained to listen from the other side.

'If the family decides that it's time to acknowledge that he's not going to get any better, then we would be looking at with-holding medical treatment if he got another infection. We could withdraw nutritional support but that would mean going to court. For certain families this is a more difficult decision to make than switching off a machine.'

'Understandable.'

Mr Lomax continued, 'Of course, it can get more difficult, the longer you leave it. It always strikes me that it has a lot to do with guilt.'

'Guilt?' Dr Carmichael inserted a finger into my mouth and lowered my bottom jaw. Poked around on my tongue. I tasted antiseptic and rubber – a gloved hand.

'Yes. Families who feel guiltier are always less ready to let them go. They want the chance, I suppose, to make things better. Families who have had a good relationship with the patient tend to be more comfortable considering it. Although, evidently, it is always a very traumatic decision.'

'You think that's a factor here?'

'I'm not sure. With this patient's family, I can't work it out. They want to keep him alive but there is no big family rift that they have mentioned.'

I'd never thought about it like this. Did Dad and Philippa feel guilty? Or Bea?

'Have you spoken to them recently?' Dr Carmichael closed my jaw, and rested a hand on my shoulder.

'The last conversation I had with them, they said they wanted to give him more time. The sister is more resistant than the father – she isn't quite ready yet. But I have a feeling it won't be too long.'

Won't be too long.

They finished their checks, moved on to talking about a new government initiative they disagreed with.

Won't be too long.

*

If they really were going to let me die soon, I needed to get my act together and work out who had done this to me. I needed to know who would be held responsible for my murder. Just like the police, I was trying to work out plausible suspects and motives, but with significantly fewer resources.

I imagined laying all the facts out on the floor, like I had done with all my notes on Holly King. What did I have? Where were the holes? What were the patterns?

The first thing to consider was a series of photos. All women. I turned them over, one by one, to read the text scribbled on the back in my handwriting. First, a pale face, dark thick fringe, big brown eyes, thin lips. 'Clare. Second year uni. Few dates. Sociology? Saw her once more, third year. She didn't see me. No baby with her.' Then three more photos in quick succession, out-of-focus, poor-quality images. A blonde (Kate), a girl with long dark curls (Susy), a petite redhead with freckles (Sophia). Only their names on the back of each print. On the back of a photo of a girl with tattoos down one arm, were the words: 'Vicki. Could drink me under the table. Nice laugh.' And finally, I flipped over the photo of another blonde, this one strong-shouldered with chalky hands. 'Rachel: really good climber, from Exeter Uni. First year. Level-headed. Can't be her?' And that was it. Those were the only ones I could really remember. There were other names that I couldn't even match to faces – Erin, Dani, Georgia. I didn't feel proud of myself – if I'd paid more attention, been a bit less of a dick, maybe I wouldn't have ended up where I was now. But try telling that to a randy nineteen-year-old.

These few faces, and these sparse facts, were all I had on this line of my investigation. Yes – any of them could have sent the letter, if somehow I had managed to get one of them pregnant. But could one of them have tried to kill me? It had to be unlikely. Wouldn't there have been some better revenge to take? Wouldn't it have been better to get money out of me, or even just an apology?

Which led me to the next thread of my suspicions. Work-related grudges. I imagined sitting down at my computer and trawling through my cuts: every story I had ever written. I wasn't perfect, but I had never pissed anyone off that badly, had I? I'd always seen myself as the kind of reporter who could talk to anyone – from brickies to barristers, from little children to nonagenarians. I found it easy to get on with people, to such an extent that Bill used to sneer across the office after listening to me charm someone over the phone, 'Alex bloody Jackson. Thinks he's everyone's best friend.'

But that wasn't completely true. There were plenty of people I had written stories about, who later called in to complain. Court cases I'd covered that went online and made it hard for the defendant to get a job once they came out of prison. Interviews that people felt had misrepresented them. All of us in the office had had a couple of death threats in our time, but they were rarely taken that seriously. One guy who didn't like the story I wrote about his restaurant getting a low food hygiene rating called me up to say, 'I hope you sleep well tonight and don't lie awake, thinking about me coming round there with a meat cleaver'. I couldn't even remember his name, though – that was the last I heard from him, and it was at least two years before my fall.

One threat I did take more seriously, and which Bill made me report to the police, was from Rita Younge, a woman in her forties who we knew had been sectioned several times. The story I had written wasn't about her, but about her twin brother, who had been caught exposing himself to children in a park in St George. He'd been sent down, but Rita didn't like the way I had written about him, and began a nasty vendetta against me. She wrote in to the letters pages under false names, slandering me and saying I was a paedophile; we recognised her handwriting from the notes she stuck to my car windscreen detailing how she would go about torturing me. She would call my office landline and repeat, over and over, 'You won't get away with this. He wasn't a bad man, my brother. He's innocent.' I tried reasoning with her, the first few times she called. I explained that I wasn't the judge that sent her brother down, that he had pleaded guilty, and I'd written a very reasonable account of what he had been caught doing. It was, in fact, a very dull article, buried in a left-hand hamper on page twenty-four. I wasn't afraid – it was clear that she wasn't well and I didn't think she would see her threats through. But when she wouldn't stop, Bill called the police. An officer was sent to speak to Rita and I never heard from her again. It couldn't be her, could it? Why would she go quiet for months and then reappear to do something to me while I was climbing? It didn't seem plausible. And the letter – it wasn't her style. The wording didn't fit. Neither did the photo of the baby.

But then, the letter appeared to have nothing to do with the Holly King case, either. Apart from the fact that there was no child involved, the letter had arrived at our flat before I'd started doing any interviews. I was pretty sure about that.

The other doubt I had was that killing me wouldn't have killed the Holly King story. True, the rest of the articles in that series we were going to run were still unwritten – interviews with relatives, Ormond's lawyer. (As I left the office on that final Friday afternoon, Bill had shouted after me: 'I want the next one filed by Monday at eight sharp, princess. Get those fucking interviews out of your notebook.') But anyone in that office could have followed my trail and done those interviews again – and besides, for all the murderer knew, the shorthand scribbles in my notebook had all been typed up and turned into page leads. It would have been a massive assumption on his part to think that killing me would stop the paper running more.

No. If Holly's murderer was behind this, then he must have been banking on scaring the rest of my team so badly that nobody would touch the story, that even the editor would be afraid to take it further. He obviously didn't know how a journalist's mind worked.

For all the question marks that lingered over the Holly King case, it remained the most probable lead I had. For someone to try to kill me, they had to have a reason to punish me. Or, they thought and acted differently to most decent people. Someone who didn't have a problem with killing. There had to be a link between this case and my letter, I just couldn't see it. It was too much of a coincidence for me to receive such a threatening note within weeks of someone trying to kill me.

I never knew what happened to the rest of that case. Was William Ormond out of prison? Had they caught the real murderer? If only I knew.

But there was one more person to consider. Eleanor. If only to rule her out once and for all. Practically, I couldn't think what she could have done to make me fall the way I had. And then there was the question of motivation. There were only two ideas I could come up with. One: that I'd done something that day to piss her off and she'd done something on impulse. Two: she genuinely was in love with me, though God knows why, and decided that if she couldn't have me, then nobody could. That, quite frankly, seemed ridiculous.

It made more sense, if she really did care about me, for it *not* to be her. I remembered how angry she had been when she saw Bea with Cameron. If anything, her target would be Bea, not me.

Out of everyone I was lining up as a suspect, I knew Eleanor the best. I trusted her. She wouldn't try to hurt me. She just wouldn't. I couldn't bring myself to believe that one of my closest friends would do that. What kind of a man did it make me, even allowing myself to consider it? And besides, whenever she visited, she not only went over the day of my fall repeatedly – an unlikely thing for my attacker to do – but she bombarded me with a never-ending stream of confessions. Wouldn't this have been one of them? The biggest of all?

I picked up the pile of imaginary notes about her from the memorised brown carpet tiles around my office desk, and put them in the imaginary bin, along with week-old banana skins, crisp packets, and chewed-to-death Biros.

Over those weeks, the nights felt longer than the days. Lonely, and more painful than ever. My body experienced a series of excruciating cramps. My legs. My back. Arms, toes, hands. The muscles contracting and stiffening against the fabric of my thin pyjamas and the bedsheets. And as I lay there, unable to sleep, I thought about the person who had tried to murder me, coming back to finish the job. I was jumpy every time someone came into my room. What was taking them so long? It could only be a matter of time. I'd been here for more than eighteen months. If they came, there would be nothing I could do.

23

'. . . it just makes you wonder if any of us is safe. Ever.'
Philippa had high-heel-clipped her way in, thrown a new bunch
of flowers onto the table next to me, and was now telling Connie
everything she knew about the police investigation, as Connie set
up my food pump for the night.

'Well, indeed.' Connie gently rolled me over onto my back –
obviously aware that she needed to treat me a bit better in front
of my sister.

'Then the liaison woman came round yesterday to see how we
were, and she told us something that the other guy, the detective
or whoever he was, hadn't told us before.' Philippa paced in her
heels. Clip, clip, clip.

'Oh yes?' I heard the buzz of the controller for my bed as
Connie raised my head and torso. The upper half of my body
hinged upwards and forwards.

'Apparently, the day Alex was out climbing, some birdwatcher
was at the top, up by the Downs. And they saw someone right at
the spot where Alex should have finished his climb. Standing
there, right on the edge of the cliff.'

The buzzing stopped and I felt Connie pull my bed sheet
down and roll my pyjama top up to expose my stomach. I wanted
her to stop, to let me concentrate on what Philippa was saying.

Doing what? Watching me?

Connie tugged sharply on the tube stuck into my abdomen, an inch or two above my belly button, causing an intense stab of pain. I felt coldness inside me as she flushed liquid through the tube into my stomach.

'Anonymous tip-off, they're saying. The birdwatcher. Didn't leave a name.'

'But what does that mean?' Connie asked, out of breath from the effort of taking care of me. There was the sound of plastic being fiddled with as she attached my feeding tube to the pumping machine. 'Did she explain?'

For once in her life, Connie was proving useful – asking the questions I wanted answered. I heard a tap and the machine droned into life. The fourteen-hour feeding cycle had begun, and cool liquid started to trickle into my stomach.

'No. That was it. She was definitely talking like this person that was seen up there was a suspect, although she didn't come out and say it in so many words. I think she probably wasn't meant to have said anything, so when we started asking more questions she shut down. What were they doing up there?' Clip, clip, clip. 'Meanwhile, that girlfriend of his carries on as if nothing has happened, as if he doesn't exist. I told you she's got herself a new man, didn't I?'

'Yes, you did – shameful. I can't believe it.' Connie held my head forward as she fluffed up my pillows. This did not form part of her usual routine – it was all for show.

'He loved that girl. Why, I don't know,' Philippa said.

I didn't know what made me angrier – her sharing details of my private life with Connie, or the way she had it in for Bea. I didn't want my girlfriend to be with someone else, but I could understand why she was doing it. Why couldn't Philippa?

'If I see them together, I swear I don't know what I'll do,' Philippa said. 'I tried talking to Dad but he thinks it's a good thing! I don't know what's got into him recently, it's like he's forgotten Alex is his son.'

Clip, clip, clip.

'I suppose I'd best be getting off.' The door clicked shut and cut off Philippa's voice.

This was big news. Why had this tip-off birdwatcher guy only just come forward? Was that the only new information the police had?

I knew the spot where twitchers congregated to watch for falcons. Had he been there? If so, I could see the ledge where this other person might have been standing, a ledge where several routes finished. Anyone could easily climb over the low mesh fencing running alongside the path at the edge of the Gorge. There was a good bit of land on the other side. It would be easy to look down at climbers beneath you. So someone was standing there, right at the point where I would have topped out when I finished the climb? What did that mean? People were always there, ignoring the danger of the cliff edge. It wasn't unusual.

There had to be more. For them to be talking about this person as a suspect, as Philippa seemed to think they were, they must have been doing something.

Had they thrown something at me? Kicked me? Pushed me as I got to the top? What else could it be, for the police to be interested?

One person was ruled out, if what Philippa said was true. Eleanor couldn't have been at the top. I was leading the climb – she'd told me so. She was somewhere lower down on the rock, beneath me, waiting to follow me up.

So who else could've known I was there?

24

One of the worst visits I had after finding out about the tip-off was when Bea brought in a selection of music for me.

'I was talking about you to . . . a friend,' she said, standing next to me, chewing her gum noisily. My face ached with the absence of her kiss. How long had it been since she'd touched me with any affection? But at least she hadn't dragged the chair down to the end of my bed this time. Did that count as progress?

A friend? I'm not an idiot.

'I've brought my iPod.' I felt her put it on my chest and heard the quiet rattle as she untangled the wires of the headphones. 'He says it might spark recognition in your brain, bring you round in a way that talking won't.' She spoke quickly and abruptly, like she always did when she was in a bad mood. Or upset.

Dad had already tried music therapy, I wanted to tell her. The doctors recommended it to him months ago. Did they never mention it to her?

'He suggested a few songs we could try,' she said. Chew, chew, chew.

What's up?

I'd known her long enough to know that gum meant she wanted a cigarette, which meant she was on edge about something.

'I just need to know we've tried everything. I need to know for sure that you're not—'

Not conscious?

Is that what was upsetting her?

'Your dad's on a mission. Says we've got to do something. But I can't – you know – I can't until I'm sure it's the right thing.'

Something wasn't right here. If she was upset because of the thought of me dying, she would be more teary. More emotional. That wasn't how she was talking. She was worked up about something.

What's happened?

Minty breath fell onto my face as she leaned across me, pressing the headphones in so roughly that it hurt. Her touch jolted me after so long going without it – it was like electricity shivering through me. But I didn't feel able to enjoy it.

'So, here's the first one,' she said. Chew, chew, chew. 'This band is playing in town next week. We might go. They're not very well known. My – my friend saw them supporting this other group . . .'

Indie rock filled my ears. It was too loud and hurt my eardrums. It was repetitive, catchy – I could see why they might like it. Once, I might have liked this kind of music, too. But not today. Never would I like this song. This song that he had picked.

Worse, it was a love song. I couldn't bear to think of them listening to it together, holding hands, singing the words to each other.

' "You begged me to stay when I had to go," ' a cocky kid with a Manchester accent sang each time the chorus kicked in. ' "And you told me your name so I'd always know." '

Bea pressed the headphones in again, but I could just hear her speak through the music. 'It's his favourite.'

Fuck you, dickhead. Fuck you.

'No?' Chew, chew, chew. 'Let's try this.'

Hip-hop.

Really?

She knew I hated this kind of music.

'We thought this one might jar you a bit, you know. The rhythms and the lyrics . . .' Expletives filled my ears, drowning out her words.

Heat was rising to my face. After so long feeling only over-whelming love for her, the unfamiliar anger sent a tremor through me.

She watched me for a while longer, then I heard the faint sound of her sitting down in the chair next to me. The music continued loudly, through a random selection of tracks I didn't want to listen to – each presumably chosen by her 'friend'. It blocked out the rest of the noises in the room, until one of the headphones slipped out.

Bea was muttering to herself. I hadn't realised she was still talking until my right ear was released from its musical torture. I could hear the flickering of paper, too. Pages in a notebook?

What have I missed?

'. . . then yesterday . . . May twenty-seventh . . .' She spoke slowly: her diary-writing voice. '. . . windscreen smashed . . . brick lying in road . . . both wing mirrors kicked off . . .'

Her stalker? This was going too far. The violence of what she described shocked me.

'. . . first I thought it might be the usual . . . students on their way home . . .'

It's too much of a coincidence.

'. . . but mine was the only one targeted on the street . . . nothing missing, either . . .'

She mumbled more words, scratched her pen on the page. In my left ear the track had changed to classical music of some kind.

The heat came back to my face – of anger directed not at Bea this time but at whoever was making her feel like this. Her car must have been what was making her sound so agitated today.

'. . . don't know what they want from me . . .'

It has to be your stalker. You're not safe.

'. . . police sent someone out last night . . . glad it wasn't that Halliwell guy again . . .'

Finally. So they're taking it seriously?

'. . . what'll I get home to find next?'

Don't let it get to you. That's what they want.

'. . . freaking me out . . . keep thinking . . .'

I'm sorry. I wish I could help.

'. . . is it the woman who sent Alex the letter?'

I think it's linked to the letter, but . . .

What did I think? Someone was trying to scare her. Or warn her. It had to be related to what had happened to me. But was that really down to a jealous ex of mine? There was no way of telling Bea about my suspicions about the Holly King case.

Again, police evidence photos of the girl's body flashed into my mind. It would be all my fault, if –

If –

Had I led him to Bea? Had he come after me, then had his attention drawn to her? If he'd known where I climbed he'd know Bea was my girlfriend. But why start to persecute her two years after trying to kill me?

She sat at the end of my bed for what felt like a long time, in silence. The iPod kept on playing into my ear, shuffling through track after track. I didn't know any of them.

Please. Stop. Leave her. It's me you want.

Don't hurt her.

Please, I'd do anything.

Come here, kill me if that's what you want. But leave her alone.

Eventually, Bea stood up, and went as if to pull the remaining headphone out. But she stopped briefly before she did so, and I could feel her eyes on my face.

'Alex?' She rested her fingers on my ear. 'Nothing . . .'

She removed the headphone and I heard her drop the iPod into her bag.

'Nothing.'

Her footsteps padded away from me, towards the door.

Be careful. Please.

I imagined her journey through dark streets. I saw her arriving home to find her door kicked in and a masked man with a knife, waiting for her. Pushing her to the floor, cutting a gash in her cheek. Tearing off her clothes. Raping her. Leaving her for dead in the bedroom.

The vividness of it convinced me I was having a premonition, or a vision of the present. My heart pumped fast, my underarms felt damp and drops of sweat rolled down my temples from my forehead.

I can't—

I gasped for air. Choked on the saliva pooling in my mouth.

I must have exhausted myself after several hours of panic. I found I was asleep, trapped in the same vision – watching from the corner of our flat, trying to help her, trying to shout to her but realising that saline drip lines bound my wrists and ankles, and the sponges used to clean my mouth were stuffed into it, gagging me.

When I woke up I was shattered.

I lay there, waiting for someone to come in and tell me Bea had been found.

25

You need to go to her flat.

I wanted to scream at the nurses every time they came in.

Bea is in danger.

'Time to clean you up, Alex.'

You've got to get her some help.

'Let's turn you onto your side, shall we?'

There's nothing I can do.

'We need to get rid of some of that phlegm in your throat for you.'

She's dead. Bea is dead.

'Fucking donkey. Look at this mess.'

She's dead. It's my fault.

This went on for what felt like days on end. The only visitors I had were hospital staff. Bea lay lifeless and cold on the floor in her flat. When would they find her?

By the time Rosie and Tom next visited I was furious that nobody cared enough to notice her absence. Tension and aches plagued my body.

Why haven't you checked on her?

Rosie sat in the chair on my left, and from the direction of Tom's voice it sounded like he stood next to her by the window. When they walked in, the smell of food hit me – spices, meat, salt, fat. The torturous smell of meals served to other patients on the ward came and went every day. But this seemed stronger, closer. They must have eaten just before coming in.

'I can't stop thinking about him,' Rosie said. 'How could someone do this? There's a guy in one of my classes who looks like him. Red hair. Freckles.'

'Huh.' Tom cracked his knuckles.

Don't worry about me. What about Bea? Why haven't you been to see her?

'It could have been you,' she said.

'We've been over this. Whoever was behind this, they were after Al. For whatever reason.'

Leave. Go. You've got to go and find her. There might still be time.

'I can't get it out of my head, though.' She paused, changed tack. 'Oh crap . . . did you bring forks?'

'Yep,' Tom said.

'Feels a bit strange eating in here.'

I heard a plastic bag being crumpled, followed by several pops that coincided with a new, intense smell wafting over to me.

'Where's the peshwari naan?' asked Rosie.

'You didn't ask for one.'

'Don't you remember me saying not to get a plain one?' She sighed. 'Never mind.'

Was this really happening? They were going to eat an Indian takeaway in front of me. The food smelled delicious. My mouth watered. I was already thirsty, as always, and now my stomach rumbled jealously.

How can you do this?

Through mouthfuls of what I imagined to be tender lamb bhuna and perfectly spiced pilau rice, charred tandoori chicken and sweet mango chutney, they carried on chatting.

'When does Bea reckon her car will be sorted?' Tom asked.

'A week, if she's lucky? They could only start on it this morning.' Rosie stopped, swallowed.

Relief flooded me. Bea was alive. There had been no one waiting for her that night when she got home from hospital. I felt my muscles relax slowly, starting with my shoulders, moving down my spine to my legs, as if I'd downed a shot of neat whisky.

'So is she going to the police again?' Tom chewed his food noisiliy.

Rosie took a forkful of curry before she carried on, almost unintelligible. 'This is the thing I don't get . . . she did tell them about the car, but not about the phone call.'

'Maybe she just hasn't got round to it. It's not even been twenty-four hours.'

'No – she says she's not going to bother.' I heard cutlery scraping against plastic. I imagined wiping up the last bits of curry sauce and chutney with my finger. Rosie went on. 'I don't know . . . she says all this stuff is happening, but . . .'

'What do you mean, "she *says*"?'

No reply.

'Rose?'

'It's just that she's – she's acting in a certain way.'

'Meaning?'

'She's refusing to go to the police. Saying they'll fob her off again.'

'And?'

'Do you think there's a chance that she's making it up?'

'Rosie Phelan! You're meant to be her friend.'

Why would Bea make this up?

'I know, I know, but what if? It's all so strange. She seems to think there are several people following her. She thinks the car being totalled is linked too, but that kind of thing goes on all the time round there. It'll be students.'

'But how would you explain that call? Phone rings as soon as she walks into the flat, and then the line goes dead – sounds to me like someone keeping pretty close tabs on her.'

'Oh, I don't know. Maybe she isn't making it up, then. But she could be imagining it. She is under a lot of stress.'

'Rosie . . .'

'And the other strange thing is she doesn't want to tell her parents about any of it.'

'So?'

'But she normally tells them everything, they talk all the time, like – every day or every other day. She doesn't want to bother them with this, though. I feel like there's more to it.'

'She could just be telling you the truth.'

Tom coughed, and his mouth slurped at a drinks bottle. The noise shot me through with longing. It sounds crazy but I fantasised daily about those stainless steel bottles we used to take out climbing, to the point that I thought I could taste the faint metallic sharpness that the liquid always took on. I wanted a drink so badly.

'I don't know. Something doesn't add up,' Rosie said.

Bea was safe – for now. But for how long? My inability to do anything was unbearable. If the police wouldn't help, she hadn't told her parents, and her best friend was doubting her, who was going to protect her?

Someone had to take action, I kept telling myself.

Someone has to do something.

I have to do something.

26

Everything shifted.

I had wanted to know who put me in this hospital bed since I found out it wasn't an accident, but now I wanted more. More than the five Ws, as we called them in the newsroom. What, when, who, why, where.

My feelings of frustration at my inertness became something else. I didn't just want to gain some kind of peace before I died. I wanted to look this person in the eyes. I wanted the chance to help Bea, to save her from the fate I could feel her careering towards. She hadn't been hurt, yet. How long before her stalker went to the next level? I might be the only person who could help the police work out who had tried to kill me, and who was putting so much effort into intimidating her. Lying here, thinking about it all while I waited for death, was no longer an option. My mounting fear for Bea was the catalyst that made me see how stupid I had been to accept my demise without a fight.

Adrenalin coursed through me, excitement making my limbs and heart feel strong as I let myself believe for the first time in months that I might actually be able to beat this peculiar sickness. I let myself think things that I had been blocking, turning away from, ever since I found out that my accident was no such thing. I had spent all those months before that moment thinking that fate had put me here. If it was fate, it meant I deserved it, and that nobody could have done anything to stop it. It was always going to happen. I got it into my head that I was destined to slip, to have hit my head. It was karma. And so, resigned to this fact and overwhelmed by the situation I found myself in, I had decided I wanted to die. And when I found out that wasn't true, that someone had deliberately tried to end me, I had been too stubborn to see what that meant for my death wish.

But now. Now! I finally gave myself permission to acknowledge that this new information flipped my perspective upside down and inside out. I'd been cheated of my life and my chance to make up for things I'd done. I'd been cheated of so much. And I wanted to get it all back.

Everything shifted.

I was not ready to die.

Whatever route you climb, wherever you are, whatever the difficulty, there is always a crux – the hardest section, the point of the climb where the most danger exists. On many climbs, the moves before and after it are easy in comparison. The crux is where you prove yourself. I had thought for some time that my fall, my descent into this mysterious illness, waking up trapped inside my body – this whole thing was the crux move of my life. Without a doubt, it was the hardest thing I had ever had to go through.

Now I saw that even the string of months I had been hospital were just part of that build-up. Now I had reached my biggest challenge. Usually, you would stand at the bottom of a route and identify the hardest sections, prepare for them, make sure you saved enough energy to complete them. But I hadn't been able to plan for this. All I could do was stay calm, work out my strategy, and commit to it. You couldn't beat a crux unless you believed you could – it was a mental challenge as much as a physical one. Out on the rock, you had to know you could do the moves and trust that on the other side the climb would be more straightforward again and you would have energy to get to the top. Right now, I had to trust that the hard work I was about to put in would pay off, and I would get my life back. I was going to find a way to show someone – anyone – that I was awake.

It wasn't going to be easy.

For a start, I was running out of time. For many, many months I had silently willed Dad to let me die, and it had finally started to look like he would.

The day after Rosie and Tom had their curry, Dad and Philippa visited. They had barely been here five minutes when the door opened again.

'Oh, great,' Philippa said. 'Look who's decided to show her face.'

'Philippa,' Dad warned.

'Your new boyfriend busy, is he? Got a spare few minutes to visit your old one?'

Bea?

'I can go. Come back later,' Bea said. 'I didn't know—'

'What? That he would have a visit from people who actually care about him?'

'Enough!' Dad shouted. 'You don't need to go anywhere, Bea. Stay.'

Bea mumbled a thank-you and the three of them remained in an awkward silence for a few minutes.

Bea, I'm going to get out of here. I'm going to sort this out.

I felt invigorated after my change of heart. I was really going to do this. I would find a way to communicate, then one day I'd get out of this hospital.

I'm finding a way back to you.

'Have you heard anything else from the police?' Bea asked. 'I called them, but they say they can't tell—'

'I'm not sure we should discuss it,' Philippa cut in.

Bea didn't rise to my sister's rudeness. She was clearly feeling sheepish about Cameron, otherwise she would have been giving as good as she got.

'Sorry, but there might be reasons they've told us one thing and you another,' Philippa said, coldly.

Bea tried again. 'But they must know we will talk to each other?'

'I'm surprised to see you here, if I'm honest,' Philippa said.

Don't talk to her like that.

'Don't take it out on Bea.' Dad spoke calmly but firmly. 'Life is complicated, Phil. It isn't always as black and white as you'd like to think. How many times do I have to tell you that?'

There was silence again. Dad's limping footsteps moved towards the chair on my right, and he pressed a hand on my bed to steady himself as he sat down. He reached out his fingers to stroke my face.

Bea was the next to speak. 'I think I'm going to leave you to it.'

'Stay,' Dad repeated. 'While we're all here, we should talk about what happens next with Alex.'

You need to keep me alive. Give me more time.

'Bea might have come round to our way of thinking, now that she's replaced him,' Philippa muttered.

Bea ignored her. 'You really want to do this?' she asked Dad.

'Yes.'

'You as well, Philippa?'

Exactly what I would have asked. Since when had Philippa sided with Dad on this?

'It's the best thing to do.' Philippa didn't sound convinced to me. 'Dad's right.'

'You never met Diane,' Dad said. 'But when she wanted to die, Alex supported her in that decision. I've been trying to think of anything he said during his life that would give me an indication of what he'd want me to do now.'

No. Don't do this.

'Philippa, back me up here,' he continued. 'Alex didn't want his mother to have all that extra treatment. He wanted her to have a dignified death, didn't he? That's what he would want for himself.'

I couldn't blame him for what he was doing, but I was horrified at how my words were being turned back on me. I'd said those things about Mum – not me. That wasn't what I wanted for myself.

'But are you sure we've tried absolutely everything?' Bea's voice sped up. 'And I was thinking, with the criminal investigation. Shouldn't we at least wait until we find out what happened to him?'

Yes, this is good. Keep going.

'Nothing's changed as far as his condition goes,' Dad said.

Things have changed. THINGS HAVE CHANGED.

Pain stabbed at my temples.

'But I think Alex would want us to be totally sure. He wouldn't want us to give up on him yet.'

'But when?' Philippa jumped in. 'When would we finally be able to do that? What do you propose we do in the meantime? They can't keep him in hospital for ever. What do you want us to do? Bring him home? We can't afford to modify the house, buy all the equipment they say we'd need. Dad's arthritis is getting worse.'

Dad made a noise of protest.

'What? It is. You forget things, too. And look at those glasses! They're filthy. You can barely look after yourself, let alone him. You'd have to give up your job, and I can't be there, and we can't afford to pay anyone, and there's no space in the only nursing home in Bristol that could take him, so he'd be miles away and—'

She stopped abruptly and within seconds the door slammed. Had someone walked out? Come in?

'Sorry,' Dad said. 'You wouldn't always know it from the way she talks but she is really upset that we can't care for him at home. She doesn't want to give up her job, and I wouldn't let her anyway. She's struggling with it all, to be honest. She's only recently accepted the idea of – of this.'

'I could take care of him,' Bea said.

'You know you couldn't,' Dad said gently. 'It's difficult. We're planning to go ahead with this.'

Dad, please. Don't do this.

'Please think about it some more,' he said. 'We want your backing, too.' From the direction of where he was sitting, I heard the soft thud of a glasses case opening, shutting, opening, shutting.

Neither of them spoke.

Opening, shutting. Thud. Thud.

'I'm going to head home.' Bea sounded exhausted. 'You staying?'

'For a bit. Philippa will calm down and come back soon, I imagine.'

'Okay. Look, I'll think about it,' Bea said. 'But I think he'd want to keep fighting, I really do. I think he'd want us to take more time. Be sure about what we are doing. Get them to do more tests, at least.' The door clicked open and shut.

I heard Dad shift in the chair, but he didn't speak for a while. *Don't do this to me.*

If I thought it enough, would the message get through?

Don't do it don't do it don't do it.

He leaned on my bed again as he eased himself out of the chair, then walked behind me, towards the wall where the devil suctioning machine was kept, where I had listened to the nurses washing their hands in a sink and pulling paper towels out of a dispenser to dry them. For something I had never seen, I had quite a clear picture of what it all looked like.

And then, out of the silence there came a terrifyingly loud and sudden noise. A guttural roar from Dad, followed quickly by a clattering, smashing sound. As I tried to understand what had happened, the room went totally silent once more. What had just happened? Had he hit something on the wall? Kicked a chair? Or had he fallen?

Are you okay? Dad?

I heard him move back towards me, and as he got closer I could make out the heaviness of his breathing. It was the way people breathed after physical exertion, but there was something else in it too – the stuttering, irregular rhythm that gave away tears.

As he passed my bed on his way to the door, he briefly stopped to touch my shoulder. I could feel him shaking.

27

Bea was back the next day, reeking of cigarettes.

She was sitting on the edge of the bed, her hip against mine, her leg jiggling up and down, her foot tapping on the floor. I felt the movement through the whole mattress.

'They're still watching me.' Her body shivered against mine. 'I called the police last night, and I mentioned your letter – again. At least they've got it now.' Her leg kept bouncing. Tap, tap, tap. 'And I asked again if they'd found out any more about who vandalised my car, but they said it was unlikely they would ever pin it on anyone.'

Why aren't they helping you more?

'What I don't get is why the woman who sent that letter to you, who did this to you, why she would be doing this to me, now? What have I done to her? Nothing. It has to be linked, but I don't see why she is doing it.'

I think you're on the wrong track. Don't assume it's some jilted woman.

'Am I losing it? I know that's what Rosie thinks.'

I hope you are. It would be better that than have the person I think it is following you.

'I feel totally powerless. The guy in the car, watching the flat the other day. I went out there, ready to confront him, ask who the hell he was. But he saw me coming and drove off. What can I do? I just have to sit it out and wait for the police to charge someone?'

She was talked out, and sat quietly. I saw an opportunity to put my crux plan into action. If I wanted to show any of them that I was awake, I needed to get their attention. Of course, I had tried to do this for all those months before I gave up on my fight for life. But maybe I hadn't tried hard enough? Now, I had renewed focus. I was going to make it happen, I was determined. I tried to make a noise. Maybe I could grunt, or cough. I concentrated hard but nothing happened.

Come on, Alex. COME ON. Get her attention.

Still, nothing. How did you do it? I couldn't remember. I tried to find a muscle in my chest, mouth, neck, that would react when I tried to tense it or move it. I tried to scream. Tried to blow out air from my mouth.

Still, nothing. Bea wasn't noticing my efforts. I kept trying to grunt.

Arghfh. Harghb.

She starting talking again. 'I've been thinking about . . .'

I ignored her. I needed to try something else.

I made myself think about all the regrets I had about my mother's death. I thought about not telling her I loved her enough when I was a kid. I thought about telling her I hated her too often when I was a teenager. I thought about never taking her to the theatre, like she'd wanted me to. I thought about finding excuses not to visit her when she was in hospital. I thought about my decision to back her up when she said that she wanted to be allowed to die.

It worked. The tears started coming, dribbling down my face.

Look at me. Can't you see that I'm awake? These are real tears.

'I can't just sit around waiting for this to go away. I've got to do something. I'm going to head down to the Gorge this afternoon, see if I can find the spot Tom showed me,' she was saying. 'Take another look at where it happened.'

Bea. Look at me.

How was I going to do this? I screamed another silent scream. *AAARGH. Listen. I'm here.*

The next morning, I put the second part of my plan into action. I had to get them to run more tests on me. When Dr Sharma did his ward round I tried my grunting routine again.

Arghfh. Harghb.

'Let's have a quick check of your heart,' he said, and a cold piece of metal slid under my pyjama top onto the skin of my chest.

Arghfh. Harghb.

'All sounding good . . .' I stopped listening to him, instead focusing all my energy on my mission.

Pfffffsk. Help. Me.

There was no noise.

Run the tests. Run the tests again. Let me show you this time. Run the tests. Run the tests. The tennis test. The house test. Let me show you.

I said those words over and over and over in my mind.

Run the tests. Run the tests. Run the tests.

I was vaguely aware of him talking, but I tuned it out and kept on with my mantra.

Run the tests. Run the tests. I want to find a way to communicate with you. I want to talk to my family. Run the tests. Give me another chance. I'll try this time. Run the tests.

The door clicked shut. He'd left the room.

I was due a miracle, and it came through. The next day, two days after I found the will to live again, Dr Sharma came back in with Pauline. Nothing unusual in that.

I resumed my chant.

Run the tests. Run the tests.

I tried to speak.

Gahhhf. Froooomn. Cahgbod.

And to my surprise, he said, 'His dad has given us the go-ahead for another round of our tennis scans. I've got some time later today – can you get him ready for about two o'clock?'

'No problem, Dr Sharma,' Pauline said.

'We've refined the tests a little. It'll be interesting to compare his previous results to today's. Although I'm not expecting to see much of a change, if I'm honest.'

Wait until you get me in there.

Later that day, Pauline came to wheel me out, down the corridors, back to the room with the MRI scanner.

Dr Sharma gave me the same instructions, and the nurse assisting him put headphones into my ears. My heart was pumping fast, my mouth dry. They slid me into the machine. Could this be the moment they finally realised?

The music started and so did the whirring, mechanical drone patterns of the scanner, alternating with electrical clicking sounds. Dr Sharma's voice came in through the headphones and he asked me to imagine playing tennis. I did it. I served, I returned shots, I jumped up and down and ran around, all in my mind. I threw myself into it. I envisaged them watching all this impressive mental activity on their screens. But when they spoke to me over the sound system, they didn't betray any emotion. Dr Sharma said, 'Now, imagine walking through the rooms of your house. Go into one room, look around. Think about what you would see. Then move into another room.'

I found myself on the doorstep of my parents' home, not the flat I had shared with Bea. I stood outside the front door, which was painted red with glass panels. I twisted the handle and stepped through the door into a magnolia-walled hallway with wooden floors. It smelled like home. Like Mum – hairspray and red roses perfume. Like dinner on the table. Like football kit that needed washing. There was a bowl of potpourri on the small table on the left.

I carried on walking through, towards the back of the house. My feet paused on the tiled kitchen floor, which always felt cool underfoot. There was a table on the left where we would sit to have dinner, with a vase full of pink lilies on a crocheted mat in the middle of it. I saw the big seat Philippa and I used to fight over. The boiler on the wall. Pine cupboards. And there, on the right, by the gas hob, stood my mother. She turned to smile at me, stirring beef stew in the saucepan in front of her. Then she turned away again.

Out of the kitchen and then doubling back on myself to the left, I was in the back room. Tiled floor, again. Full of things; junk, you might call it. The big stereo that was outdated now. My old sports equipment: hockey stick, cricket bats.

I walked into my dad's study. On the wall was his volcano calendar, which Phil and I had given him several years ago and he'd never taken down, pinned open at April and showing a huge ash cloud exploding out of a volcano somewhere in Papua New Guinea. Behind the glass door of a display cupboard was his collection of rock specimens. His prized possession was a slice of beautiful Cotham Marble which he once told me he had found and polished up when I was just a baby. 'Not easy to find, this,' he had said to me, proudly. 'And you only get it round Bristol.' I used to love stroking the smoothness of its surface and looking at the detail in it – its patterns like a perfect landscape painting, complete with rows of silhouetted elm trees and ploughed fields. I opened the door to reach in and pick it up—

'Thank you, Alex,' Dr Sharma spoke through my headphones. The thrumming of the MRI stopped. 'That's it for now.'

Did you see anything?

My head was hot, and I could feel the adrenalin pumping through me.

Has it worked?

As they pulled me out of the scanner and took the headphones out, I heard Dr Sharma whistling.

Please, tell me. You saw my brain working, didn't you?

He sounded happy. Didn't he?

A door clicked open and I was wheeled out into another room where I could smell something sweet – Pauline, waiting to take me back to the ward. 'How did it go?' she asked.

Dr Sharma stopped whistling, and sighed.

'Same as last time.'

28

When the man came in, I was distracted. He interrupted a vigorous training session I was putting myself through. I'd moved on from sound to movement. I had already tried to flex each muscle in my body in turn, or at least every limb, toe and finger, eyelid and lip, and now I was focusing on two small areas. Perhaps I could build strength if I concentrated my efforts.

It had been a bad night, after the scan. I had nearly lost faith again. How could they not have seen anything? Last time, I had deliberately not done anything they'd asked me to do. I had evaded their scanners and tests. This time, I had done everything I was told. I'd really gone for it. Why could they not see that?

Unless: I never had any control over any of it. When I thought I was resisting their tests, my actions had been pointless. They wouldn't have been able to see the truth anyway. They couldn't detect my brain activity. Something was preventing them. My brain wasn't working right, or their tests weren't working right. Hadn't Dr Sharma said they were unreliable?

But as I heard the sounds of the hospital getting ready for a new day, I'd dragged myself out of my self-pity – it wasn't going to get me out of here. There had to be another way round this; it was simply a matter of methodically trying different things. So, after moving through my body, here I was, focusing on the little finger of my right hand, and my left eyelid. One part for each side of my body, in case my condition affected one side more than the other. I concentrated so hard on trying to move each of them that I became slightly delirious, and started to hallucinate that they moved.

When the man walked in, I was abruptly pulled out of my reverie. I assumed it was a man, from the roughness of the breathing. He said nothing. It didn't sound like Dad, or Tom. I smelled the strong burning scent of Deep Heat rub, and I got the feeling of someone watching me intently.

Sweat started pricking my underarms. What if it was him – the guy who tried to kill me? Finally here, to finish what he started.

Who are you?

He didn't speak. It wasn't a doctor or a nurse – I couldn't hear any chart-rustling. No one approached the bed.

Say something. Who are you?

A cough. Definitely a man.

It's you, isn't it?

'I'm in. Nah, no problem.' He spoke in hushed tones. An East London accent that I recognised.

'Not much. Just lying there. Tubes and shit.'

It was a young guy, someone I knew.

'Mmm. Talked to the police press office on my way over. Nah. Not happy.'

Press office. So you must be –

'He said he was going to call Louise. Exact words were, "I don't think your editor will want to jeopardise an attempted murder investigation. How are plans coming along for those awards of yours that we're sponsoring next month?" Yeah, exactly. Tell Louise to expect the call. Don't let her back down.'

I placed the voice. It was Jacob, the new guy at the paper. I felt light-headed with relief.

'Okay, hang on. Let me get my notes.'

The familiar sound of a notepad being flicked through. Who was Jacob on the phone to? Bill?

'The bit he was against us using were the quotes from my officer contact, the stuff about the tip-off and who they think did it.' He paused. 'Of course I didn't.'

The birdwatcher tip-off?

'Yeah, I got Jo back in the office, going through Alex's blacks to see if there's any stories in that year before he fell, or was pushed – or whatever happened. See if there's anything in there that could have upset someone enough.'

They were going through my old stories. Surely it was obvious – it must be the Holly King case.

'She said there was that one time, that web comment – remember? The kid who threatened to kill Alex because he covered the court case about his mum being put in prison for dealing?'

He was just a kid.

'Okay, well. She's still going through the rest.'

What else has she come up with?

'Obviously we thought about the Holly King case, but—'

But what?

'Exactly. The only person who might have it in for Alex after the campaign would be Barker, and he's banged up.'

Barker?

'The dates don't work. Barker was already in prison for that other assault when Alex was – well, when whatever happened to him.'

The name was new to me. Was I following this right? Barker must be Holly King's real killer. But he was already in prison for attacking someone else when I got hurt. Did that mean William Ormond had been freed?

This was good and bad news, all at once. Good news that the paper's campaign had paid off and that Holly's murderer was being punished. Good news that he couldn't be stalking Bea. But I'd lost my prime suspect. And the police weren't likely to be inclined to help my case, given I'd been party to exposing their incompetence.

Jacob coughed.

'Okay, so yeah. The police are waiting. On the record, we're allowed to say that they're reinvestigating the circumstances of his accident. They don't want us to call it attempted murder.'

What are they waiting for? Why don't they make their move?

'Anyway, I'm here now. What do you think Louise wants? I can describe what it's like, if you want. It's fucking bleak. Hang on, I'll send you a photo.'

He paused. I heard a fake camera shutter, on a phone.

'Got it? He doesn't look good, does he? Shame – he was a decent bloke.'

Don't talk about me in the past tense.

'Okay, so you want colour, detail, atmospheric stuff.'

He paused.

'Speak to who, the doctors? I don't know – I could try, but won't they call the press office?'

The conversation was making me miss work. I was even feeling sentimental about Bill and his shiny head.

'No, no family. Do you have a number for the girlfriend? I can call her after I get out of here.'

Bea would hate that.

'What do you mean? Why should Ollie do it?'

Ouch. They wanted him to share his scoop.

'Insensitive?'

He no longer seemed to care about speaking quietly.

'How do you know if you won't let me call her?'

He swore under his breath.

'Fine. I don't want a joint byline, though, guv. This is my story.'

He swore again.

'So what do you want me to do about what my contact told me? We running with it?'

What did he say?

'It's just such a good line. I think we should risk it. Everyone is going to assume it was a bloke what done it. But my contact is adamant. The witness definitely saw a woman.'

A woman?

'Okay, yeah. Bye.'

Jacob muttered more expletives. 'Insensitive? He can fuck the fuck off.'

The scribble of a pen on paper. Pages flipping over. I tried to remember what he looked like. Always smart, even in his footie kit. Took pride in his appearance. Flash gold cufflinks and a signet ring. Hair slicked back with Brylcreem. I listened to the sound of him moving around the room. What kind of story would they run? One of their own people in a coma, then it turns out it's an attempted murder case – they'd go big on it. There would be pages and pages. Witness appeals. Colour pieces with details about the scene of the accident, interviews with friends and family. It was weird, being the subject of the story rather than the one writing it.

And then, without a word, he was gone. The door snapped shut. I knew I should get back to my muscle exercises, but my mind was elsewhere.

Definitely a woman.

My assumptions about who was to blame were unravelling. Holly King's murderer was behind bars and had been when I fell. The police's main suspect seemed to be a woman.

Was it really an ex who had done this to me?

I'd come full circle – right back to the letter.

Visits were all over the place. Tom and Rosie appeared at least twice a week – I hadn't spent this much time in their company since being in hospital – and Eleanor seemed to come in more often too. Bea was here less. Then there were the random arrivals of people who had stopped visiting me months ago. 'We saw it in the paper,' said other climbing friends. Cousins. Even my doctors and nurses seemed to be different when they came to check on me. They must have been intrigued by the crime drama unfolding around this room.

Only Bart kept up his usual routines, mopping my floor, singing to me, and saying nothing to suggest he had a clue what had happened in the outside world. But one evening, he wasn't his usual self. He seemed agitated.

'Hello, friend. Bart is here to clean room,' he said as he walked in, but his voice was more rushed than normal. I smelled the same disinfectant, but there was no mopping being done. Instead, I could hear him muttering. 'Where is it,' he was saying to himself. 'Where is the thing. Come on, where is it.' He clattered around the room and I heard papers rustling, chairs moving.

'Ah!' he shouted, sounding immediately happier.

The TV came to life, blurted and unfinished sentences and clips of music hitting my ears in quick succession as Bart apparently flicked through the channels. What was he after? He never watched the TV in my room. Then it finally settled, and I heard the unmistakable drone of crowds cheering, singing, shouting. Airhorns being blown. The voice of a football commentator, steadily increasing in volume and speed, '. . . in there! Flag's up. Flag's up, it's not going to count but he doesn't know yet. But Poland have not taken the lead . . .'

Bart let out a small yelp. 'Very, very exciting, my friend. Very exciting game.' He sounded like a small boy – incredibly excited and tense. 'They can't let England score! No goals yet, my friend. No goals, no goals. Both ends.'

What was it? I worked out in my mind what year it was, what competitions would be happening. The World Cup would be on this year. So what was this – a friendly?

When I heard Bart sit down in the chair at my side, I knew my floor probably wasn't going to be cleaned tonight. He stayed with me for what felt like a long time shouting at the TV, slapping a hand down on my bed every now and then, and muttering to himself in Polish.

I couldn't help but get carried along by his excitement. It felt like watching a game with my dad. Poor Dad. He hated having to watch his beloved Liverpool play with me. I suspected it was because he didn't like anyone else seeing how agitated he got. Sometimes I would turn up anyway. Without fail, his face would drop as he opened the door. 'Oh,' he'd say. 'I thought maybe you'd be going climbing this afternoon.'

I couldn't resist. It was hilarious to see him sitting right on the edge of the sofa, jumping up and down when a goal was scored, shouting at the referee that he was 'no better than a cabbage' (whatever that meant).

Bart, however, seemed happy to have someone to sit with as he shouted encouragement at the TV. After only a few minutes I was rooting for Poland to win, too. As the game neared full-time, the commentators were sombre – it was still nil–nil and England hadn't delivered. Typical England, they were saying. Some sparks of quality but not enough. Bart, on the other hand, sounded like he might be about to have a heart attack. He was very happy with the score. If he was like this for a friendly, how did he cope during a crucial qualifier?

'Come on, boys,' he yelled. 'Where you gone? Where you—'

He stopped short, and I heard some noise in the corner of the room by the door.

'Just going,' he said quickly, and the television went silent. 'Just leaving. Sorry – just having quick break with—'

He tapped my arm.

'Alex,' Pauline said. 'You were having a quick break with Alex?'

'Yes, yes. Alex.' Bart shuffled around the end of my bed, clearly embarrassed to have been caught slacking. 'Must go, leave you in quiet.'

Where was he going to watch the last few minutes up until the final whistle? More to the point, how was I ever going to find out what happened? I heard him wheeling his bucket out of the room.

'Thank you.' This was Bea's voice; she must have walked in with Pauline.

The door slammed shut.

'Should he be watching the football here?' Bea asked Pauline.

Suddenly, my eyes opened a little. The vision in one was partially blocked by the pillow squashed against the side of my face, but I was still able to watch Bea walk back and forth in front of me.

'I'll have a word,' Pauline said. 'Let's see this photo, then.'

'It's on my phone, not the best quality . . .' I could just make out Bea's shape in front of me, bending over as she went through her bag. 'Do you think I would be allowed onto the maternity ward, to take a look? Or could you get me a bracelet?'

Why do you want to go to the maternity ward?

She sounded excited, more buoyed up than I'd heard her in a long time.

'Let me look,' Pauline said. 'We might not need it. I used to work down there, I should be able to tell you what you need to know.'

What did Bea need to know?

The two of them stood hunched together, presumably looking at Bea's phone. What had she found?

'I had to hand over the original to the police but thankfully I'd already taken this.'

'Oh bless, it's a cute baby, isn't it?'

'Yes, I suppose so.' Bea's voice faltered. 'But I need to try and work out who its mother is. It could really help with—'

'Can you zoom in?'

'Yes. See, that's the thing. Back then, when I found it, I didn't have such a good phone so I couldn't do all of this. But when I moved all my files onto my new one I noticed I could zoom much closer in and sharpen it up, and look – if I put this filter on it, you can just make out these letters here – see? "L.A."?'

L.A? I couldn't remember any text in the photo. Where was it? On the cot?

'Yes, I see. Hmm.'

'So what do you think? Is that where they'd write the hospital name? The mother's name? Or what?'

'It could also be part of the baby's name,' said Pauline.

'Is there no way of being sure?' Bea asked. 'From its position on the bracelet?'

Pauline sighed. 'I'm sorry, my love. I don't think I could say for definite. It's not that clear.'

'Could I not get one, to look?'

'They won't let you down there.' Pauline sounded genuinely sorry. 'And to be honest, I don't think you'd get much more. It would depend on the hospital, the midwife, any number of things. And look, it's handwritten – I think they might have computer-generated ones here these days.'

I heard a smack: Bea's hand against the wall, or windowsill. Pauline seemed to move towards her again, comfort her.

'I'm sorry, my love. I'm sure they'll work out who did this to him.'

'I thought I could have gone back to the police with something, something to make them listen to me,' Bea said.

L. A.

There was only one name that might fit, out of the list I had come up with so far. And even that relied on it being the mother's name visible on the bracelet, not the baby's and not the hospital's.

L. A.

Clare.

29

The next day, Philippa walked in, mid-conversation with Pauline.

'. . . police say when they called?' Pauline asked, as the door whined open.

'They've arrested someone,' Philippa said. Clip, clip, clip.

Who? Tell me who it is.

'That's good, isn't it? Hmm?' Pauline asked, gently. 'Do you know them?'

'I wish I didn't.'

'Oh, you poor love. It's what they say though, isn't it – that you're more at risk from someone you know than a stranger. How are you holding up?'

'It's a relief, I suppose, to start to bring this to a conclusion. But I feel so betrayed, angry on his behalf, you know?'

Who is it?

'It just goes to show, you don't know anyone,' Philippa continued.

'You didn't say who . . .'

'It's his girlfriend. Calculating little—'

'Surely not?' Pauline gasped.

No.

'But she always seems so lovely. She was here only yesterday.'

No. This is crazy. Bea would never—

'Lots of people say that. I never got what he saw in her.'

They've got it wrong.

I felt dizzy, like my bed had been tipped backwards and I was sliding, head-first towards the floor.

'And they've arrested her?'

'How could she do this to him?' Philippa was ranting now, ignoring Pauline. 'I can't get my head around it. I never liked her, but I didn't think she was capable of this. That little bitch. How could she?'

'It's hard to take in.'

'He's my only brother, you know?'

'I'm so sorry, my love.'

Philippa sounded like she was treading the fine line between fury and tears.

This can't be true.

'No, *I'm* sorry – maybe I shouldn't have come here. I'm not thinking clearly. You don't need this, you've got enough to be getting on with.'

'The police are sure it's her?'

'They told Dad they aren't looking for anyone else.'

No. Bea would never do this to me. It must have been one of those girls I screwed over. Clare.

'How is Graham taking it?' Pauline asked.

'Graham?' Philippa said, confused – as if she didn't know our own father's name. 'Dad? He's fine. I mean, he isn't, but . . .'

'Oh, my love. I'm going to get you a cuppa. You're upset.'

'I'm beyond upset,' Philippa snapped. 'I'm sorry. I don't mean anything against you. But I can feel my heart racing – I could punch a hole through this window. I just can't comprehend what would make someone want to do – do *this* –'

She placed a hand on my leg.

'– to another human being.'

As she pulled away I heard her take a deep breath, trying to compose herself again. 'These need replacing.' Rustle. Thud. The crackle of cellophane as she put new flowers in place. Clip, clip, clip as she walked around the room.

They've made a mistake. Don't trust the police.

Pauline tried again. 'Let me get you a cuppa.'

'I just feel so stupid for not realising it earlier. That two-face bitch.'

How can you believe this?

My head was spinning. It was impossible. What evidence could they possibly have?

'They think she'll confess once they tell her what they have. If she even tries to deny it, I swear, I'll . . .'

They've got the wrong person.

As the initial shock started to wear off, I was left feeling completely disoriented. I could barely keep track of where they were in the room. How could this be happening?

'But did they say *why*?' Pauline asked. 'There must be a motive.'

'They've got a letter, which Bea says she found a couple of weeks ago. But the police think she actually found it much earlier, and she was so upset by it that she did this.'

No. She only just found it. She would have said something if she'd seen it before.

'But what did it say?'

'It's cryptic, but it suggests he had an affair. The thing is—' Philippa broke off, muttering angrily to herself. 'I *remember* that little liar telling us about it, a few weeks ago. She put on this whole act of being upset and confused. It was all a performance, everything she has said and done since he was put into that ambulance. She's been trying to cover her tracks for months.'

You know full well that Bea didn't do this to me! You've got to help her.

She continued, 'He didn't have an affair, of course. He wasn't that kind of guy. But she didn't even give him a chance to tell her that, did she? Police reckon she flipped out and when he was climbing that day she pushed him off the top. Or she threw something at him. Made him lose his footing somehow.'

No. This is impossible. She wasn't even in Bristol. Where is she now? Is she okay?

They say the most likely explanation is that she threw a rock, or – I don't know what they think she threw. And that's why he fell. Crime of passion, police are calling it.'

Impossible.

Philippa laughed, bitterly. 'And the other thing – the *other* thing. We've just found out the full story about the witness who came forward. The birdwatcher who saw her on the cliff. They recognised her photo in the paper back when it happened, but didn't want to get involved. Didn't want to get involved! Their conscience only got the better of them recently, they told the police. How could you keep quiet about something like that? All this time we've been welcoming her into our family. We could have been saved all of these months.'

More dizziness hit me, and then something else. I suddenly got a strong urge to relieve myself. It was nothing unusual – I had no control over when it happened. I could always feel the warm stream of piss go through me, out of my body via the catheter and into a bag which the nurses changed regularly. But this time as I felt the flow of liquid there was also something else. Dampness. Warm dampness against my thighs.

You've got to be kidding me. Now? This has to happen now?

I made futile attempts to will Pauline to notice.

My catheter. Check my catheter.

I knew what she would find. I tried to feel for it. Normally I could just about feel the plastic inside me; not painful, but there, nonetheless. But at that moment I couldn't feel anything – it had come out.

Pauline. My catheter.

She was oblivious. 'Bea always seems so lovely,' she said again, sadly.

I wanted to think more about what Philippa had said. What was going to happen to Bea now? Where was she? But my piss was still flowing freely and gave me a more immediate emergency to deal with.

Couldn't they hear it? See it? The mattress cover felt wet and hot under my skin.

'I hope she rots in hell,' Philippa spat. Her voice wavered as she repeated the words, then there was the unmistakable sound of her sobbing.

Pauline. My catheter – please?

It was no coincidence that this had only happened a couple of times before, and every time it was just a few hours after Connie had fitted me with a new catheter in her eminently professional manner.

'Are you sure I can't get you some tea?' Pauline tried again.

Philippa didn't reply. There was more sniffing; uneven breathing.

'Come on, my love. Come with me.'

Wait – can't you see –

I heard the door close.

The damp sheets started to cool and my skin itched. The ammonia smell got stronger as the minutes passed, and with it came a familiar feeling of embarrassment.

When I was a boy, I used to wet the bed. I didn't remember having bad dreams: I just woke up, drenched and ashamed. I would call out for Mum and she'd arrive in my bedroom bleary-eyed and warm from her bed. Without saying anything or putting the light on, she'd peel my pyjamas off, then change my sheets. She never told me off, never got cross.

Mum.

My throat tightened.

What would she think about this? What would she make of Bea's arrest?

Mum.

It didn't take me long to work out exactly what she would say. 'You've got to trust the people you love.' I could hear her voice saying the words. 'Trust is everything in a relationship.'

I miss you.

On her deathbed she wrote three letters: one each for me, Philippa and Dad. I never read theirs but I'd read mine every day for a year or so. In it, she talked about the day I was born. 'My life changed more than I ever imagined it could.' She told me she was proud of me. 'You've become a fine young man, you remind me of your father when I met him.' And she gave me her advice for living a happy life. 'Don't worry too much about anything. Work at your friendships. Always try to see things from other people's perspectives. Let yourself fall in love, but remember: you've got to trust the people you love. Trust is everything in a relationship.'

I had to trust Bea. There was no way she had done this to me. It was one thing for Philippa to believe it – she had never liked her. But I wasn't going to let anyone poison my mind against her. That was the only thing I could do for her: stand strong with her: I couldn't help her in any other way. Where was she? In custody? She must have been afraid. Who would be looking after her? Her parents. Tom and Rosie, I hoped. They wouldn't abandon her.

Shivers passed through me, goosebumps travelling up my torso and arms from my rapidly cooling groin and thighs. The sound of Bea's disappointed voice kept playing, over and over, in my head. 'I thought I could have gone back to the police with something,' she'd said yesterday. 'Something to make them listen to me.'

'Make them listen to me,' I heard her say, on repeat. My brain was playing tricks. Why wouldn't it move on from this phrase?

Make them listen to me. Listen to me.

And then I understood why my mind was so stuck on that moment: that was the last time she had been here. Would it be the last time she ever visited me? Would it be the last time I ever got the chance to hear her voice? Was that our goodbye? What if she went to prison? Even if I got better, would I ever be better enough to visit her? In these last few weeks, since the letter, she had been one of the constant things in my life. I relied on her. I needed her.

I was desperate to remember everything about our last moments together, just as I had been after Mum died.

Did you touch me? I can't remember. When was the last time you touched me?

I scanned my body, trying to force the memories: her hand on my leg, her lips on my forehead, how she held herself against my back.

If I'd known, I would have paid closer attention. What was the last thing she said? Did she kiss me?

As I tried to replay that day, the images jostled for attention with what I could remember from my mother's final hours.

The shape of Bea's body, pacing back and forth in front of my face as I lay on my side with my eyes part-open.

Mum's breathing, getting shallower. Me, propping up the pillows behind her head and adjusting her duvet, just to have something to do.

Bea's excitement when she thought she had made a breakthrough with the baby photo. Why hadn't I made more effort to listen to her?

Mum's eyes, closed, as she said, 'Look after your father. Look after Philippa for me. She's not as tough as she seems.'

Bea, asking Pauline to help her get onto the maternity ward.

Mum, laughing feebly as I reminded her of funny stories from when we were kids. The pet snails Philippa used to keep, each one called Penny, which always managed to escape. My home-made spacesuit constructed out of three rolls of tinfoil and a glass bowl over my face.

The sound of Bea's hand smacking against the wall, or the windowsill. The image of her, bending down to go through her bag. Her saying, 'Back then, when I found the photo, I didn't have such a good phone . . .'

Wait.

Back then?

What had Philippa said the police's theory was about the letter?

'. . . the police think she actually found it much earlier . . .'

When was 'back then', Bea? A few weeks ago, or nearly two years ago?

My mind went back to the day when Bea told me she had found the letter. She was angry. My face tingled with the memory of her slap. There was no way that was staged. There was no way she would have been able to resist having it out with me if she'd found the letter before.

She wasn't calculating like that.

She was impulsive.

You've got to trust the people you love.

30

How could they arrest her? What were they thinking? The anger gave me extra motivation.

Move. Move. MOVE.

I had spent the last few days focusing all of my emotions onto the little finger of my right hand.

Someone tried to kill you, and now the police want to take your girlfriend away.

Nothing.

You need to get out.

Nothing.

You have to find a way to help her.

As I tried to move, Connie was shuffling around the room doing some of her usual checks.

'How are you today, you old donkey brain?' She laughed, and started rolling me onto my side. Grunting with the effort, she lifted up my left shoulder and pushed at my back.

I used my anger against her as fuel.

Move. Move.

'Con, you'll want to come out here,' a voice said from outside my door. It was one of my other, younger nurses.

Connie stopped what she was doing, leaving my upper body twisted sideways but my legs lying flat, side by side. 'I'm busy.'

'You'll want to see who's here,' the younger nurse said, with emphasis. She giggled.

And she was gone, the door clicked shut behind her.

I continued my attempts to move my little finger as I listened to the faint noise coming from the corridor, of women laughing.

Move. You need to help Bea.

Nothing.

More laughter from the corridor. Who was this guy they were so excited about?

A few minutes later, the door opened again, and almost immediately that familiar aniseed aftershave hit me.

You.

Quiet Doc must be a real looker to have the nurses this excited. I hadn't heard them getting so flustered about any of the other men they worked with.

He began his routine. I heard him pick up my charts and flick through the paperwork. He seemed more upbeat than usual, whistling a tune as he worked. What was that? I recognised the song, but I couldn't afford to be distracted. I wanted to keep my focus on moving my finger, I needed to give it all my effort if I was going to succeed.

Just a small movement. Anything.

He touched my forehead, then pushed my head to one side and the other. I smelled the faint remnants of eucalyptus shower gel on him, and used it to make myself even angrier.

Move. You can do this.

Pinning my right elbow joint to the bed, he lifted my wrist.

Move. MOVE.

He stopped whistling and dropped my arm quickly, pushing it away from him – as if I'd given him an electric shock. 'No,' he said, softly. He brought his hand down onto mine – the same arm he had been lifting a moment ago. He pressed down on my skin, flattening my fingers against the bed. 'This can't be happening,' he said.

Had I moved? Had I done it?

Maybe he was realising he was wrong, that it had in fact been worth keeping a vegetable like me alive. But I could hardly shout out, 'I told you so!'

I wasn't out of the woods yet. I panicked. Could I do it again? My head filled with questions and anticipation.

Move. MOVE.

His hand was still resting on mine, still pressing it down into the mattress.

Move. Do it again.

I hadn't felt anything. Had I really managed to move?

Move. This is your chance.

Quiet Doc sighed, and lifted his hand away.

'Maybe I was imagining it,' he said.

No. I moved, you saw me!

He pressed a finger to each of my eyelids and lifted them. I was blinded by the sudden flood of light and couldn't make out any features on his face. I desperately tried to move my eyes around, to show him a sign of life that would convince him.

He slid my eyelids shut again.

'Are you trying to come round, Mr Jackson?'

He slapped me hard across the face. The force of it shunted my head slightly across the pillow.

What are you doing?

'Are you trying to wake up?'

He slapped me again. My cheek was throbbing. He was trying to stimulate some kind of reaction.

'Can you hear me, Mr Jackson?'

And then he was gone.

I thought I heard him laugh as he walked out, and I wished I could smile with him. It must have felt like a huge breakthrough for him – to have witnessed such a development in a patient no one expected to wake up. But no one could be more excited than me. Tears began to well in my eyes and tipped over onto my cheeks.

Finally.

When the door opened again I thought it must be him, back with Mr Lomax or Dr Sharma. I strained to listen, my heart still pounding.

The usual whine as the door swung on its hinge didn't happen straight away. When it came, it was slow – someone pushing it open unhurriedly, as if trying not to wake me. Footsteps, soft and dawdling. It didn't sound like a doctor. Whoever it was approached my right-hand side, and the door clicked shut again behind them.

A strong floral smell hit me, as if a bowl of my mum's pot-pourri had been carried into the room. A woman, then.

Hello?

There was a sniff, and my visitor blew her nose. Took a deep breath.

'Bea said.'

Another deep breath.

'Bea said.' She spoke nervously, quietly. It was a croaky voice, an older woman. 'Bea said.'

Bea's mum.

I started trying to move my finger again. If I had done it once, what was stopping me doing it again?

Watch my hand, Megan.

Maybe the doctors had told her what was going on. The nurses were probably out on the ward right now, chattering about it. I was surprised none of them had been in to see me yet.

I imagined the look on Connie's face when Quiet Doc told her he thought I was awake. I wished I could have been there to see the moment when she realised her cruelty would be exposed.

Megan tried again, clearing her throat. 'Bea said I should talk to you. Directly.'

Haven't the doctors told you what's happened? You need to get a message to Bea. Tell her.

'I left her at home with Rick,' she said. 'Oh, I don't know if I can do this.' She sighed.

Tell her to come in and see me, I have to try and show her.

'Do you know what's been happening, Alex?' Her speech wobbled. 'Bea was arrested on Monday. They kept her for three days. They think she tried to k-kill you.'

Megan blew her nose again.

'She said your father might have already told you. So I'm to tell you that she didn't do it. She would never have wanted to hurt you, Alex.'

I know that.

I was impatient. She seemed oblivious to what had happened in this room earlier today. It didn't sound like anyone had told her.

'She can't come here,' she continued. 'They've given her bail conditions.'

Of course.

Bea wouldn't be able to visit. I couldn't show her my finger moving. I was going to have to be patient. Maybe Quiet Doc was consulting with Mr Lomax. They wouldn't want to get my family's hopes up until they knew I was definitely aware of my surroundings.

'She's been in such a bad way,' Megan said. I tried to focus on what she was saying and put my anticipation to one side. 'She won't eat; she has to take sleeping tablets. She's not working, we've had to lend her some money for rent again so she doesn't have to move out of the flat.'

Thank you for taking care of her.

'Rosie came over, and Bea's friend Cameron.'

Friend, is it?

'But she's in a state. The police really went at her. So many questions. Rick's furious.'

My Bea. I hated thinking of her going through that.

'They said she'd been making things up to make herself look l-like,' Megan stammered, 'a victim in all of this. Someone smashed her car up the other week and they accused her of doing it herself.'

No wonder she'd felt they weren't listening, if that had been their attitude all along.

'They've been following her, watching her. They knew everything about her, everywhere she'd been for the last few weeks.'

So that's who her 'stalker' was. She wasn't imagining it.

Megan broke down and started sobbing. 'And they found the – the ring.'

The ring . . .

Under the loose floorboard in the living room. They showed Bea?

She blew her nose again. 'They tore the flat apart. Then they – poor Bea.' She gulped the tears down. 'They threw this plastic bag in front of her with the ring inside, when they were interviewing her.'

That wasn't how I planned to propose. Bastards.

'She didn't know anything about it,' Megan sobbed. 'She had no idea.'

It was meant to be a surprise.

How dare they do that? I was overcome with the urge to throw something at the wall. Hit something. Break something.

'Then they asked all these questions about your relationship. They taunted her with the ring. Wh-why didn't Alex propose? they asked her. Why would Alex hide the ring?' Megan breathed in and out quickly, in a stutter. 'Wh-why did Alex change his mind about marrying you? they asked her. You were arguing, weren't you? they said.' She blew her nose. 'Th-they said she had found out something about you, that you'd had an affair, and she was a-angry.'

They're twisting everything.

'But she told them you weren't arguing. Everything was fine.'

My brain stirred. Had we been arguing?

The scent of Megan's perfume was filling my mouth and turning bitter. She sat there a little while longer, blowing her nose, weeping.

Had we been arguing?

Finally, I heard the sound of her smoothing her clothes over her legs, and the click of her knees as she stood up.

'I'd best be getting back to them,' she said. 'Rick isn't himself, he's worried to death about her.'

I could imagine. My anger with him for not approving of me seemed petty now – irrelevant. He adored her. How would he cope if they convicted her?

'But if you can hear me, you've got to believe her,' Megan said. 'She didn't do this to you. They've got it all wrong.' Tentatively she put a hand on mine, just fingertips at first, as if she was testing the temperature of a bowl of hot water. Then, committing to it, she grabbed me hard. Squeezed until my bones ached. Her skin was warm, soft, fleshier than Bea's. 'If they're so sure she did it, why haven't they charged her?'

She released me. Her footsteps moved slowly towards the door, it creaked open, and she walked out.

Something nagged at me; something Megan had said. Were Bea and I arguing? I asked myself, over and over, as I waited for Quiet Doc to come back and tell me what the plan was for getting me out of here.

And every time I thought about Bea now, a new memory

trickled back to me from our last weeks together. She was lying to the police. Everything hadn't been fine.

I thought again about what she said she had done that final day: gone hiking alone and turned her phone off. The Bea I knew might have done those things, if she was angry enough with me. Only now was I properly recalling how bad things had been between us back then.

There's a saying, about not having to go to every argument you're invited to. We didn't play by that rule in those few weeks. Everything became a difficult conversation. I couldn't remember many details – only the feelings of frustration, exhaustion and sadness.

We might as well have sat there every evening, writing detailed invites, listing our complaints, and then cheerfully RSVPing to each other that yes, we were available to yell and wail and spar all night long.

Darling Bea,

Would you care to join me for a three-hour debate on whether we should redecorate the kitchen? On the agenda would be funds, who should organise quotes, what we think should be done. I suggest we aim not to agree on any point and descend into a slanging match, probably resorting to an argument over something completely different which happened about six months ago which you are still angry about.

It really would be awful to have you there.

Love/hate

Alex

x

Alex,

Sounds like fun! Let me cancel my other plans. Why don't we round it all off with really nasty comments about each other's personalities, and then go to bed exhausted but fuming, only

Could it be true that the letter was behind the arguments? Had she really found it all that time ago? No. She would have confronted me about it. But the police were right: we had been at each other's throats.

Another memory that came back to me, suddenly and clearly, was the morning of that Saturday in September, two years ago. The day I went climbing. We were arguing about something particular, weren't we? It wasn't just another bickering row. What was it? She wouldn't say goodbye. She refused to kiss me. That was the last thing I remembered.

No. She couldn't have done this to me. There was no way.

I couldn't stop thinking about the rows, now that I had remembered them. Was it just a rough patch, or would we have split up if it had continued like that?

Maybe Bea had been thinking about ending it with me. Maybe that's why she went walking that day, to work out what to do. If she had wanted to finish with me then, what did that mean for us now? I couldn't be sure if she would even want to be with me, if I ever recovered – especially with her new man on the scene. Had she only stayed by my side for the last two years because my fall had forced her to?

A loud sneeze announced Eleanor's presence at my bedside. I must have fallen asleep, and hadn't heard her come in.

'Excuse me,' she said, before sneezing again. 'Excuse me.' She was close to me, on my left-hand side.

'It wasn't Bea,' she said.

Nothing from her, either, about what Quiet Doc had seen earlier. When were they going to examine me again?

'I saw her afterwards, when you were in intensive care,' Eleanor said. 'She was a mess. She wouldn't have been so upset if she'd done that to you.' She sneezed again, three times. 'Bloody pollen,' she muttered, touching my arm.

Please don't do that.

'Did you see her there, that day?' she asked. 'Rosie told me what they think she did. But you would have called out if you'd seen her at the top of the pitch.' The words gushed out. 'You would have shouted her name. I would have heard.'

I couldn't remember.

'I mean, I can see how she could have done it.'

No. You've got to believe her.

'There's that slab section at the top of Transgression, isn't there?'

Transgression. So we'd been on Transgression that day? It fitted with what Philippa had said, about the police tip-off. Transgression finished on that ledge, the one that was visible from the area where birdwatchers liked to stand.

We had done that climb loads of times. About eighty metres, completed in four pitches. I could see the top pitch – not at all steep, so you could scramble up those final nine metres and over the fence at the top.

'I wish you'd got some protection into the rock after you left me.'

I never bothered with any there. It was an easy climb up that final slope, you could almost walk it. Whoever did this to me must have known I never put protection in there, they must have watched me before. We did that route almost every time we went out in the Gorge – it would have been easy to see us there.

'You must have been at the top, because I'd let out about nine metres when it happened.'

Which means I fell eighteen metres – nine back to you and then another nine on the rope. A long way to fall.

'I can't believe she's strong enough to overpower you and push you, but . . .'

Exactly.

'I suppose she *could* have thrown something at you, like they're saying.'

I could see every move on that piece of rock. Why couldn't I remember leading that day?

'But then I would have seen something fall.'

And you didn't?

'The police got me in, asked me to describe the climb to them. They kept asking if I saw Bea there. If I noticed anything unusual.'

But you didn't?

'They said she had been back there a few weeks ago, to the spot on the path along the top. They asked me how she would know where it was, so precisely, if she hadn't been there on the day,' she said. 'I didn't know. I couldn't tell them.'

Hadn't Tom taken her there? Didn't she tell me he had done that? That's how she knew.

Eleanor changed tack. 'I'm worried I've made things worse for her.'

You could only tell them what you knew.

'They tricked me into it. I didn't know until it was too late. They asked me what I made of your arguments.'

And? I couldn't see where she was going with this.

'I told them what had been going on – I told them it wasn't major, but that you weren't getting on. And then they said, "So they *were* arguing."'

No, no, no.

That was it.

That was why Bea hadn't kissed me, the day I fell.

It was coming back to me.

I had let slip that I'd told Eleanor about us fighting.

'That's our private business,' Bea had said. It was the night before I went climbing. Or a few nights before? I was in bed, she had jumped out when I'd told her that Eleanor thought we should take a weekend away, try and patch things up.

'And you haven't told Rosie that we've been arguing, I suppose?' I asked.

'That's different,' she had said. 'It would be different if you told Tom. But Eleanor—'

'Eleanor what?'

'I just don't feel comfortable with her knowing our business. You spend so much time together.'

'We're just friends. Get a grip.' I'd said that. I'd really said that. I felt like such a shit. Had she known that Eleanor had a thing for me?

If we hadn't had that particular argument, would we have been on better terms that morning? Would she have kissed me goodbye?

Why wasn't she telling the police the truth? Could she have blocked it from her memory, like I had – some kind of reaction to the trauma of all she had been through? Or was she trying to protect herself? She must have known it would make her look bad. But it would make her look worse if they could prove she was lying.

Eleanor's voice brought me back to my hospital room.

'I thought they already knew about it, but they didn't. They were just guessing, trying to find out.'

She sighed.

'But there's no way Bea would have done this to you, I told them that. Even after everything with this guy – this Cameron guy. I don't believe she'd want to hurt you, would she?'

*

As I tried to make sense of my day, later that evening, I kept coming back to Bea.

I'm so sorry.

I desperately wished we hadn't been arguing. I wished we had sorted things out before all of this had happened. But I knew, I absolutely knew it couldn't have been her who did this to me. I refused to believe it. If I had little trust in the police before, I had even less now. They'd tricked Eleanor into giving them the information they wanted. They'd used cheap tactics to upset Bea – what did the engagement ring prove? Just that *I* wasn't ready to get down on one knee. It said nothing about her. I hoped she'd had a lawyer when they questioned her. Megan hadn't mentioned one.

Please tell me they didn't make you admit to anything, Bea.

I had to find a way out of here, I needed to help her. When was Quiet Doc going to come back? I couldn't believe I had managed to move; even when I felt at my most determined, I didn't think I was actually going to do it.

But what was taking him so long? Surely they'd be in to see me first thing in the morning. The tune Quiet Doc had been whistling continued to keep me company as it had done most of the day, an earworm I didn't stand much chance of shifting, not without some other music to replace it. What I needed was Bea's iPod. I'd even listen to some of that terrible hip-hop if it would just give me something else—

Bea's iPod.

Suddenly I felt very much awake, my heart rate accelerating.

That music Quiet Doc was whistling was really catchy. Repetitive.

A Manc accent crept into my head, adding lyrics to Quiet Doc's wordless melody. ' "You begged me to stay when I had to go, and you told me your name so I'd always know." '

It was the song Bea had played me. The one Cameron had chosen.

241

What was it that she had said when she brought her iPod in? She was excited, because this band was relatively unknown.

It was a coincidence, I told myself, trying to calm down. Just a coincidence. It was absolutely possible that two different people, in the very small circle of people I had contact with, could be into this emerging indie rock group.

Just a coincidence.

31

I was being paranoid.

This was ridiculous. It was just a song. Maybe the band were more popular than Bea thought. There was a better explanation – a more reasonable explanation than –

Than –

It was Cameron's favourite song.

Quiet Doc had been whistling Cameron's favourite song.

I'm being ridiculous. Quiet Doc can't be Cameron.

I've got more important things to be worrying about.

Bea's the police's prime suspect. I've got to help her.

I ignored myself, and racked my brains, trying to go over everything I knew about both of them.

I didn't know Quiet Doc's real name. It could be Cameron.

But Cameron wasn't a doctor, was he? Did I know that? Bea had hardly ever spoken about him. She'd never mentioned what he did for a living, had she? Had Rosie and Tom? Someone would have said if he was a doctor.

And if he was *my* doctor, they'd definitely have told me. He'd have had to declare it or something.

Something doesn't make sense.

If Quiet Doc was Cameron, had he met Bea here? Was the story about grief counselling just a big lie?

My mind was working overtime, making connections and

breaking them, trying to piece together something that was remotely logical.

What did she say about him, when she first met him?

He had spun her that story, about his wife dying six years ago. She'd said he was well-built, no – what were her words? 'Strong-looking'. And then I remembered – she *had* mentioned a job. He had to be strong in his line of work, she'd said. He was a builder.

I was just getting wound up over nothing.

He was just a builder. Fixing up people's extensions, knocking through walls. Painting flats in Clifton in shades of Farrow & Ball. Not operating on people's brains, not doing ward rounds, not checking people like me for eye movement.

I was embarrassed, even though no one had been privy to my crazy thoughts. As my heart rate slowed again, I tried to laugh at myself. Would it even have mattered if Bea had started going out with Quiet Doc? It wouldn't have made any difference, I lied to myself. It wouldn't have mattered if the man sleeping with my girlfriend was also one of the doctors messing around with my weakened body. That wouldn't have been humiliating, or degrading.

It was a stupid thought to have had. Bea wouldn't have lied to me like that. She wouldn't have made up the grief counselling. She would have just told me the truth. And when Eleanor and Rosie saw them together they would have recognised him as one of my doctors.

Unless . . . was it possible none of them had ever seen Quiet Doc? He wasn't one of my main team. He wasn't here every week. He wasn't part of the big briefings they would sometimes have around my bed. He always seemed to work alone. Whenever he was with me his scent was uncontaminated by anyone else's. That memorable smell of white spirit –

Bea's voice came into my head again. 'He's a builder or something . . .'

A builder? Or a painter?

The phantom chemical scent wafted into my nostrils.

Shit. Shit.

Why would a doctor smell so often of gloss paint and white spirit?

What else did I know about them?

Quiet Doc didn't seem to think I should have been kept alive. He thought everyone would be better off with me dead. I'd thought he felt sorry for me. But maybe he just wished I'd left Bea free and totally unattached.

What else did I know?

He's methodical.

He doesn't like talking.

He sometimes smells of coffee.

I didn't know if Cameron drank coffee, did I?

He likes my shower gel.

It was the turn of my own phrase that tripped me up. He liked *my* shower gel. If I'd thought: *he likes the same shower gel as me*, maybe I wouldn't have made the connection.

He likes my shower gel.

Did Bea still have my shower gel out in the bathroom, at our flat? Had Cameron been using it? When did I start smelling the eucalyptus and pine on Quiet Doc? It hadn't always been there, had it? It was a more recent thing.

Shit.

There were too many coincidences. But I couldn't work out what they all meant. If they were the same person, someone wasn't telling the truth. Was Bea lying to me or was he lying to her?

I was suddenly very afraid for Bea. He had pretended to be my doctor – he was some kind of con man. If he had concocted such an intricate web of lies, what else was he capable of? What else had he told her? I'd never liked the sound of this Cameron guy, and I'd never really liked Quiet Doc – not until he saw me move and, overjoyed, I labelled him as my saviour.

A new punch hit me full on in the gut.

If I was right about this – if Cameron and Quiet Doc were one and the same, and if this bastard wasn't actually a doctor – then he wasn't going to tell anyone about me moving. He wanted Bea: an ex-boyfriend who was about to wake up didn't fit into that plan. What was it that he had said? 'This can't be happening.'

I had only managed to move once, and it was in front of the one person who wasn't going to help me.

32

I was going to have to try and show someone else my new trick.

What the hell was going on? There was still a chance I was imagining all of this, my capacity for suspicion sent into overdrive by the events of the last month. But no – I had a gut feeling about him. Something definitely wasn't right. Why was he coming to see me? What was he trying to achieve? And why pretend to be a doctor? Was it just for some twisted kind of kick?

After my success with my finger, I moved on to my feet. I tried to wiggle my toes. I tried to lift my heel. Move my whole foot from side to side. Occasionally I thought I had managed it, but there was no way of knowing for sure; not unless someone saw me do it. Quiet Doc hadn't been back since yesterday. With every hour that passed, I lost a little more hope that I would be proved wrong about his identity.

I tried to keep myself busy, tensing each group of muscles in turn. My toes, my feet. My calves, my thighs. I couldn't feel anything. What *did* it feel like to successfully tense a muscle? I couldn't remember. My glutes. Abs. Nothing. My hands, arms, shoulders. Neck muscles. My jaw.

Come on, Alex.

Back down to my feet.

'You can go in, if you want?' Pauline said, out in the corridor. My door must have been open.

'I was waiting for my girlfriend.' Tom, sounding flustered. 'But I suppose I could.'

'Go, on, my love. It's always nice for him to have a visitor,' Pauline reassured him.

Flip-flops smacked along the floor and immediately Tom started cracking his knuckles. I couldn't remember a time when he'd visited alone.

Say something, then.

He didn't sit down – the joint-cracking remained isolated by my feet. My bed juddered and I heard flickering paper. A clunk as the bed shook again. Was he looking at my charts?

Tom. Talk to me.

More footsteps squeaked in. 'Oh, I'm sorry.' It was Connie. 'To, errr . . . interrupt.'

'No, no, go ahead,' Tom said.

'Got to clear his trachea, see. It's been bad the last few days and we have to check it every couple of hours.' There was the sound of rattling plastic as Connie detached the devil machine from the wall behind me.

'Of course,' Tom said quickly, glad for an interruption to save him from talking to me.

Connie fiddled with my tracheostomy, breathlessly panting custard cream breath over my face, then inserted the tube into my throat. The agonising wire wool scratching began, and I lost the ability to pay attention to anything else.

Aaarggghh.

The razor blades dragged up and down, up and down.

AAAAARRGGHHH.

Through the noise I could just make out Tom and Connie, chatting.

Fuck you.

Then she switched it off, removing the tube and leaving my throat burning like it had been cleaned out with bleach.

'. . . but it doesn't hurt?' Tom was saying.

'No. It vibrates a bit in my hands, but other than that, it's fine.'

'Not you. Him. Doesn't hurt him?'

'Oh, I see. No. He can't feel anything.'

I can't feel anything? It doesn't hurt?

If she really thought I couldn't feel this, then I couldn't deny it to myself any more. Quiet Doc hadn't told anyone what he'd seen. He had no intention of telling them.

The plastic fittings behind me rattled as Connie reattached the devil machine to the wall.

'Good.' Tom seemed relieved. 'Because it looks uncomfortable. I wouldn't like to think of him being in pain.'

'Oh, no. Don't you worry,' Connie giggled. Flirtatiously. There was a rush of water as she rinsed her hands. 'Like I say, he can't feel anything, and anyway,' she lowered her voice into what I could only imagine she believed was an alluring whisper, 'I'm very good at what I do.'

You're embarrassing yourself.

'Right,' Tom said.

There was the rumble of paper towels being pulled out of their dispenser as Connie dried off, and a loud rattling noise. 'This bloody thing. I've been telling them to sort it for weeks – about to fall off the wall, it is.'

'Want me to fix it?'

'I couldn't ask you to do that,' Connie said.

'I'd be happy to. Let me take a look. You got a flat-head screwdriver?'

'I'll go and look, dear,' Connie purred. Then I heard the thud of bodies clashing to my right, near the doorway, a confusion of words: sorry, oof, whoops. Metal clattered to the floor. The scent of coconut filtered through the air towards me.

'Are you okay? I'm so sorry.'

Rosie.

'No, no. I wasn't looking where I was going,' Connie said. I knew she'd be muttering insults as soon as she was out of earshot. She clumped off, squeaking down the corridor.

'Sorry,' Rosie said. 'I ended up chatting to Cameron when I dropped Bea off at his place and I just totally lost track of time – did you know he's a painter and decorator? I thought we could ask him to do the hallway. Save you trying to reach from the ladder.'

I was right.

The burning sensation in my throat intensified.

'Depends how much he costs,' Tom said. They shared a quick kiss. 'Any news?'

They were both still standing at the foot of my bed. The frame jolted as one of them leaned against it.

'Her mum and dad are still around – they're driving her mad. I don't mind them, but she—'

'I meant, from the police?' Tom interrupted her.

'No. But she's convinced they'll charge her,' Rosie said.

'They won't.'

'The whole thing is messed up.'

'She'll be okay,' Tom tried to soothe her. I heard the friction of skin on material as he rubbed her arm, or back. 'She'll be fine.' He was interrupted by an insistent buzzing noise that made my bed vibrate.

'Who is it?' Rosie asked. 'Don't answer.'

'Hey,' Tom said before she could finish her sentence. He whispered, 'It's Bea,' to Rosie.

'Did you?' he said into the phone. 'She must have it on silent.' He whispered to Rosie, 'She tried to call you.'

He spoke into the phone again. 'Hang on, slow down, I'm going to put you on speaker.' He mumbled as he tried to find the right button. 'Okay, go on.'

Bea whispered, echoing over the line. 'I'm freaking out,' she said.

My chest tightened as I was hit by the sound of her voice for the first time since her arrest. She sounded scared.

It's him, isn't it? What's he done?

'What's wrong?' Rosie spoke loudly, as if to a deaf elderly relative.

'Cameron,' Bea whispered. 'Something weird is going on. He knows stuff –'

My chest constricted more. I knew it.

'Why are you whispering?' Tom asked. 'Where are you?'

'In the bathroom,' Bea whispered back.

'His bathroom?'

'Yes,' she hissed.

'Where is he?'

'He's sorting out his tools, in the van.'

'Okay, so what stuff does he know?' Rosie asked, sounding dubious.

'Little things,' Bea whispered, her voice crackling over the line. 'About the questions the police asked me – things I haven't told him.'

'Like what?' Tom asked.

'We were talking about what my chances were of getting charged, and he said, "You've got to face facts. It's hard to see how they won't, given you were seen there that day."'

'And you hadn't told him that?'

'No. The police said someone saw me – even though that's impossible – but I know I never told him. I didn't want to talk to him about the interview – the ring—'

'Maybe he guessed,' Tom said.

'How could he?' she whispered.

'So someone else must have told him,' Rosie said. 'There must be an explanation. You're stressed – you're not thinking straight. It's my job to tell you when you freak out over something that you shouldn't, and this is one of those times, okay? It's not weird for him to know that someone thinks they saw you—'

'It is. Please, you've got to believe me,' Bea said. Instead of getting angry at what Rosie had said, she sounded desperate. My heart was beating faster and faster with frustration; she was scared and I couldn't help her. Why were Rosie and Tom assuming she was imagining it? This guy couldn't be trusted. 'Something's not right,' she went on. 'There've been lots of little things he has said. I can't think of everything, but he's acting really strangely.'

'Okay, so let's say he's found things out from somewhere else, and not from you. Let's think logically about this.' Rosie spoke slowly. 'Just ask him how he knows. What's the worst he can say?'

'I think he's working with the police.'

Feeding them information?

How did this fit in with what I already suspected, about him pretending to be my doctor? Was that some sort of cover?

Rosie muttered something under her breath, then said, 'We're coming over there. You need to eat something. You need to sleep.'

'You don't believe me.'

I believe you.

'I – I don't know that you've got the evidence to back this up,' Rosie said. 'Why would he be helping the police?'

Because he doesn't care about her? Because he's been lying to her from day one? Because he's the kind of psychopath who pretends to be a doctor?

'Well, how else does he know so much? There are other things, like I'm sure he mentioned the route Al was on, but that's never been in the paper, and I never told him.'

Tom stepped in. 'Slow down. Rosie's right, Bea – think about this logically for a minute. What could he be telling the police? He didn't know you when this happened to Alex.'

'I don't know,' Bea whispered. 'Maybe they've asked him to keep an eye on me, or – I don't know. Do you really think I should talk to him?'

No. Just finish with him. Get as far away from him as possible.

'If you think it would help,' Rosie said.

'I need to think about it. I thought – I really thought we were getting on. I thought he liked me, you know?'

Bastard.

There was a moment of silence. Tom shifted his weight again on the bed and it creaked. In my mind I was busy punching Cameron in the face, repeatedly.

You shouldn't . . .

Punch.

. . . have fucked . . .

Punch.

. . . with my girlfriend.

'Shit, hang on,' Bea whispered. There was the sound of water flowing – a tap being turned on.

I could just make out a man's voice in the background. '. . . are you? You still in the washroom?'

'Be out in a minute,' Bea shouted.

His voice was muffled, but it could have been Quiet Doc.

Bastard.

'You still there, Bea?' Tom was whispering now. 'Look, just try and relax. I'm sure there's a good reason for everything.'

'Okay.' Bea's whisper was barely audible over the sound of the running water.

'Do you want us to come and pick you up?' Tom asked.

Silence at Bea's end.

'Yes,' she said after a few seconds. 'I'm sorry.'

'It's okay. But you need to get some rest,' Rosie said. 'Promise me? It'll make more sense if you try and sleep. Stay with us tonight.'

'See you in a bit.'

The line went quiet.

Tom and Rosie left quickly, rerunning the conversation between them and trying to work out how they could help Bea see sense. They thought she was overreacting.

I was the only one who believed her, the only other person who knew something wasn't right about Cameron. And the only one who couldn't do anything about it.

33

Who was this guy? Was his name even Cameron? Was he helping the police? That still wouldn't explain why he was visiting me, pretending to be a physician.

As I went over everything I knew, I hit upon a simple fact that I had overlooked earlier. I had been getting visits from Quiet Doc – who I was now certain was Cameron – since long before Bea had met him at grief counselling. His interest in me pre-dated his interest in her. Why?

I thought about how creepy he was, about his lingering touch, the way he spoke to me and moved me around.

Was he the man who had killed Holly King? But they'd arrested someone for that. They couldn't have got it wrong twice. Was he the man who had tried to kill me?

He knew the name of the climb I had been on that day. But then he also knew things about the police investigation into Bea.

There had to be some other clue, somewhere in my memory.

I started to go over everything Bea had said in that frantic conversation in the bathroom.

In the bathroom—

Wait.

'You still in the washroom?'

He hadn't said bathroom, or toilet. He'd said washroom, hadn't he? My mind wasn't playing tricks on me.

Why would he use that word? It was one of the things the Canadian staff at camp always took the piss out of us Brits for, calling it the bathroom.

He had an English accent, but could he be from abroad? Were any of my exes from North America? Could Cameron be the brother or new partner of one of those girls I never called back?

You will pay for breaking my heart twice over.
We deserved better than you.

Maybe. That could be it, couldn't it? But would he really be angry enough to try to kill me over something so far in the past? He'd have to be an insanely jealous person to go that far.

Washroom.

I felt I was on to something with Canada. Hadn't Cameron – or Quiet Doc – mentioned Canada, once? I thought he had. What was it? He'd been there . . . or he knew—

That was it. When Bea met him at counselling, he'd said he'd been to the Rockies.

This was getting closer and closer to home. Had we known him, when we were in Alberta? If so, why didn't Bea recognise him? Why didn't I know his voice? Was his British accent just part of a disguise?

I kept trawling through my memories of everything anyone had said to me in the last few months about how I came to fall, about the police investigation.

The police said it was a woman who had done it – but that was just because of the anonymous tip-off.

What else did I know? What else had I heard? Who would have done this to me? What had I done to them to make them hate me so much?

It was Bea's words that finally did it.

'All you've ever done is try to help people.'

256

That's what she had said when she found out it hadn't been an accident.

A wave of horror washed over me, totally obliterating the anger I had been feeling. I knew who Cameron could be.

All I had ever done was *try* to help people. But it hadn't always gone to plan.

34

Sleep didn't grant me any relief that night. I lay closed-eyed but awake for hours. In the morning, I submitted to the usual routines. A suppository to empty my bowels onto a waiting plastic sheet. The nurses turned me, wiped me, turned me, wiped me. Changed the bed sheets. Cleaned my mouth. Sucked the crap out of my throat.

I fell asleep later in the day, exhausted. When I woke up, I couldn't work out what time of day it was – I thought I could sense daylight on my face but I could have been wrong. I spent a few minutes working through my routine of trying to make a noise in my throat, trying to move a finger or a toe or wrinkle my nose. Still nothing. This must be possible. I had to find a way to move again. That was – if I had ever moved at all. Had Cameron really seen something happen? Or was he just toying with me? He was clearly capable of anything.

I wasn't getting out of this place alive, I saw that now. He was going to kill me. It must have been his plan all along. Now, if he thought I might be about to recover, he wouldn't waste any more time. Who would stop him? Pauline? Connie? I didn't stand a chance.

And Bea – what was going to happen to her? Where was she? I hoped she had stayed with Rosie and Tom last night rather than going home alone. What if—

Something shuffled in my room. A tapping, shushing noise. Enough to catch my attention. Then, silence again. The harder I listened, the louder the blood pumped in my ears. Whatever it was, it had gone quiet now. Maybe a piece of paper had fallen to the floor, or a bird had hit the window. No. The noise I heard was a human sound. Then a spicy scent reached me – black pepper, smokiness.

I knew you'd be back.

A noise, again. A crack, a click. Like bones in your neck when you tilt it from side to side, or the pop of knuckles.

This is it, isn't it? I'm out of time.

A crack, a click, again.

The hairs on my arms stood on end. I tried to form a word – tried to roll my tongue and push air out through my mouth.

I hadn't heard him come into the room, so he must have done so when I was napping. Which meant he had been here for a while, watching me as I tried to move and talk.

I'm sorry for what happened to you.

Had I guessed right? Was he who I thought he was?

Killing me won't change anything. Please don't do this.

Footsteps, now. Quiet. As if he didn't want to make a noise: it was a soft tread, but audible. Soft-soled shoes. A slow, deliberate step – a creep – across the floor, coming towards my bed. Closer now, approaching along my right-hand side, until the steps stopped next to my head.

He put a hand over mine – over the finger he saw move before.

Still, he said nothing. I heard an occasional intake of air through his mouth, his nose. Rough, heavy.

The door banged in the corner of the room as it was pushed open wide against the wall.

'Oh. I didn't realise.' It was Connie, sounding flustered.

He said nothing. I imagined a wordless exchange. A turn – a

smile, perhaps? A gesture to explain what he was doing? A finger to his lips?

She spoke again. 'I needed to – but I can come back later. No problem.' A silly laugh. 'You're ever so good to visit him, dear,' she flirted.

That wasn't how she talked to doctors. Quiet Doc definitely wasn't a doctor.

'It's what family's for,' he said.

'Oh, of course,' Connie giggled. 'You're his cousin, is that right? Or uncle?'

'Cousin.'

So that's what you've been telling them.

'I see. I'll leave you two to, well, catch up.' Another silly giggle, and she left the room.

His hand touched my lower arm and ran down away from my elbow. He twisted my wrist, and bent each of my fingers in turn, to form a fist. He did all of this silently, and slowly.

Instinctively I went to flex the muscles to pull away.

Just make it quick.

He dropped my hand back on the bed, leaving my right arm twisted at an awkward angle, with my wrist facing the ceiling. He lifted the bed sheet. A chill drifted down as the cooler air reached underneath it, down my chest, stomach, legs. The sheet pulled against my toes where it was tucked in under the mattress, and caught under my arms as he lifted it up. He dropped it again, carelessly, onto my chest. He didn't pull it back up to my chin, he didn't rearrange it.

Then my tracheostomy tube moved in the hole in my neck. The tube tugged against my skin and the inside of my throat.

What are you going to do?

I felt a wetness in my armpits. Why didn't Connie come back to check everything was all right? It was the first time I had ever willed her to return.

His hand scooped underneath my head, lifting it. My chin dropped down to my chest and my neck was pulled out of place. I was like a baby, in one of those moments when you see parents telling their unpractised friends to support its head as it lolls around with no muscles to keep it straight. It all happened quickly: he lifted my head, and with a smooth movement dragged the pillow out from underneath it. He let go of my head and it fell back against the mattress, rolling to the left, towards the window. I winced. Saliva escaped from my mouth and dribbled down the side of my face. My skin was hot beneath it – burning up with the humiliation, the fear, and the adrenalin.

He grabbed my chin roughly and nails dug into my flesh. His movements became more ragged, quicker, more urgent. With one yank, he pulled my head back to a central position, the pressure of the mattress firmly on the back of my scalp.

Connie! Someone?

So much pain consumed me that my thoughts skewed. My mind flew from the twisting strain in my badly placed arm, to a flailing attempt to locate Cameron, back to the tilting stretch in the front of my neck making me feel like my head would fall off backwards.

Overwhelmed by all of this, I didn't feel the air change.

I didn't feel the air change around my face as he brought the pillow down onto it.

It was cool, when he brushed it against my mouth and nose. At first, I thought it was a piece of material being draped over me: he swept it so lightly across from the right temple to the left. But then, with a gentle pressure, he held it still, and I felt its weight.

Fuck. Get off me. HELP! Help me!

I struggled. I took myself to the place in my head where I could push him away, where I could twist, turn, bite him. He pressed the pillow harder against my face and I tasted the starched cotton case on my tongue.

But he had missed one thing.

Tracheostomy. My neck. You haven't – covered my neck – I can – still – breathe.

And then, as if he had put the pillow on my face by accident, he lifted it off again. His heavy aniseed-tinted breath hit my face – he panted as if he was the one who had been suffocated.

We stayed like that for several minutes, side by side, until his breathing slowed.

Think about what you're doing. Please. I never meant to hurt you.

Cameron put his hand under my head again. Fingers spread wide like the claw on a digger, lifting me up as he stuffed the pillow back underneath. Again, he let my head drop, but this time he didn't correct its position when it fell to the left.

As I waited for him to make his next move, noise ripped into the silence. Rain began pelting the window – a sudden, heavy shower that resonated like shingle hitting the glass. It filled my ears and dulled my ability to hear what has happening – but I felt suddenly that he had moved away from me. Where to? I scanned the room, listening.

All I heard was the creak of the door as it opened, and then a thud as it shut quickly.

'Bea,' he said.

Bea? Here?

'You shouldn't be here,' he went on.

'You can't tell me what to do.'

'They'll come after you. You're already in enough trouble as it is.'

She was breathless. 'Why are you here?'

'You need to go. Before someone sees you. We can talk later.'

Get out of here, Bea. He's dangerous.

'We talk now. You've been lying to me.' Fear and adrenalin charged her voice.

The rain continued to attack the window. My body tightened

in agony as cramps passed through my awkwardly turned right arm. More spasms came as I lay there, unable to stop them. I felt like an asylum patient strapped in for electric shock therapy, shackled at the wrists and ankles to my bed, prevented from moving, no matter how much pain I was in. I writhed around inside my body. I wished Bea would come to me and move me.

'Who are you?' she asked him, again.

35

'You know who I am,' Cameron said.

'You're working with them, trying to pin this on me.'

'With who? The police?' He laughed.

Bea held firm. 'Are you?'

'Come off it.'

I felt pressure on my leg, through the sheet. From the weight of it, the broadness of the touch, I could tell it was his hand, not hers. 'Thought I'd come and see this ex-boyfriend of yours. You talk so much about him.' He squeezed my shin and pulled away. 'Thought I'd check out the competition. It's tough, you see – being the second man in a relationship.'

'You don't know him.' Her voice moved closer to me. I smelled the cigarette smoke on her and felt soft skin brush against my upturned palm.

'Maybe I do.'

'What does that mean?'

Both of them stood close to me now, near the right-hand side of my bed. The rain continued to beat against the window on my other side.

He ignored her question. 'Are you sure no one saw you come in? We could still get you out of here.'

Do what he says. Go.

'Who? Your colleagues? Admit it.'

'For the last time, I'm not with the police. You've got it all wrong.'

'Okay then, but you are telling them stuff about me, aren't you?'

'You've got to sort out this paranoia.'

I wanted to hit him so badly. No matter what I'd done, Bea didn't deserve any of this. A right hook to the side of his face would be all I needed. I'd offer myself up for an extra hour of chest suctioning if I could see his pulped nose, and a few teeth spat out onto the floor. I listened to the rain and imagined the pattering noise was his bones splitting into tiny fragments.

'Paranoia?' she asked. 'Remember yesterday? You said that I'd been seen by the Gorge on the day Alex fell.'

'Yes. You can see why the police would be suspicious, to be fair to them.'

'But I didn't tell you about that.'

'I'm not a policeman, a detective, or whatever you think I am. You think I've got an inside contact?'

'Maybe. Yes.' She hesitated.

'You're confused,' he said. 'We'll talk about this properly. Let's just go home, get out of here without being seen. You go first, and I'll follow in a minute. We'll draw less attention that way. You're breaching your bail conditions.'

She wasn't about to give up. 'No.'

His voice changed. He became impatient, bordering on angry. 'Nothing's going on.' He almost shouted the words at her, then swiftly changed tack. 'I love you.'

She laughed.

'I do.'

'Don't change the subject.'

'Bea. I've shown you how crazy I am about you.'

I imagined the way he looked at her as he said this. I imagined what intimacies his words made them both remember in the moments of silence that followed. My heartbeat sped up again. The rain had stopped, and sun hit my eyelids through the window, as if it had emerged from behind a thick bank of cloud. It warmed my cheeks, spreading down to my neck. But it did not calm me as it sometimes did. Nothing could calm me right now.

The fury crushed me, ground me up. My breaths came quicker, quicker, and my arms tingled. I heaved my legs over the side of the bed. Rolled my shoulders once, a backwards roll like someone digging their fingers deep into my back muscles, as I sat on the edge of the mattress. Cameron and Bea hadn't seen me yet – they were busy with each other, so used to my inertness, to there being nothing of interest on this side of the room, that they didn't even register the movement. I stood at the moment he turned and saw me, like a skeletal zombie emerging from my shallow grave. His face melted in horror, his jaw dropped, as I moved towards him. Bea whimpered, whispered my name, but I didn't look at her. I was only interested in him. He backed away from me but had no space to move into. He pressed against the wall. I felt crooked, stooped after months of inactivity, but strangely strong. My breaths came out in rasps, and with every one more power returned to me.

I kept stepping, slowly, across the room until we stood face-to-face. I could smell the spice of his aftershave again, a liquorice insistence on his breath. I looked into his eyes. And then I rocked back quickly, with grace, whipped my right arm behind me and snapped it forward. My clenched fist connected with his nose, the pain a shock to me as it dashed my knuckles and sent shards of sensation up to my shoulder. Cameron brought a guarding arm to his face, turned away. Blood ran down into his mouth. Bea screamed now but I pushed him to the floor and knelt on his chest, clawing my hands around his neck and pushing, squeezing, amazed at my own power and adrenalin. His eyes bulged, his face darkened into deeper and deeper shades of red, purple, blue, as he realised what I meant to do. His arms flapped at his side, scratching me, and his feet kicked at the floor. He was like a beetle on its back, flailing its limbs to try and get up. He was strong, too, and not quick to surrender. But if I had learned anything in the past two years, it was patience, and I could wait for him to go. Bea's shrieks continued, but she didn't try to pull me off him.

He went slack; the tension fell away. I released my grip on his stubbled throat and stood up, wiped my hands on my pyjamas, and walked back to my bed. I lay down, pulled the sheet over me, closed my eyes.

The sun left my face and almost immediately my skin cooled, as if the light and warmth had never been there.

The spell cracked, then shattered, as Cameron spoke again, oblivious to his grisly fate in my mind's cinema.

He talked softly. 'I've really fallen for you.'

'Stop it. Just tell me what you're doing.'

'Fucking hell!' he shouted. 'You really want to know?'

'Yes!'

He sighed, and when he spoke his voice had lost all its angry heat and his measured composure had returned. 'Do you ever get the feeling that we've met before?'

36

This was the most I had heard him say. As Quiet Doc, he'd never spoken this much. Now I knew I was right. I had heard this voice, once – a long time ago. That time, he'd been distraught, shouting, drunk – but it was definitely him.

I had to lie there and listen as he played games with Bea and she slowly pieced it all together for herself.

'What are you saying?' she asked.

'I'm sorry I shouted. You see what a hold you have on me.'

'Don't touch me. Get off.'

'I didn't want to upset you. I just want to be close to you.'

'You're hurting me. Cameron, please.'

'I can't watch you cry.'

'I – I've changed my mind. I'll go. We can talk about this later. I'll – I'll meet you later. Just let me go.'

'I can't do that. You should have listened to me earlier and gone when I told you to. You can't go now, when you're this upset.'

He wasn't going to let her leave; I could see that now. Not now that he knew she wasn't buying his lies. She was on to him.

'You wanted to know why I'm here?'

'I do. But – we can talk about it later.'

'Why do you keep looking at the door? I don't know why you're suddenly so scared of me. And you don't want to call for security, remember?'

'Please. I'm not scared. I'm just tired.'

For a moment, neither of them spoke.

'You don't remember me?' Cameron asked.

'We never met before grief counselling,' she said, confused.

'It's true that we never spoke, and maybe you never even saw me,' he said.

Here it comes.

'You were too busy with your work. But I saw you – beautiful Beatriz.' He affected a Spanish accent to say her name. 'I saw you even if you didn't see me. You were so good with the children. They adored you. Beautiful Bea.'

She whispered, almost silent. 'What children?'

'Abigail would come home every day, asking if she could take you gifts. She would ask: "Daddy, is everyone pretty like princesses in England? Like Bea?"'

And then Bea was there. She had caught up with me. She inhaled sharply. 'Abigail.'

'She was such an innocent little thing. Clear green eyes, like her mother.'

Her heavy breaths quickened.

'Soft blonde hair, chubby little legs, freckled skin.'

His voice had become airy – the words emerging from a deep memory. In my own mind I saw Abigail, in a striped swimsuit. Running with her friends. Pretending to be an aeroplane, arms reaching out on both sides. Pink-cheeked and breathless. Laughing under grey skies, the promise of rain coming down from the mountains. Not a nice day for a swim.

'What are you telling me?' Bea asked.

He's Abigail's father.

'She would've been eighteen, this year.'

It took a few seconds to sink in.

'Your daughter?' she whispered.

'But he—'

My heart jumped as Cameron shouted the words – a jolt in the calm quietness of his reminiscences.

He continued, more quietly; coldly. '*He* killed her.'

'Alex? No—'

'He broke my heart.'

Not deliberately.

'What are you talking about? Alex didn't kill her.'

'First, Abigail. Then, Layla.'

'Layla?'

'My angel. I would've done anything for her. I moved to Canada for her . . .'

A strong hand grabbed my shin again, digging fingers into my calf through the sheet. 'First, Abigail. Then, Layla. When I walked into the house I couldn't understand what I was seeing . . .'

'I don't understand. Layla was your wife? What has Alex got to do with her?'

'. . . the feet hanging in mid-air, next to the banisters . . .' He gripped my leg harder and pain spread up to my knee.

Aaarrghh. Let me go.

'. . . bare feet, red toenails. Pretty toenails. At first it just confused me. But then I started screaming and lifting her, holding her around the legs, lifting . . .'

I felt Bea's softer touch on my thigh, sliding slowly down my leg until it reached his crushing grasp. His hold released, one finger at a time, but it left behind bruised flesh. She rubbed at my leg a couple of times, up and down.

'It was two years after Abigail,' he said. 'Heartbreak, I told the coroner. Don't say it was just "suicide". It was heartbreak.'

'I'm so sorry. Losing your daughter – I . . .' She faltered. 'But it wasn't Alex's fault.'

Cameron's tone changed abruptly. He snapped back to the room, and snarled at her. 'He. Killed. Them.'

'No.'

'Abigail Conway. You remember?' he shouted.

'Yes I do,' Bea said sadly. She paused and I felt the weight of her body against my legs as she sat on the bed. 'But Conway. That's not *your* name.'

'New life, new identity.'

'We did everything for her. I'm so sorry.'

'She drowned when he should've been watching her.'

'It all happened so quickly.'

'I never got to say goodbye. When I saw her in the hospital, she was blue. Her hair was tangled around her.'

I thought about the day after Abigail died, when Cameron – we knew him as Harry Conway – had shown up at Bow Camp, drunk. Shouting. The management kept me away from him, but his voice echoed around the camp premises. I remembered his English accent – unusual for a local parent. Another counsellor told me his story: how he had left London to be with his girlfriend in Alberta, set up home with her there.

'He had to pay, don't you see?' Cameron said. 'I did what any father would have done.'

'*You will pay,*' Bea said under her breath, strangely. She wasn't saying it to him, but to herself. 'He didn't have an affair.'

Cameron said nothing.

'He broke your heart twice over. Abigail, Layla.'

Again, nothing. What was he doing?

'Tell me it wasn't you.' She was crying now, choking back tears to speak. 'The photo—'

'My baby girl, hours after she was born. My perfect daughter.'

L.A.

Layla.

'You made me think he'd—'

'He killed them,' Cameron said. 'I didn't have a choice, can't you see?'

In a flash of movement I heard Bea lunge for the wall behind me, and a couple of his heavier steps move after her. She cried out, 'Let go of me!'

'I can't do that. Not if you're going to try and press that panic button again.'

Fight him. Get help.

'You stupid girl.'

'I won't try and press it again, please – just let me go. I won't tell anyone what you've told me. They wouldn't believe me, anyway.'

'You know I can't do that.'

She whimpered. He was holding her where they stood, to the right of me.

'Stop moving,' he said.

She made a noise but it was muffled – he must have covered her mouth.

'Shut up. No one is coming. They can't hear you out there.'

I listened to her struggle as she tried to pull away from his grip again. She freed her mouth from his hand. 'I can't believe you did this to him. You got the wrong person.'

No.

I immediately knew what she was going to say.

There's nothing to be gained by doing this.

'It wasn't Alex's fault.'

'He should have been watching her,' Cameron snapped.

'You're hurting me.'

I heard him breathing, thinking.

'If I let go of you, you have to promise not to shout again.'

'I promise.'

She sighed, and I heard her footsteps at the end of the bed. It had worked. He'd released his grip.

Run, Bea. Get out of here. Don't worry about me.

I listened as he moved too – towards the door. He was blocking her escape route.

'Alex isn't the one you should be angry with,' she said.

'He was on duty,' Cameron said. 'It's in the coroner's report. He didn't even come back for the inquest – they sent some manager.'

'He wasn't at the pool.'

'What're you talking about?'

You don't have to do this. You're only putting yourself in more danger.

'He was ill. He went to the bathroom. He left me watching the pool. Me.'

It was still my responsibility.

I felt sick. I was sure he had planned to kill me today. What would he do to her?

'When Al came back, he saw her under the water,' she said. 'Cameron?'

He said nothing.

'I'm sorry. We did everything we could. But Alex didn't deserve this.'

'How could you not have seen her?' he shouted. 'Excuses. Always excuses. It was both of you, then.' A noise, the slam of a fist against a table, came from my right – over by the door. 'Both of you,' he growled.

Bea moved around to the other side of my bed, away from him.

Get out of here. Just run. If you're fast he won't be able to stop you.

'I was right to come after you as well.'

Go, Bea.

'I did it to get at him, take away all the good things in his life—'

'Did what?' she asked. 'You mean pursuing me?'

'Pursuing?' Cameron laughed. 'You were so easy to get at.'

Bastard. She was vulnerable.

'All I had to do was watch you for a while, see what you liked, pretend to be into the same things. Scare you with a few creepy phone calls. And you came running into my arms. No problem.'

She gripped my left shoulder. I felt her nails press into my flesh.

Get out. He's going to hurt you. He's going to kill both of us.

'Why did you leave it so long? Abigail died so long ago.'

'Why did he get to be happy?'

'What?'

'Why did your precious boyfriend – or you, for that matter – why did you get to be happy? When my life was ruined? Abigail, Layla. Then Kelly walked out on me—'

'Your girlfriend? So that was true, what you told me when we met?'

'After she left, I moved back to England, moved here. And I watched you both, for a year or so.'

A year? You watched us for that long?

Had he followed us? What had he seen?

Bastard.

'Then, two years ago – Abigail's sixteenth. We'd have had a party with her favourite banana cake, and sixteen candles. I thought about that day even before she was born. I imagined my little girl – all grown up! She would have been beautiful. A heartbreaker. I should have been able to see it for real.'

Instead you were here, stalking us.

'It seemed like the right time to do something,' Cameron said. 'It was him who gave me the idea, arrogant prick. Always refusing to wear a helmet. I saw the damage I could do to him, with so little effort.'

'But you left him alive. Why are you doing all this now?'

'You call this living?' he asked. 'I've enjoyed watching the life drain out of him, so very slowly.'

'And watching me . . .'

'You're not the victim here.'

'I—'

He laughed. 'If you had just stopped coming here, I'd never have bothered with you. But you kept coming back, and back, didn't you? You kept loving this pathetic man. I couldn't let him have that.'

Bea inhaled, still squeezing my shoulder. 'And now what? Now you're finally going to kill him?'

'Now here's the funny thing. I wasn't going to,' Cameron said. 'But this is where it gets interesting. He's coming round.'

So I did move?

He waited for her to take it in. 'No.'

'I saw him move.' He touched my right hand again, trailing up my wrist. My hairs stood on end.

'You must have imagined it. I've been here almost every day for—'

'I know,' he said. 'Strange, isn't it? I'm the person he chose to show that he could move.'

I didn't choose you.

'And I can't let him wake up,' he added. 'So now's the time to finish what the pair of you started when you let my daughter die.'

'I don't believe you,' she said. 'You're trying to manipulate me.'

'Believe what you want.' He started picking up each of my fingers, then dropping them down, one by one. 'Alex, am I lying? Tell her.' He laughed.

You fucking bastard.

His heavy footsteps moved around the foot of my bed, slowly approaching the spot where Bea stood by my left shoulder. She held onto me. I felt the heat and sweat from her palm.

'Everything you said. That you loved me—'

'You were just part of the—'

Her hand lifted off my shoulder and simultaneously there was a loud crack, followed by a surprised cry and a grunt from Cameron.

Bea let out a smaller yelp. She was struggling, in pain.

I heard her push against him, her feet scuffing the floor, her body banging against the bed.

'You don't want to go assaulting a police officer.' He laughed. 'I can't believe you thought I was a cop.'

'You're their witness! Their birdwatcher. You convinced them you'd seen me there that day.'

'They weren't too hard to persuade.'

'You're trying to frame me for his attempted murder—'

'Only attempted?'

'Shit, Cameron. Why have you got that?'

He chuckled softly, and I heard her suddenly stop struggling.

What? What is it?

'I think we should look at new options. Murder-suicide – what do you think? I can see the front pages: Devastated woman stabs comatose victim before slitting her wrists. Totally plausible.' He laughed again. 'How about – New lover speaks about knife attack: "I tried to stop her, but I got there too late".'

A whimper from Bea.

'What do you think?' he asked. 'Here? It would be quicker if I went down the vein, but more likely that you'd have gone across, don't you think? More believable?'

A knife?

'Your wrists. I love your little wrists. So thin. Delicate.'

'Let go of me.'

'These hands.' After each word, I heard a noise that made my throat contract, ready to vomit. A kiss. The touch of his lips on her skin.

If you hurt her –

'Your pretty neck,' he whispered.

Another kiss.

'No,' she whispered.

There was a gentle thud, as if he had pushed her against the wall. She let out a small cry. 'Please.'

Cameron inhaled deeply. 'That smell of you.'

Bastard. Get off her.

37

Then, everything exploded into chaos.

The door slammed open. 'Fucking hell,' I recognised Rosie's voice in the doorway. 'Get away from her.'

'Rosie,' Cameron said. 'Thank God you're here.' His ability to flip his temperament so quickly was chilling. 'We need to restrain her.'

'Bea?'

'She's going to hurt Alex. She just admitted to me that she did it.'

Bea sobbed. 'Don't listen to him. Everything he's said is a lie.'

'Has he hurt you?'

Bea didn't reply.

'We need to get her out of here before the police come,' he said. 'Help me. Every time I try to stop her she gets violent.'

'That's not what it looks like to me,' Rosie spat at him, before she screamed into the corridor, 'Someone call Security! This man has a knife.'

'No!' Cameron said. 'They'll take Bea away. What did you do that for?'

Nurses shouted in the corridor and people started running. A woman yelled, 'Security! Security!'

'Come over here,' Rosie said, as Bea wept by my side.

'Stay where you are,' he said.

'Bea would never hurt anyone.'

'I know it's hard to believe, but—'

'Liar.' Rosie stood firm. Bea sobbed.

'I had to stop her.' Cameron spoke in a semi-whisper, as if confiding in Rosie.

'You're delusional. Put that down. You don't want to hurt her,' Rosie said, calmly.

Heavy footsteps came in at speed. 'Step away from her,' a man shouted. 'Step away!'

I heard movement by my side.

'Get behind me, miss,' the man said. 'Right. Now, you're going to have to give me that.'

'It's only a penknife,' Cameron said, as he tried to turn on the charm. I heard the blade being flicked in and out.

'All the same,' the man said. 'Hand it over. Just give it to me – you don't want any more trouble. Let's make this easy.'

'I only had it for self-defence. And I was trying to protect him,' Cameron said. I heard the slap of metal on skin as the knife was passed between them, and then a sudden series of thuds and grunts as something heavy hit the floor.

'What you doing?' Cameron's voice was muffled.

'You can't come in here with a knife and expect not to be restrained. Greg, c'mere,' the man said to someone else in the room. 'Make sure he doesn't get up, would you?'

Cameron grunted.

'Keep still, mate. If you know what's good for you.'

'Shhh.' I could just make out Rosie's voice in the corner of the room, as she pulled Bea close to her. 'It's okay, it's okay. What the hell happened? I left as soon as you told me you had followed him here, but the traffic was so bad.'

'I thought – you'd never – get here,' Bea said as she wept, gulping in breaths. 'I had – to keep him – talking. He was going – to kill – Alex. Couldn't get out.'

'Why didn't you call for help?'

'I was scared I'd – get in trouble – then – I don't know. I didn't think anyone – would believe me. I was so scared he would hurt us.'

'Okay, okay. Shhh,' Rosie said. 'I'm so sorry, I should have listened to you.'

'She's lying,' Cameron shouted up from the floor. 'She's a manipulative little bitch.'

'Would you be so good as to keep this gentleman quiet, please, Greg?' the man said. Cameron groaned.

A radio fizzled, and the man spoke into it. 'Yes, we're here. No, should be fine. Under control. We'll bring them down.'

Pauline's words in my ear drowned everything else out. 'He's still breathing, he's still okay.' She turned my head from side to side, holding me under my chin.

'Officer!' Cameron shouted.

'No, mate. I'm security. Police on their way.'

Pauline busied herself at my side, rearranging my arm, pulling the sheet up to my neck. 'I'd like you all to leave,' she said. 'I need to look after my patient.'

'Sir, she's a murder suspect –'

'Save it. You'll all have to come with me,' the security guard said. 'You too, ladies.'

Pauline cleared her throat. 'Can everyone please get out of this room,' she said.

'You heard her,' the security guard said. 'Let's move this into the corridor.'

The door thudded shut behind them. Pauline stayed with me, flicking through my charts, checking my pulse.

She went to roll me over, and my mind lurched away, following Bea and Cameron out of the room. She was safe, wasn't she? The police would have to believe her now.

Adrenalin pulsed through me, but the endorphins were kicking in too. I was still alive, and all the pieces of this puzzle, which had plagued me for weeks, had fallen into place.

He couldn't hurt me any more.

He couldn't hurt Bea.

38

'... there's nothing to him ...'

I woke up to a confusion of smells and sounds. Chanel No. 5. Cheese and onion. Soap. My eyes were partially open, but a greyish shape close to my face blocked out everything else.

'Liquid food doesn't do much more than stop you disappearing.' Connie's voice, right over my face – that's where the cheese and onion came from. I tried to stop my nose from inhaling.

The skin on my chest tingled as my hairs stood up, and as I felt the clamminess of Connie's hand on me I realised she must have taken my pyjama top off. Shapes in the rest of the room appeared suddenly as her greyness leaned backwards to stand at my right-hand side.

Clipped footsteps skirted around the bottom of my bed and I saw a tall, dark figure moving from the door towards the window. Philippa.

Suddenly my face flashed with heat as I tasted the ghost flavour of starched cotton, smelled the smoke and spice of that aftershave.

The quiet moments of peaceful ignorance after I had woken up vanished.

Where's Bea? What have they done to her?

'Pauline says it all kicked off last night after I went home.'

'Hmm,' Philippa said. Clip, clip, clip.

Tell me she's okay.

'She says the trust have launched an internal investigation. She should never have been able to get in.'

'It wasn't her,' Philippa said, simply. She sounded exhausted.

'But they arrested her, didn't they? Breached her bail, I thought?'

They must have arrested him too. Tell me they aren't just holding Bea?

Philippa seemed reluctant to be drawn in. 'The man that was here—'

'The one with the knife? *Is* he your cousin?'

'No!' Philippa sounded disgusted. In the corner of my room her black figure distorted as she appeared to fling her arms out. 'He bloody well isn't.'

'He seemed so charming. I never suspected a thing.' Connie's hand rested idly on my chest as she chatted, although the familiar soapy smell nearby told me she should have been giving me a wash.

'Well, now you know.'

'It's been big news round here. Is it true that he came here to—'

'Maybe,' Philippa cut in, agitated, 'if you all gossiped a little bit less and noticed unusual visitors a little bit more, this wouldn't have happened.'

'Oh, we weren't gossiping.' Connie didn't have the sense to shut up, even for a moment. 'I only meant we were shocked. That's all.'

Philippa sighed, relenting a little. 'He's the one who – who put my brother in hospital in the first place. Tried to kill him.'

Connie gasped. When Philippa didn't immediately volunteer more information, she prompted her. 'How . . . ?'

'He pushed him,' Philippa said, quietly.

'He was so friendly—'

'Alex got all the way to the top and he just . . .' Philippa paused. '. . . he shoved him over the edge.'

So that's what happened.

'You think the girlfriend was involved?' Connie asked, patting my chest.

'They let her go.' Philippa's voice had dropped to a whisper. 'I got it so wrong.'

I drifted into my own thoughts. Bea was free. They had him.

'I'll be gone in a moment, leave you in peace,' Connie said.

'No, don't worry.' Philippa's shape had already begun to move towards the door. Clip, clip, clip. 'Dad and I have a meeting with Mr Lomax.'

I kept asking myself: when did this start? It began long ago – ten years earlier in Alberta under grey skies. It started when I applied to work at Bow Camp, which came after I decided to take a gap year after school – a decision I made following Mum's death, which happened because I supported her choice not to continue treatment. I traced it further – would I have gone to Bow if I didn't climb? It started when I went to Isaac Beaumont's fourteenth birthday party at the indoor climbing wall in St Werburgh's Church. It started when Dad bought me my first pair of climbing shoes.

If I hadn't gone to that birthday party, if Dad had refused to buy me my own kit, if I had told Mum I wanted her to go through another round of radiotherapy, if she hadn't died, if I hadn't felt the need to take a gap year, if I had chosen a different place to go, if Bow hadn't offered me the counsellor job.

If I hadn't been on lifeguard duty that day. If there hadn't been so many children allowed to pile into the pool.

Abigail was only seven years old: one of the local kids whose parents dropped them off at the start of each day while they went to work. That day, she had been laughing happily with those friends, laughing under grey skies which promised rain was on its way from the mountains. The legs of those same friends later kicked around her as she drowned. There were too many children in the pool. No one saw Abigail's body, in her striped red and white swimsuit, slip under the water. No one noticed her long blonde hair floating on the surface.

When we did finally see her, I jumped into the pool, fully clothed. I picked up her limp body, lighter than I expected it to be but still dragging against the resistance of the water. Children were screaming around me as I half-lifted, half-dragged her out of the pool and rolled her onto her back. Other counsellors were shouting, Bea was screaming for someone to call an ambulance, but the noise felt distant. As I put two hands onto tiles at the water's edge and heaved my own body out, I looked down and saw Abigail's lips – thin and blue – and her eyes rolled back in her head. One of her arms trailed over the edge, her fingers dangling into the water.

I brought my mouth down onto hers and breathed into her lungs, pressed on her chest, started the routine we had been trained to perform. She was freezing cold, already turning grey. It felt like hours went by before I was being pulled away by black-suited paramedics, who took over the desperate attempts to revive her lifeless little body. I knew she was gone. Staggering backwards, exhausted, I somehow found myself walking into the main camp building, watching the windows in front of me reflect the chaos that continued behind my back. I walked down the corridors, shivering, treading on red lino tiles. I was barefoot – we never wore shoes for lifeguarding duty – and I could feel biscuit crumbs and crisp fragments collecting on the hard, damp skin of my soles as I walked. My body felt heavy, inert, and impotent. The weight came from my sopping wet shorts and T-shirt, and my dripping red fleece, but it felt deeper than that, too. My whole body felt heavy and useless.

Would she have been scared? Did she understand what was happening? Would a seven-year-old know what drowning felt like? I hoped not.

Was this condition chosen for me, as a kind of karmic retribution for the way she died? I had felt several times that my existence resembled a long, slow drowning. I waved my arms, slapping down on the water's surface, but they made no noise. I kicked, but my legs were tangled in weeds, pulling me down. I screamed for someone to see me but nobody heard. My head went under, but I managed to keep myself afloat. Just. As the time somersaulted along, those spells under the water felt longer and longer. I struggled more and more to keep my mouth above the surface, to keep the air coming in.

I had to get out of there. I tried to move again.

Move. Move.

Nothing.

39

The next day Bea visited me herself.

The door swung open with a whine, and I listened as she walked around my bed to sit down next to me. The citrus in her hair was strong – she must have just washed it. There was no trace of vanilla.

'Alex?'

She scratched her leg: nails on denim, then lifted her hand and waved it in front of my face – like you do to see if someone is awake. My eyes were closed but I sensed the very slight change in light through my eyelids, heard the chime of metal bangles on her arm as it moved.

'Alex?'

Yes?

'You're not, are you. You're not here. He said you had moved – he was making it up, wasn't he?'

No. I moved. I really did.

She took hold of my left hand in both of hers. I tried to push my thumb against the pressure.

Come on, Alex. Move.

'Everything is so much clearer, now,' she said. 'Everyone is treating me like I must be traumatised but I don't feel that way – I feel . . .' she searched for the word, stroking my fingers. 'I feel calm. For the first time in months.'

I knew I should be pleased. So why did I feel so apprehensive?

'I've written you a letter, okay?' She let go of me and I heard a piece of paper shake in her hands. 'I want to make sure I say everything I want to.'

She sounded so different. The tension was gone. The fear had disappeared.

'Part of me wishes he was right, so that maybe you could hear this,' she said. 'But there's a bigger part of me that hopes you can't. It would be better for you, that way.'

I can hear you. You've got to believe that.

'So, here it is.' She took a deep breath and cleared her throat.

'I love you. But I need to let you go.'

No. Look at my hand. I can move, I know I can.

'I have always done what I thought was the best for you. I have fought for you.'

She took another breath. 'But the fight has changed and I think that what is right for you has changed, too. I can't keep hoping that you'll wake up. I need to listen to the doctors now. We have to face reality. We can't keep you alive for our own selfish reasons.'

Don't do this.

'I'm sorry that you took the blame for me, and that you landed up here because of it. I'm so, so sorry. I'm sorry that I didn't believe in you, that I didn't trust that you hadn't had an affair. I'm sorry for everything before this, for whatever was stopping you asking me to marry you. I think I understand, and I know we would have worked it all out.'

The ring.

Oh, Bea.

We were having a rough patch, and I had panicked about proposing to the woman I was bickering with. Now I saw that it wasn't clear which of those two things had come first. Were my nerves what started the fighting?

I wish I'd just done it.

'I know that, because of the wonderful life we had together. You made me so happy, do you know that? Thank you for all those years.'

Please. Don't do this. Don't say what you're about to say.

'And so, I hope if you can hear me, you will forgive me.' She grabbed hold of my hand again. 'After I read this to you, I'm going to talk to your dad. You know what I'm going to say to him.'

I had one last chance, as I saw it. The tears came easily once I let them flow.

Look at my face, Bea. Watch me. This is no coincidence.

'I – I will always love you. For the rest of my life.'

Don't go.

'Bye, Alex.' She whispered the words over my face and kissed my lips. A spearmint-masking-cigarettes kiss.

Then she saw my wet cheeks.

'Oh, Al.' She wiped them, gently smoothing the skin just below my eyes. 'Don't be sad. We've got so many amazing times to remember.'

Although I knew she thought my tears were involuntary, in that moment it felt like on some level we understood each other.

She kissed me again, a longer, lingering kiss – but then she stood up.

Don't go.

Footsteps moved away. The door opened, shut.

I had to step up my game. Bea had been the only one keeping me alive. If she stopped resisting Dad and Philippa's plans, what would happen?

What can I do?

I started going over everything that had happened, trying to remember the order of events. And I started telling myself the story of it all. I began resurrecting the dead and gone days, bringing them back to life.

'More colour, Alex,' I can hear Bill saying. 'More details. More colour.'

I'm not sure how much more colour this story could take, Bill.

It feels like it has taken me about six days to get through everything. During that time, not much has happened. Tom and Rosie visited once, as did Dad. Bea has been in a couple of times, and either stayed silent or spent the time talking about happy memories that we have shared. She seems relieved.

But now, I've hit the present day. I have no stories from my past left to tell. I don't know what happens from here. From now on, it's just me in this moment, experiencing what happens right now.

Now. Now. And now.

I lied.

Something *has* happened in the last six days. I've been pretending it is nothing, hoping it might go away. But it's getting worse.

I have a headache. It reaches from the base of my skull, grips around my head to my brow. I need painkillers. My mouth is dry, my lips drier – with each breath in and out I feel the tug of the cracked skin. My throat is sore and throbbing.

Pauline came in earlier, she propped my door open – maybe to get more air moving through. It's particularly warm and stuffy today. I can smell food – leftover lunch or the next evening meal being cooked up in the kitchens. It always smells the same. Boiled vegetables, stewing meat.

But today it doesn't make me hungry. I have no appetite. The headache. My mouth, my throat. It all points in the same direction. I know what this is.

Footsteps in the corridor. Coming closer. Clip, clip, clip.

Philippa?

'My feet are killing me.'

Philippa. The sound of something clattering onto the floor.

'That's better. My toes are so swollen.'

I smell sweaty feet.

'Hottest day of the year so far, they're saying.'

Is she talking to me? She never talks to me.

A hot hand on mine.

Philippa, touching me?

'How are you?'

Why are you talking to me? You haven't spoken to me for months.

She sounds uncertain. Her grip tightens on mine. My body rolls a little to the right as weight drops onto my mattress.

'Do you remember that time when we were little?' She's talking softly. I've never heard her like this.

'With the bikes and the dogs?'

Vaguely. When we lived out in Thornbury, the house with the green wallpaper.

'It was a hot day. Maybe that's why I've been thinking about it this week. You could smell the grass, baking. The tarmac melting.'

Those kids down the road with a tree house. We wanted to play with them but they were older.

'That day, we took our new bikes out.'

She squeezes my hand.

What's going on? Why are you being like this?

'You said to Mum that you would look after me.'

I tried to be a good big brother. My duty, Dad said. I had to.

'We cycled down that steep lane. We weren't wearing helmets – you stashed them in a hedge.'

That was when I still had my black Raleigh Wildcat. Your bike was pink – it had silly streamers coming out of the handlebars. We cycled to see the house with the Alsatians in the garden.

'You told me we should go and see the house with the dogs in the garden. The ones that barked whenever we went past. They couldn't get out, but it still scared us, it was exciting.'

She sniffs.

Are you crying?

'But before we got to the bottom of the hill, you skidded. I was behind you.'

A rabbit ran out in front of me, I braked.

'I saw you come off, slam your head on the kerb. You lay there in the road. Your wheels kept spinning. I shouted at you but you didn't move.'

Another sniff.

It knocked me out, the bang to the head.

'There was blood on your face.'

Liquid drips onto the skin on the back of my wrist, and she brushes it away.

'I thought you were dead. I remember thinking – I don't want him to be dead.'

She sobs now, properly crying, sniffing.

'It's always been me and him. We are brother and sister. I can't be an only child.'

What's got into you?

'I know . . .' She trails off. 'All that stuff with Mum.'

She clutches more tightly at my fingers.

'But you were always my big brother.'

She coughs. The sound reminds me how sore my own throat is. Swollen.

'I've been so mad at you. I can't get a handle on it, some of the time – I just feel so angry at the world. But I was talking to Dad about it yesterday and he said something.'

Why couldn't you have talked to me like this more?

'I told him, I didn't know why I was feeling so wound up. And he said, "You know what I think it is? I think you are angry with yourself for never accepting his apologies over your mum's death. You never made up with him, and you've been taking that out on everybody else." He said he thought I did the same with Mum, I was angry with her, but then I was angry with myself for being angry with her and I couldn't get out of that cycle.'

She is still crying onto my hand.

'How could he see that, and I never could? He's right. He's always right. I'm sorry. I guess I thought I would have all the time I wanted to make up with you, when I was ready. I didn't know . . .'

She sighs.

'That there would be a time limit.'

I thought you were just angry with me for being reckless. For leaving you on your own to look after Dad when he gets old. I thought you still hated me for letting Mum die.

'I suppose what I'm trying to say is,' she takes a sharp breath. 'Despite all our differences. I'm going to miss you.'

I'm waiting for her to say something else.

She is crying.

Still crying.

Uneven breaths.

More tears fall on my hand.

First Bea, and now Phil. I'm running out of time.

40

All the oxygen has drained from my room. Every time air sucks in through the tube in my neck it barely reaches my lungs. And the heat. My head itches from the sweat trickling down from my scalp on either side of my face. I smell of a night's hot, soaked sleep. Fresh air – imagine that! A breeze against my skin. But this window never opens, and they won't take me outside. Once, they wheeled me round the garden – unless I dreamed it – and a water fountain splashed me with its mist. The claw grips my head from back to front, pressing in. In. My lungs sit heavy, filling up, begging me to cough. I'm drowning in fluid: soon there will be no room left for air.

Stay with me. I have to keep talking to you so they find me, and send a rescue team to dig me out from deep inside my body.

Keep talking, Alex. Don't give up.

I'm no fool. I've felt like this before. Pneumonia. My opponent in the ring, breeding its blackness inside my body to attack me from within. This is the seventh? eighth? ninth? time we've faced each other, in two years.

The tickle in my throat, then the stuffed nose. I spent days ignoring it, convincing myself it wasn't this.

It's only a cold.

Not a sore throat, maybe an ulcer on the back of your tongue?

You're imagining it.

But there's no denying it – not with all these symptoms piling in.

I can't get ill. Not now.

What if they don't let me get better this time?

41

'. . . his obs are okay. Slight temperature but nothing too . . .'

That's Pauline talking, as she walks in. They're doing their big ward round. These are the ones that seem to happen once a week, or something like that. When Mr Lomax checks how everything is going with me.

'. . . pressure areas are intact. Everything under control, Mr Lomax.'

Everyone is here. Mr Lomax. Pauline. I haven't heard other voices yet but Sarah the physio is usually here, probably some other doctors, another nurse.

One of them must be looking at my arm, my hand. *Move, thumb. Move.*

'Thank you, Pauline.' The boom of Mr Lomax's voice. 'We will keep this brief, although I do have slightly more to say than usual. I want to fill you in on the latest in this case.'

I focus on the whole of my right arm.

Move. Move. Move. If I can just show you all.

'I have spoken with Patient's family.' He speaks slowly, with self-importance. No one dares to interrupt.

'They all now agree that there is no sign of improvement, despite the tests we have run and our ongoing treatment.'

The room is full of new smells. Coffee breath, a floral

perfume. Armpits. I try to ignore them all and focus everything onto my arm.

Just a twitch. A flicker. Come on. Move!

'I held a best interests meeting with Patient's family and we
talked through all the options and outcomes. We talked about
how we can take things forward.'

My heart rate climbs steadily. My mouth is dry – it feels full
of grit. I'm thirsty to the point that I think I can smell the water
in the air around me, the moisture on the gathered group's skin.
I'm certain I can smell an open bottle of water in someone's
hand.

This can't go on. I have to show them.

Move. Move. Move.

'We discussed what Patient would have wanted. We talked
about his past wishes and feelings. Unfortunately, they hadn't
discussed the possibility of this type of situation before he was
injured – but they believe he would not wish to be kept alive in
this condition for any longer.'

*So I was right. When Philippa said she would miss me. When
Bea said goodbye.*

'Now, they don't want to go down the road of withdrawing
Patient's nutritional support . . .'

*They don't? They're not going to – what? They're going to keep
me alive?*

'. . . because, as we all know, that can be a cruel way for things
to end. But.'

He takes a deep breath.

No buts. Please. Watch me. Look at my arm.

'When he is next ill – the most likely scenario we're looking
at here is that the pneumonia returns.' He coughs. Splutters.
'Excuse me.' He hacks away again. Someone near my head tuts.

'Where was I?'

'When he is next ill.' I recognise Connie's voice.

'Ah, yes. When he is next ill, we will not be treating him. Now, let's discuss . . .'

No. I need more time. I NEED MORE TIME.

How long did I spend wishing they would do this? Wasted hours. I should have used that time to prove I was conscious. I need to show them.

Last chance. Move. MOVE.

'. . . this is not to say that we will not give him pain relief. If there is any indication that he is in pain, continue as normal. But no antibiotics. All decisions on treatment should be referred to me or Dr Sharma. Under no circumstances should anyone allow the dramatic events of the last week to have any bearing on deciding the best path for Patient.' He coughs again. 'Everyone clear?'

Murmurs of 'yes' and 'okay'.

'Good. That's today's ward round done, then. Thank you, everyone.'

It's happening.

Chest tightening. Head throbbing.

I don't know if I'm ready I don't know if I'm ready.

Relax, Alex. You're still alive. Stay calm. It's not over yet. Think of good things. Remember . . . when you were sixteen? You spent the summer climbing on the garage wall, you'd nailed four wooden blocks onto it, remember? Relax. You would climb a little way up, traverse from one end to the other using those blocks and the tiny features on the bricks to hold onto. Relax. You'd swing along, hanging on with your fingers, your trainers smearing on the wall below you . . .

I'm reaching up, right. I grab hold of the top of that brick with the chip in the corner. Cling on. Keep my arms straight. Move my right foot along, edge it up against the wall. Bring my left foot through between my right leg and the wall, and move my hands along to follow . . .

My breathing has slowed. My chest is still tight and my head aches but the panic has receded.

What now?

Maybe it's time.

Who's there?

Hello?

Footsteps. Uneven – limping.

Dad?

The door shuts with a click.

Dad?

A zip purring open.

The soft sound of strings being strummed.

My mattress sinks under the weight of a steadying hand, and a body sinks into the chair on my right-hand side.

A couple of chords, strummed slowly.

Dad?

The beat of his fingers on the wooden body of his guitar, and more strums. Up, down. Up and down. His foot tapping on the floor.

'You know, we never wanted to have to do this,' Dad says quietly. His foot stops.

'I just hope things start to get better, for Philippa, for – for me. It feels as if a weight is lifting, now that we've decided.'

He clears his throat.

'It's not just you. It's everything with your mum. I need to – you know.'

What?

'There's a song that makes me . . .'

What?

'I – I'll just play it.'

He clears his throat again. Resumes his foot-tapping and picks out a tune on the guitar strings.

I know this one.

He sings 'Blackbird' gently.

I don't understand.

A knock on the door interrupts my confusion.

'Come in,' he says. The door whines. 'Oh – Pauline, hello again.'

The scrape of chair legs, the acoustic echo of the guitar as it hits something solid when Dad rushes to stand up. I feel his hand on the mattress.

'Ooh, steady now. You didn't need to get up on my account, Graham,' Pauline says.

'Only polite.' He wheezed, seemingly exhausted by the small effort.

'I was listening to you play, outside. You stopped?'

'I'm sorry, I didn't mean to disturb you.'

'No, not at all, my love. I like it.'

Dad laughs. 'You're the only person who does, apart from him,' he says, and I sense a nod in my direction. 'His sister hates it, finds it embarrassing. So I don't subject her to it any more.'

'I think you have a hard time, trying to keep everyone happy, all the time, hmm?' She speaks softly. 'Not an easy job.'

They stand in silence for a moment, before Pauline breaks it. 'You were saying earlier, outside, before we were interrupted.'

'Oh, yes, I was wondering. If you'd like to, you know . . .'

'Yes. I'd like that. I'll catch you before you leave and we can work out a date – got to get on now.'

'Okay. Yes, okay. Great. I'll – yes. I'll see you when I leave.'

The door clicks shut. Dad doesn't move.

What just happened?

'There's a turn-up for the books,' he mutters, then lifts his guitar and settles slowly back into his chair.

He starts picking at the strings again.

Did you just ask Pauline out?

Help me. Make the pain stop.

My mouth feels like it is full of painful ulcers – swollen and burning. I can only take shallow breaths, as if my chest isn't there and I'm breathing no deeper than into my throat.

I've stopped trying to move. Please, just help me.

Aches pound around my nose, under my eyes, behind my eyes. Toothache-type pain in places I have no teeth.

The doctors haven't noticed yet. Normally, by now, they'd have seen the rise in my heart rate. They'd have seen me sweating, and noticed that their suctioning didn't seem to have done anything.

Help me. Give me morphine.

I think I'm ready.

42

Death. I want to claim it – make it my own. It can be – will be – what I want it to be. I will fly if I want to. I will live my final hours as a blackbird, soaring in the sky, looking down on everyone. I've always wanted to fly. I will dive down, rise up, marvel at my speed and agility. Then I will close my eyes, and fly through into eternity.

If I decide that I want to die with Bea in my arms, I will do that. She will be warm, smooth, as we lie together on the sofa. I will smell the fine down on her neck, kiss the pinkness of her ear. Hold a hand on the rise of her hip. Then I will close my eyes and take the touch of her with me.

If I want to go while sitting above the blue-green Grassi lakes, then I will. I will hike up there at dawn and sit amongst wild flowers and imagine diving; no – I *will* dive into the freezing water, because its iciness will hold no danger for me. As I sink under, I will roll over onto my back and look up at the cloud-free sky through the lake's rippled surface. Then I will close my eyes and let my body float upwards – and away.

I can do anything and be anywhere.

The room is getting hotter, hotter, hotter. Steamy, as if I'm in a sauna and each time a nurse comes in she is pouring a ladleful of boiling water onto a pile of rocks at the end of my bed.

Hotter, hotter.

The heat is inside me, too, rising up.

It's him. He's calling me, drawing me into the ring.

In the BLUE corner it's PNEUMOOOOONIA.

The door whines and – clack – shuts.

Hello?

Pauline's familiar marzipan smell hits me before she starts humming a tune I don't know.

She stops and runs her hand over my forehead. It slips through the moisture.

'You don't look good, do you, my love? Let's see.'

She presses a finger to my wrist.

'Hmm.'

She touches my forehead again.

'Very hot.'

She's never done this before – she's – stroking my hair.

'Poor love.'

'Think this might be the last time you get ill, my love.'

She pats my shoulder.

'I'll see what I can find to make you more comfortable.'

Her footsteps are leaving the room.

Pauline – hey, Pauline?

Pauline.

She's gone.

So let's welcome him to the RIIIIING. In the RED corner, it's Alex Jackson . . .

I'm stepping in. If Pauline thinks I'm hot then I'm stepping into the ring, aren't I? This is it? I'm up?

Are you happy, now, Cameron?

Where is he? Sitting in a prison cell.

Do you really think this is what Abigail would have wanted?

I'm going to die in this bed, but that's okay.

You didn't break me.

I've had a good life. A happy life. I've known real love. Real love with a beautiful, funny, intelligent woman. My Bea. My girl.

You didn't take that away. Nobody can take away what I had before all of this. You can't touch it.

. . . voices? Whispering voices.

Speak up. How am I meant to hear you?

Shwshwhshwhshhh. Whispers. Sshwhshshwhshhh. Psshwhsh. Coconut. Lemony-sweetness. Who smells like that?

Oh, I know who you are. You're those art dealers, aren't you? The ones I called earlier. Hey, you know what? I have something you might want. Under my bed. Look under my bed. There's cave paintings under there. Medicine men with hoops. Hoopla! Worth a few quid, I think you'll find. I can grant you access if you want, let you take them away for the right price.

Shwhshswhshwhsh. '. . . can't believe they're going to do this to him . . .'

Tom? Mate, look at these cave paintings, buddy. Hoop men with medicine and bears and snakes. You can look for free. No charge for you.

'. . . do you want to say anything to him?'

'I don't know, Rose. What kind of thing?'

'Anything. Things you need to say. Memories?'

Chalk dust smell in the air. Cracking knuckles. Crrrr-ack. Crrrr-ack.

They are thousands of years old. Untouched. I found them. No one ever thought to look under my bed but they were there all along.

'. . . I was thinking about that day we went deep-water soloing at Berry Head . . .'

Yes! Berry Head. What a place. Down climb the cliff from the top, right down to the sea then traverse left to climb back up – no ropes – if you fall you drop into the sea but we didn't we climbed to the top no ropes – free and easy.

'. . . remember it? Rainbow Bridge. The water was so clear and bright, like we were in the Med. And deep. That was the best climb of my life . . .'

Let's go again tomorrow. Let's take your car though, mine's in the garage.

'. . . I've never felt adrenalin like it, knowing I could fall at any minute but I would just plunge into that water. That rock – remember? Orange and grey and black and white – technicolour. The final overhang with those massive dinner plate holds. The feeling when we topped out – climbed up over the last section. I'm so glad we did that climb together . . .'

I might need to borrow some gear, too – I can't think where mine is – it must be somewhere but I can't think where I put it.

'. . . I promise I'll live my life to the full, mate. I'll do everything to make it count.'

'Come here, Tom. Come here.'

Pick me up at seven, will you? . . .

. . . a spider walking across my face. I feel its eight legs, little pins walking over me. It crawls up my nose, out of my ear.

Or is it a bird? There are feathers now, soft against my face. A beak, tapping at my lips. Tap. Tap. Did the bird eat the spider? She swallowed the bird to catch the spider, that wriggled and jiggled and tickled inside her.

I feel it, the crunching of the bird's jaws and teeth as it devours little eight-legs. Without seeing it I know it's a blackbird. I can tell from the gurgle of his stomach as he sits on my forehead, and digests.

What does spider taste like? Bitter. No, sweet – like honey.

Honeycomb. Crunching in my mouth, melting onto my tongue . . .

. . . you came all this way, to see me.

'You sound surprised.'

It's so nice to hear you. And you look good. Healthy – you've put weight back on.

I breathe in – hairspray and red roses perfume. Mum.

'Yes. I'm doing well. But I miss you.'

We've missed you too.

'You can stop fighting now, my darling.'

You think so?

'You can let go.'

I'll think about it.

'Don't just think about it.'

I like how you've done your hair. You like it when I say that, don't you? You used to tie it up like that when we were kids.

'Come and find me, my darling.'

How will I know where to look for you . . .

. . . 'I think you may be right.'

'It's dropped slightly, hasn't it?' A hand against my head. Marzipan.

Cool air on my chest – sheet pulled down and pyjama top pulled up.

'He still feels hot, though.'

That's better. Thank you, Pauline.

The sound of plastic and metal. She tugs at the tube in my stomach.

Coldness inside me.

'This'll make it all a bit better now, my love.'

She strokes my forehead. Feathers on her fingers . . .

*

. . . the blackbird on my face. Pecking at my throat. Peck. Peck. Peck.

Moves down my neck. Peck. Peck.

He picks a hole in me, in my chest, with that sharp little beak. I can feel the hole.

He is tunnelling. Where to?

I understand! I understand, little bird. You're trying to let me out. I can climb out of that hole, yes?

They sent you, finally. Keep going, keep pecking at me, I can stand the pain.

Keep going until you reach me – I'm a little bit further in, to the right and deeper down.

Keep pecking, little blackbird . . .

. . . Bea is on my bed with me, curled up at my side, her leg hooked over mine.

My gorgeous girl. My Honey Bea. You know I love you?

'Quiet, now. Not much longer.'

I was thinking, we should go away for a weekend. A cottage in Wales. Log fires. You and me. Sheepskin rugs. Blankets and sofas you sink into. A few bottles of wine. Fish and chips.

She doesn't answer.

Don't you want to come?

'Quiet, now. Shh.'

She keeps stroking my arm.

'It's going to be okay. I love you . . .'

. . . tap tap tap. Peck peck peck.

You're nearly there, little guy. Keep going. Keep tunnelling.

I'll set off a flare so you can see where I am – ready? Are you watching for it? Five, four, three, two, one.

Did you see it?

Yes – right here. I'm right here.

I can see his yellow beak, I can see the light behind him and his blue-black shadow.

You're through! You did it! Don't go – don't fly.

He's gone. But he has left his tunnel, right through my chest, my heart and lungs. I can see the light at the top.

If I climb out, then I'm free.

43

*S*oon I'll be at the top. Lactic acid pumps in my arms but I have more strength in me, I can feel it.

Not far now.

No one has ever done this section before. There's zero chalk on the rock, it's unclimbed territory. I've always wanted to be the first to climb a route and name it.

Up close to the rock you see so much more of it. The lichen and moss. The little cracks and chips that stretch out like a map: a puzzle for me to solve. It's amazing. This grey limestone was formed hundreds of millions of years ago. This here is little creatures, insects, piled on top of each other. Dust and leaves. Piles. Layers. History. Millions of years of it.

It's just me and the rock. I'm free soloing: I've got no need for ropes today. I'm at the top of my game. I run my palm over the surface of the sun-warmed rock, checking for my next hold.

Up. Up.

The holds are small and crimpy: they bend my fingers to their limits. I swap my hands over, shaking the blood back into each of my forearms in turn.

Up. Left.

I traverse left around a blank rib of rock. Smooth moves. Strong moves. Hips in. Shoulders back. Finding the balance point on each move.

Up. Up.

I tackle a small arête section. Both my hands grip the far side of the vertical edge of rock, which juts out from the rest of the wall, parallel to my body. With my feet smeared over holds on the near side, I use my body tension to stop the lethal barn-door swing off the rock. I've never climbed so well.

Up. Up.

I'm so high now. A peregrine perched on the cliffs to my left carefully eyes the birds flying and singing behind me. Her sharp golden yellow feet clutch to a ledge sprouting lollipop-like purple spheres of flowers.

Up. Up.

I can't wait to see the top. No one has been there before. This is going to be different. What's up there?

Up. Up.

So close now. One – two – four more holds max. I can see them all. Up and right. I jam my left foot into a crack. Up and right. My left hand touches the top edge – a big jug of rock to pull myself up on. One more pull and I can haul myself over and top out. I pull myself up.

Up. Over.

Look at this.

It's beautiful. It's beautiful up here.

Acknowledgements

To everyone at Harvill Secker – particularly Liz and Jade – thanks for having faith in this book, and for working so hard to help me make it better.

To Peter (and that empty chair next to me), I am so grateful. Thank you for your belief and enthusiasm, and for introducing me to your excellent team at RCW.

I couldn't have attempted to imagine the experience of being locked-in without the accounts of Kevin Weller, David and Sandra Nette, Kate Allatt, Julia Tavalaro, Richard Marsh, Martin Pistorius, Philippe and Stephane Vigand, and Jean-Dominique Bauby. Thank you for going to such astonishing lengths to put your respective fights into words.

For medical help – thank you to Rory, Sarah, Mat, Vicki, Mel, Gareth, Geraint, Dawn and Damian. Any medical inaccuracies or unlikelihoods are my own fault entirely.

For teaching me to climb – thanks Dave at TYF, and Emily at Bloc. For answering my never-ending stream of technical questions, I'm indebted to Greg and Gary; for an insight into the mind of a climber, to the autobiography of Jerry Moffatt.

I am grateful to Liz for your advice on police procedure, and Richard at the Bristol Naturalists' Society for your help with geology. Lindy – thank you for all the printing!

Gavin – I simply couldn't have got this far without your hours of reading and discussion in the early days. And to others who taught me on the Bath Spa Creative Writing MA (particularly Celia and Sam) or workshopped sections with me, thanks for your encouragement and tough love.

My first readers – Erin, Clare, John and Sophie – you were so generous with your time, suggestions and feedback.

Alison – thanks for being the Scarb to my June. I'd love to say more, but what happens in WriteClub stays in WriteClub.

To my friends and family, particularly The Syndicate, my Lovely Ladies, the Circle of Trust, and my big brother, James. Thank you, all.

Mum and Dad, I could thank you a million times and it wouldn't make a dent in my debt.

Finally, Matt. For having such unwavering confidence in me, without reading a word. For that walk in Cheddar Gorge. For all those other miles we covered, while you listened. Thank you. And Gwen, who arrived in the middle of it all – you turned my life upside down in the best possible way. I love you both.